DECEPTIONS

PRAISE FOR ANNA PORTER

Winner of the Shaughnessey Cohen Prize for Political Writing, the Nereus Writers' Trust Non-Fiction Award, the Jewish Book Award for Non-Fiction, and the Canadian Authors Association/ Birks Family Foundation Award for Biography, and shortlisted for the Taylor Prize.

"Porter's offbeat thriller yields tension and humour from its revolving perspectives as well as its deep bench of colourful supporting characters . . . . This peppy thriller from Porter (*Kasztner's Train*, 2008, etc.) bursts with banter and tantalizes the reader with half-revelations and game-changing twists." — *Kirkus Reviews* on *The Appraisal*

"[A]n intelligent and exhilarating thriller . . . Porter's stylish story vividly transports readers to Budapest and other European locales and keeps them hooked as her well-developed characters navigate corruption and deception." — *Publishers Weekly* on *The Appraisal*

"All of this is daring and mystifying fun, and includes along the way a tour through everything that's fascinating about Budapest's history, especially the appalling bits." — *Toronto Star* on *The Appraisal*

"If you want to take a quick trip to Budapest, this book is your ride. Anna Porter knows the byways and cafés of her native town and spins a web of mystery around an art heist, Ukrainian criminals, and money laundering. In short, we have everything we want in an Eastern European crime novel." — *Globe and Mail* on *The Appraisal*

"A gripping thriller set against the rich post-war history of middle-Europe where fortunes were reversed through war, revolution, and shifting political regimes and where the past itself cannot be trusted. Born in Budapest, Canadian writer Anna Porter generously shares her knowledge of time and place and impresses with detailed insights into the world of art history and appropriation, big money deals, and the quest for restitution."
— Staunch Book Prize on *The Appraisal*

DECEPTIONS

A **HELENA MARSH** NOVEL

ANNA PORTER

Published by ECW Press
665 Gerrard Street East
Toronto, Ontario, Canada M4M 1Y2
416-694-3348 / info@ecwpress.com

Editor for the Press: Susan Renouf
Cover design: Michel Vrana
Cover image: *Judith Beheading Holofernes* by Michelangelo Merisi da Caravaggio (Public Domain)

LIBRARY AND ARCHIVES CANADA CATALOGUING IN PUBLICATION

Title: Deceptions : a Helena Marsh novel / Anna Porter.

Names: Porter, Anna, author.

Identifiers: Canadiana (print) 20200384163 | Canadiana (ebook) 20200384198

ISBN 978-1-77041-538-6 (SOFTCOVER)
ISBN 978-1-77305-672-2 (EPUB)
ISBN 978-1-77305-673-9 (PDF)
ISBN 978-1-77305-674-6 (KINDLE)

Classification: LCC PS8581.O7553 D43 2021 | DDC C813/.54—dc23

The publication of *Deceptions* has been generously supported by the Canada Council for the Arts and is funded in part by the Government of Canada. *Nous remercions le Conseil des arts du Canada de son soutien. Ce livre est financé en partie par le gouvernement du Canada.* We acknowledge the support of the Ontario Arts Council (OAC), an agency of the Government of Ontario, which last year funded 1,965 individual artists and 1,152 organizations in 197 communities across Ontario for a total of $51.9 million. We also acknowledge the contribution of the Government of Ontario through the Ontario Book Publishing Tax Credit, and through Ontario Creates for the marketing of this book.

ONTARIO CREATES

ONTARIO ARTS COUNCIL
CONSEIL DES ARTS DE L'ONTARIO
an Ontario government agency
un organisme du gouvernement de l'Ontario

Canada Council for the Arts

Conseil des Arts du Canada

Canada

PRINTED AND BOUND IN CANADA

PRINTING: MARQUIS 5 4 3 2 1

MIX
Paper from responsible sources
FSC® C103567
www.fsc.org

For Lyla, Noah, Ava, and Violet.

CHAPTER ONE

She sensed him before she saw him. The smell of wet wool and cigarettes. He approached cautiously on rubber soles, a little breathless as he entered the salon and stopped a foot or so inside the door. She slipped the thin long-bladed knife from her sleeve, stretched her fingers over the handle, and waited a moment — it was, she knew, a crucial moment because sometimes a moment would be too long — but this was Paris, not Moscow, not Bratislava, and she was not working on a dangerous case. She glanced up at the large, burly figure. "Helena," he said with a note of anxiety in his voice. The pedicurist, massaging Helena's instep, may not have seen the knife, but he had. "I didn't mean to scare you."

"Do I seem scared?" she asked.

"No," he said. "Do I?"

"A little."

She noted his badly shaven face, his pale eyes still fixed on her sleeve, his burgeoning belly stretching the grey wool sweater over his corduroy pants. "Put on a little weight," she said with a smile.

"All that *rakott krumpli*," he said, "but I will lose it on delicate French food and wine." He spoke English with a soft Hungarian accent, pressure on the endings, but a great deal better than the last time she saw him. Must have been taking lessons. A pity, she thought. She had liked his accent first, even before she began to like him.

"Would you have time for a coffee? Or a glass of wine?" he asked. "There's a good place down the street."

"Le Buci," she said. "And how the hell did you find me?"

He shrugged, palms up, delighted with the implied compliment. "Am I not a detective?"

"Back with the police?"

He shook his head. His hair was cut short, his grin was as guarded as she remembered it, crinkling the skin around his eyes. More warmth there than he cared to give away. "Fifteen minutes," she said. Much as she loved looking at them poking out at the end of her long claw-foot bathtub, she could skip the lacquer on her toenails. She would have to talk with Louise about letting someone know where she was. Anyone. Even when she suspected that the person was relatively harmless, and Attila was not exactly harmless. Louise, an otherwise very sensible woman, must have developed a weakness for slightly overweight Hungarians.

She would not be the only one with that particular weakness.

Café Le Buci was on the corner of Dauphine and de Buci, a short walk from Helena's office, but she rarely went there. This neighbourhood, Saint-Germain-des-Prés, had been her father's favourite arrondissement, and he had taken her to Le Buci on her first visit to Paris with him. He had wanted, he said, to take her to all the places he loved. This was the city of art, he told her, and as a student of art, she would become as addicted to the city as he had. She had resisted then, but later, when he had exited her life, she found herself drawn here.

The outdoor seating area was on the sidewalk, where she could not have her back to a wall. Besides, this time of year there were still too many loud visitors occupying space. It was gloomy inside, but Attila found a banquette near the entrance with a bit of light, a narrow view of the street, and a seat for her against the brick wall with an old-fashioned placard advertising beer. Good to know that he had remembered her phobia, and charming that he would sacrifice his own comfort for hers.

He had obviously planned this. Two glasses of white wine appeared on the table as soon as she sat down, as well as some sort of pâté with thin wedges of bread. "The waiter says it's a Bordeaux," Attila said, "and something about it having been a good year. Will you try it?"

She settled with her back to the wall and examined the offerings. The waiter must have concluded that Attila was a tourist. The last good year in Bordeaux that was ready to drink was 2015, and the pâté looked like it had seen better days. She ordered an espresso. "What brings you to Paris?" she asked in a light, conversational tone, as if they were almost strangers, as if he wasn't a former lover, if only for a few weeks, as if he hadn't sent flowers each week after she left, as if she hadn't saved his life, as if she hadn't missed him so much she had almost returned to Budapest . . .

"A job, I think, but where I come from you can never be sure. Hired by my old sergeant at the Police Palace. You remember the man?"

"Tóth?"

"He wants me to watch over one of our esteemed Council of Europe representatives. Maybe our supreme ruler wanted to get him out of the way. Or to move him somewhere more pleasant than Hungary these days, as a reward for past service. It's hard to tell until our man has made his first speech at the CE. Our ruler has been talking about defending our Christian culture against the Muslim tide, but what he means is defending himself from anyone who disagrees with him. About anything. My man has a chance to prove himself, pushing for general agreement on agricultural subsidies."

"Agricultural subsidies," Helena said. "Is that a contentious issue?"

"Only if you want to hand over the many millions of agricultural euros to your family and friends."

Helena was not particularly interested in the Hungarian political landscape. "And he is in Paris?" she asked.

"He is. And that's the official reason I am here, but the real reason is I wanted to see you again."

"Hmm. Why is he in Paris?"

"He has meetings."

"Political meetings? And you are his babysitter? Or Tóth's spy?"

"It's complicated," Attila said, scratching the top of his head where the hair had almost begun to recede but not quite yet. "I could be both. And I am not sure why Tóth chose me for this. It's the sort of job he would offer to his favourite people, and I am not on that list. All he told me was to watch my man and report whatever I see that seems out of the ordinary. I thought coming to Paris was out of the ordinary. But maybe he is only washing some money."

"Money laundering?"

Attila grinned and stretched his hands palms up. "My English . . ."

"It's improved since the last time." Last time was at Budapest's Four Seasons Hotel, where she had overstayed her welcome, caused a major stir by confronting a Russian billionaire, and enjoyed some days with Attila walking along the Danube, watching the waves as his dog inspected lampposts. They had breakfast in bed in her room and shared dinner sitting on his dog-infested sofa in what must, at one time, have been a pleasant enough apartment in Pest, but now looked like it had been turned over by a mob. Although she hadn't noticed in the beginning, his bed had smelled of dog in the mornings, and he had shown no interest in changing the dachshund's sleeping arrangement. As for the state of the apartment, Attila had explained that his ex had taken all the good furniture, even the shelves that used to house his collection of books (that's why they were in unruly piles along the walls), but the ex had left more than a year before. To Helena, who liked order in her own life, Attila's lack of it had seemed incomprehensible. The moment she felt she thought she could belong there, she had fled. But it was still great to see him again.

"And there is this painting," he said. "Our man is divorcing his wife, and she claims her share of the painting is worth a million euros."

"Who is the painter?"

"Gentileschi."

"Artemisia Gentileschi? Or Orazio?"

"Artemisia."

"There is always a slim chance of another undiscovered work," Helena said, "but not one that hasn't been mentioned before. She has become quite the heroine for our times. Books, essays, reproductions. That massive retrospective in Milan, another in Paris, then the big one in London, two documentaries, a collection of letters by and about her. A feature film. A novel. And her value has gone up with her reputation. Her Mary Magdalene was sold some years ago for fifteen million pounds at Sotheby's. Recently, I think, her Saint Catherine went for twenty-one million euros. Is she the reason you came to see me?"

"Not the only reason," he said defensively, "but I did hope that you knew something about her."

"Nothing you couldn't have found out for yourself by looking up a few reliable sources, most of them online."

"It would take me years," Attila said. "And I thought you might be interested in a small job, authenticating. The husband, my man, claims it's a copy and worth nothing, or very little. He is talking here with some people in your business."

"Who?"

"A man at the Louvre. European Collections. It's where I left him this morning."

"Did he mention the man's name?"

"No."

Aubert? She wondered. He was supposedly an expert on the Baroque period, but he had left for London a couple of days ago on a buying trip.

"The wife," Attila said, "— and she would be your client — believes her husband is trying to cheat her out of a fortune. I thought she could use some help."

"You thought, or Tóth thought?"

"Tóth doesn't think. He follows orders. So, someone higher up who does think may suspect this. Or that she is trying to extract more from him than she has a right to expect. Why that would be their concern, I don't know."

"But you are supposed to be protecting the husband, not the wife. Right?"

"In a way, yes, but I think I am also supposed to watch over that painting. Tóth was very interested in what our man was doing talking to someone at the Louvre. He wanted me to insist I had to be there. Vaszary, that's our man, wouldn't agree."

"Do you know where they got their painting?"

"They brought it with them from Budapest."

"You realize it's quite unlikely that it's a real Gentileschi. Gentileschis don't just pop out of people's attics in Budapest."

"This one is in Strasbourg, and she'll pay you to look at it."

Since she had been left a small fortune, Helena did not need the money. What she did need was a bit of excitement, and the chance of discovering a real Gentileschi, however unlikely, was irresistible. Her last job had paid well, but it had been boring, three weeks in a Brussels lab examining paint chips with a spectroscope and x-raying bits of canvas with faded colours to date the overlays of a Poussin. A pastoral scene with shepherds. She had never liked Poussin and was somewhat allergic to his pastoral scenes.

Curiosity, Helena decided, was one of her most dangerous personal traits.

CHAPTER TWO

The great Strasbourg cathedral announced its ten o'clock mass by vigorously, and perhaps a little desperately, bell-ringing the faithful to prayers. If, indeed, it was prayers they craved on this thronging Sunday. There were no cars allowed here, and it was early October, still warm and sunny, perfect for hordes of indecisive dawdlers and harried, anxious guides. Helena ran along the Grand Rue, dodging pedestrians, cyclists, and dogs, her small black backpack bouncing on her shoulder blades. She had arrived at Gare Centrale a good fifteen minutes ago, giving herself time to drop her holdall at the hotel and scout the area before her meeting.

There was no particular reason to be cautious except for her new client's insistence on secrecy and a nagging feeling that someone had been following her. Mme Vaszary had declined the invitation to come to Helena's office in Paris since both she and the painting resided in Strasbourg. However, she said she would be happy to meet Helena's usual fee and, of course, her expenses. Paid in advance.

The woman had chosen a strange way to deliver the message and the retainer. A plain brown envelope with no return address had arrived at Helena's Rue Jacob office, where it lay unopened on Louise's desk for a couple of days while Louise assessed whether its bulk contained anything lethal. It didn't. There was a one-page document retaining Helena Marsh for the work of appraising an old painting, €20,000 in cash, a map of Strasbourg with the Place du Marché aux Poissons circled in black felt pen, and the date of the proposed meeting in the same black pen, printed in capital letters with the promise of another €10,000 when she finished her report.

∽∾

It was times like these that reminded Helena of Simon's bottomless ability to make the wrong decisions. Usually egged on by his desire for more money and another adventure. Simon had been so good at what he did that money had never been a problem. He could afford his peripatetic life, the grand house in Toronto, and his daughter's expensive education. He seemed to value money for what it proved about his abilities as the best in the business, so good that his commissions hung in the world's most distinguished museums. That he had been a rare visitor to the house he had bought for Annelise and Helena in Toronto's lush, leafy Rosedale — one of Canada's best residential areas — left Helena with the impression that he was her mother's occasional lover, an exceptionally close friend with far-flung interests that kept him from living with Annelise.

Till the end of her childhood, she had no idea that he was also her father. No matter how much Helena had insisted, how often she had brought up the subject, her mother had consistently claimed that Helena was the result of a short-lived fling, a love affair that was never meant to last. Helena began to question other visitors to the house, but no one seemed to remember him. Annelise's story was that Helena's father had departed mere days after she was born to pursue a different life with, perhaps, a different family, and that he died soon after. How was it possible, then, Helena had persisted, that he had left enough money to maintain that large house, the antique furniture, and the grand collection of art spread over three floors. He had also left ample money for Helena's private schools, her art and art history classes, and Annelise's exquisite clothes and her European jaunts.

Annelise told her all this had been his legacy. Perhaps he had felt guilty about leaving, and he had wanted to make sure they had everything they needed — except, of course, his love. It was not until she was fifteen, travelling in Europe with "family friend" Simon (a birthday gift) that the truth emerged. Even then, he wouldn't acknowledge her publicly as his daughter ("It will be our secret," he told her), and she was too angry about his years of subterfuge to even want to acknowledge him.

∽◯

The call had come early in the morning. Louise had just arrived with her café au lait and *pain au chocolat* and listened for a minute with her mouth full before she managed to tell the man that she was not Madame Marsh and that Madame Marsh would not be back from Brussels for two more days.

He hadn't left a message.

When he called again, Helena was in her office. He introduced himself as Mrs. Vaszary's lawyer — Magoci (no first name) — and that if she was interested in the offer, she should come to Strasbourg, and he confirmed he would meet her at noon the next day on the tour boat that moored near the *marché* marked on the map she had received. Madame Marsh, he said, had been highly recommended. No pleasantries, no polite introductory remarks, no explanation of the odd choice of place for the meeting. He provided his instructions and hung up. He had a Slavic accent — not Russian — and he had spoken clearly and with authority.

The Place de la Cathédrale was packed with tourists. They stood shoulder to shoulder, studying the gargoyles as their guides droned on about history, the quality of the stones, and the mastery of the craftsmen. Helena skirted the periphery, stepping around tables and chairs, children with ice cream cones, waiters with trays, and a range of well-behaved dogs. She continued to the south side of the cathedral, past the lineup for the public toilets, past the cathedral's museum where there was no lineup, and down Rue de Rohan to the quay where the tour boats waited. She bought her ticket for the Batorama boat scheduled to depart at noon.

Passengers were already waiting, four across and forty deep, chattering in a variety of languages, the children excited about a boat trip, the adults taking photographs of themselves. She took her place behind a group of noisy Swedes.

No one approached her, and no one looked like a lawyer. On the other hand, colourful jackets and T-shirts with ads for Adidas or Nike or with large Chinese lettering could be a clever disguise. But why would he bother?

The ticket-takers made their multilingual announcements, then ushered everyone onto the boat. Helena walked down the aisle between the rows of wooden seats, looking for a man with a briefcase. Instead, he wore a brown fedora, check shirt, chinos, and sandals, and carried a camera. He stood as she approached, indicating the seat next to his own, where he had placed a raincoat. He was shorter than Helena but sturdy, his back curved slightly — perhaps he lifted weights. He motioned to let her pass, but Helena demurred.

"I prefer the outside," she told him in French.

The man shrugged, moved over, and offered a welcoming smile. "You're younger than we thought," he told her under the noise of the loudspeaker advising passengers to stay in their seats during the trip, to turn to their own language on the headphones, to keep their hands inside. "You should wear the headset," he suggested. "We can talk after the engines start." He was tanned, fashionably shaved to an even five o'clock shadow, deep lines down from the mouth, maybe fifty years old, hard to tell in the shadow of his fedora. And that slurry accent. Czech? Thin overlay on local dialect?

She adjusted the headset to cover her ears.

As soon as the boat pulled away from the dock, she heard him tell her to keep looking ahead. "This will take only an hour," he added. "Please do not draw attention. Observe the buildings on either side. They are very beautiful. Please don't look at me."

"Why in hell not?" Helena asked.

"We are on a tour boat. Take the tour. Could you use a scarf or a handkerchief to disguise that you are talking? I am using my hand," he said, quite unnecessarily because she could see he was shading his mouth with his right hand. Two rings, a gold band on his ring finger and a larger chunky one with a green stone on his middle finger. Way too much jewellery for a lawyer.

She took a tissue from her backpack and started to wipe her nose.

"Thank you," he said. "We think it's best if it is not noticed that we are together. The painting is likely genuine, but there are a few strange aspects. It could be an early work. Apparently, she didn't do this sort of painting late in life. But we need to be sure." His English was very precise.

"Have you already had an expert opinion, or is this your own observation?"

They were passing under a covered bridge, grey stocky buildings on one side. "An expert has looked at it, but he was hired by the husband. He said it was a copy made in the eighteenth century, and since it is such a fine copy, it could be worth two or three thousand euros. We think it's the real thing and could be worth millions."

"He said it was a copy of an early work?"

"Yes, he seemed sure of that."

"He said it was a copy? Or a forgery?"

"Isn't that the same thing?"

"No." Her father had commissioned forgeries, never copies. Copies are a mug's game, he had told her, but to produce a new work that could have been made by the artist himself was phenomenal; to do it with the same paints, the same canvas as the original was genius. He had taken her to the Louvre to see two Monets and a Rubens he had sold them. Their experts had studied the paintings and asked no questions. Monet, Simon had told her, would have been proud to have painted these two. "A copy is made by copying something. A forgery is an original work, painted in the style of the artist, but done by someone else. It's really a tribute from one artist to another. . . ."

"Has Madame Vaszary researched its history? Is there a record of who had owned it previously? A reason you think it's a genuine Gentileschi?"

"Monsieur Vaszary bought it from someone who needed the money quickly. We don't know how much he paid, but we think it was more than he would pay for a simple copy."

"Where did he say the original is?"

"In the Hermitage. The basement."

Helena had spent a couple of years in that basement, studying Renaissance art that the Soviet army had collected to celebrate its World War II victories. It had been challenging work, authenticating Titians, a Rembrandt, a Raphael, a Caravaggio, and fifty or more Impressionists. She had reported that several of them were forgeries, but the museum had not concurred with her findings. She had long suspected that one of the more thuggish Russian oligarchs, Piotr Grigoriev, had been behind the museum's reluctance. He, after all, had sold them one of the paintings she had failed to authenticate.

"I assume your client wants me to see it?" She had meant to be ironic, but what with the handkerchief, the noise from the engine, and the insistent loudspeaker, her tone would have been lost on the lawyer.

"Today. We checked your credentials. You have a reputation for being tough. And fast," he said. "You don't look like your photograph in the journals," he added.

"Since you invited me here to see a painting, why are we taking this boat tour?"

". . . passing the old Douane building on the right. It's where in past centuries you had to deliver your goods for inspection. . . . Look for the thirteenth-century slaughterhouse bridge coming up . . ."

"Excuse this extra caution, but we wanted you to understand that your visit here has to be absolutely confidential. The husband . . ." He coughed as the Musée Alsacien slipped by on the left. "Details of your appointment are in your hotel."

"He doesn't know I'm here?" she asked.

"N—"

The lawyer dropped his hand from his mouth to clutch at his throat. He fell back, blood squirting between his fingers, trickling down his shirt front past the feathered end of an arrow protruding from his neck. Helena resisted her first impulse to pull out the arrow. She shouted at the guide (still talking about the thirteenth century in Strasbourg) to call an ambulance.

She saw a man standing at the railing of the bridge above, looking down at the tour boat, waiting. Then he pulled his grey hat low over his face, tucked something that looked very much like a longbow down the inside of his beige coat, and began to walk toward the French Quarter. Helena jumped over the lawyer and the next two passengers to get to the railing. Using it to steady herself, she leapt off the boat and landed on the embankment. She ran toward the figure retreating to the other side of the bridge who looked once over his shoulder reflexively. She could see his round flat face with sunglasses slipping down (he was likely not used to wearing glasses), his flat nose, and his thin slash of a mouth. His coat flapped open as he ran, revealing the bow now flat against his side. He crashed into a couple looking into a gift-shop window, ran down Rue de l'Ail, over the tram rails, and up to the pedestrian street, mingling with a Japanese group. He checked over his shoulder once more, shoved past the umbrella-wielding tour guide, and ran into the cathedral.

Helena closed in on him as he pushed past the indignant ticket-taker and disappeared into the darkness. She handed the ticket-taker a €20 bill, jumped the metal rail, steadied herself against a pew, and scanned the aisles. Several white fedoras, a couple of beige hats, jackets, no long coats, no one running, but near the exit line, a uniformed woman trying to stop someone who tore free and hustled out into the sunshine.

The bow was lying under a low bench near the exit. She left it there. When Helena reached the cathedral warden, she saw that the long beige coat was draped over her arm. *"Mon mari a laissé son manteau ici tout juste,"* she said.

The warden looked at her suspiciously. *"Votre mari?"* she repeated, looking at the coat.

"Il été tellement pressé . . ." Helena said as she grabbed the coat and ran out the door, looking for the man's grey hat in the crowd. She lost sight of it near the tourist office, but a moment later, as she sprinted around the side of the cathedral, there was a flash of movement up past the shops with trinkets and T-shirts, and the one shop stretching out toward the cathedral. As she ran by, she saw a display of hats — some of them grey — on a low table where casual browsers may stop and be invited in by the smiling attendant offering today's special discount. One grey hat lay casually on top of the display.

"For sale?" Helena asked.

"Je ne sais pas," the helpful attendant said. *"Il est juste returné."* Helena sprinted past the display and onto Rue de Dôme, past the textbooks shop and the alleyway that led to the small park. She balled up the coat and stuffed it under her arm. No sign of the man. She doubled back to Rue de Dôme, and up as far as Rue de la Mésange, but still no man. She retraced her steps, more slowly, looking into every shop. The sound of sirens grew louder as she approached the cathedral, but there was no sign of the man.

She stopped at the corner of the alleyway where a beauty salon's wide windows stretched both ways and a sign advertised all-time low prices for haircuts. She opened the door and asked the stylist whether he had seen anyone a few minutes ago. "He could have been running in either direction," she said. The clean-shaven stylist looked at her hair and offered her a welcoming grin. "No," he said, "no one in a hurry."

"I am trying to find a man," she explained.

"Aren't we all?" said the stylist, brushing a few bits of hair from his client's shoulders.

CHAPTER THREE

Much as Gustav enjoyed Irén's cooking and the warm, cushiony arrangements in her apartment, he was always ready to come home after a few days of her company. Attila thought it could be her lilac perfume, or her incessant fussing, but delighted as Gustav was at the beginning of his visits, Attila usually found him waiting at the door when he returned. Irén, a few years older than Attila and built for comfort, was rarely able to race Gustav to the staircase, so she would follow more sedately with one of her inevitable chicken casseroles that Gustav enjoyed more than Attila did. Too much paprika and pork fat. "My mother's recipe," she would say. "Good food is the direct route to a man's heart. Wouldn't you agree?"

Attila would nod sagely and try to make a quick getaway. Today was easier than usual because his phone was ringing and buzzing, and Gustav was aggressively pulling on his leash.

"*Csókolom,*" he shouted over his shoulder and answered his phone. *Csókolom* was an old-world greeting that covered both hello and goodbye. It referenced the old custom of hand-kissing, something Attila had never done and was not likely to start now. His grandfather had been the last hand-kisser in the Fehér family.

"Where the fuck are you?" Tóth shouted by way of a greeting.

"*Rakoczi Ut,*" Attila said reasonably.

"Not in fucking Strasbourg, then," Tóth shouted again.

"No."

"Why not?"

"You told me to be back today."

"Did not!"

"You did!"

"You had better get your ass in here." Tóth yelled before ending the call.

Attila took Gustav down to the street for a quick constitutional, encouraging him to lift a leg and leave a small deposit under the only tree left in front of the apartment building. The others had all been dug up in preparation for a sidewalk extension no one wanted or needed but, since it was paid for with EU funds, had provided an opportunity for state-sanctioned grand theft, irresistible to those with ties to the ruling party.

After Gustav's pensive tree exploration and a small memento of his visit, they went back up to the apartment in the hopelessly rickety wrought-iron elevator cage, ate some chicken, and Gustav listened resentfully as Attila apologized for having to leave again. After just a few months of their new bachelor life, Gustav had acquired some of the ex's tendencies. She, too, had worn her resentments on her face.

Twenty minutes later, Attila was at Árpád Bridge, approaching the Police Palace (so named after the government added a steel-and-glass tower to try to make the place more suitable for these proud-of-our-heritage times), showing his ID on demand to the uniformed woman who had known him for at least twenty years. It was as if he had changed his identity now that he was no longer a police officer. She then made a production of watching his wallet progress through the x-ray machine and examined his police-issue handgun as if she disapproved of his continued licence to carry it.

"Lovely to see you, too, Margit," Attila said with a broad grin as he collected his stuff from the conveyor belt. "Always surprised that you have made it through one more gruelling day."

"Hrummph." Margit pointedly turned her attention to the long corridor where Tóth was already waiting. He had acquired a large belly (delightfully larger than Attila's own) since his promotion but had not yet accepted the fact that his shirts needed to be replaced. Perhaps also his pants. Hard to know about the jacket since he wasn't wearing one.

"Your phone was off," Tóth began.

"Charging," Attila said, though that didn't quite explain why he had left his phone off after he arrived from Paris. He had needed some time to think, and it was hard to think with the phone demanding attention.

"You should be in Strasbourg, where you are supposed to be on assignment from this department, where you have an actual job, where you were sent to be useful . . ." Tóth's voice rose as he accumulated all the reasons why Attila should not be in Budapest.

"Right," Attila said patiently. "But you told me to be here for a briefing this afternoon."

"Plans changed. Everything changed. Your orders changed. How the fuck was I supposed to tell you if your phone was off?"

Tóth led the way to his office — the one that used to be Attila's — and slapped his bum into what used to be Attila's chair. "So, you don't know what happened in Strasbourg?"

Attila sat on the lower chair facing his old desk — he had made that arrangement himself, as low chairs made most criminals feel self-conscious — and waited.

"I assume you haven't had time to watch the news, but a man was killed on a tour boat. He was shot. Son of a bitch was sitting right next to a woman who jumped out of the boat and ran off."

"She is the shooter?"

"No. She is not the shooter, but she does interest the local police and should interest us if our man was interested in anything other than his belly." They were both staring at Attila's belly, which, Attila noted again with satisfaction, even from this vantage point, was not as large as Tóth's. "He was shot from a bridge above the boat. But she was next to him when it happened and instead of waiting for the police, she jumps out of the boat and hares off somewhere. The French police are all over the case, wanting to know who she is and why she left the scene, the guy bleeding to death right next to her."

"Why does that have anything to do with us?" Attila composed his face into as curious yet unaffected an expression as he could manage.

"Because the dead man was the Vaszarys' lawyer. That's why they are calling me. Plus, as I said, they now want to know who she is."

"We don't know who she is," Attila said. He breathed in and out slowly, trying to relax. *It couldn't be Helena. Could it?*

"I may not know who she is, but I have a hunch — no more than a hunch, mind — that you had something to do with this."

"I did? How?"

"Because you were our man in Strasbourg."

"But I wasn't even there!"

"Maybe not, but you might know this woman."

"Why the fuck would you think that? There are thousands of women in Strasbourg I don't know."

"But this one is some kind of art expert. And your job with Vaszary includes watching over stuff he took with him when he left here — including that painting."

"You told them . . . ?"

"That we know who she is? No. But as her picture was all over their news, it won't take them long to figure it out. I assume you invited her to Strasbourg?"

"Who told you that?"

"Never mind who told me. Anyway, I didn't tell their police. I couldn't tell them and have it all over the French papers. The French don't control their papers. It's a stupid excuse for a country and an even stupider excuse for a government. Why would somebody want to kill this lawyer?"

Attila shrugged and raised his eyebrows to indicate he had no idea, though the first thought that sprang to his mind was that Iván Vaszary would have lots of reasons for interfering in what his wife was trying to do. Not all divorces are amicable, and the Vaszarys' would have included more than a worn sofa, some books, and a dachshund.

"It wasn't Vaszary," Tóth declared.

Attila was too caught up in his worries about Helena to listen to Tóth's theories. He had suggested her to Gizella Vaszary. He thought this would be a lucrative contract for Helena, one she might not refuse, and a chance for them to be in the same city for a while. He had tried to entice her back to Budapest, but that hadn't worked. Strasbourg was neutral ground.

"He was in Paris. Wasn't he?" Tóth was asking.

"Yes," Attila said. "I was with him in Paris. He had meetings with some EU bureaucrats and a guy at the Louvre. Looked to me like he was going to spend a lot of hours in waiting rooms," Attila said. "He told me to leave."

"He could have hired the guy who shot the lawyer."

"Could have," Attila conceded.

"We can't have one of our guys involved in a murder investigation," Tóth continued. "Not even if we don't like the bastard. Vaszary may still be useful for us."

"Us?"

"Yes. Us Hungarians, in case you've forgotten where you sleep these days. Fucking moron . . ."

Tóth had never been smart enough to disguise who, in addition to the police department, was paying him. The last time, it had been a Ukrainian oligarch; the time before, a gang of Albanians looking to make an easy living off Váci Street shopkeepers. The whole reason for hiring Attila was now out in the open. Someone in the Gothic castle. Acting as Vaszary's bodyguard had been too peachy an assignment from the start.

"As for the woman on the boat, I suspect it's your friend, the art expert," Tóth said.

"My friend?"

"Marsh, her name was, last time she darkened our lives. And you, no doubt, know why she is in Strasbourg."

Attila affected a startled look. "Helena? In Strasbourg?"

"The coffee! Now!" Tóth yelled, and, as if she had been waiting outside for just such an order, a woman appeared bearing one cup with sugar on the side, placed it carefully on the plastic in front of Tóth (when did he decide to cover the desk in plastic?), and marched out of the room. She rolled her eyes at Attila as she left.

"You're on the next flight to Strasbourg," Tóth said. He picked up his cup with one pinky daintily extended and slurped. "Find out what that woman is up to."

Since leaving the police force two years ago, Attila had managed to eke out a precarious living from a few rich clients in need of information or of evidence of something fishy in their dealings with other businesspeople, but most of his jobs were short-lived and some of his clients declined to pay his meagre daily rate. Tempting as it was, he could not afford to tell Tóth exactly what he could do with this assignment.

Besides, he needed to see Helena.

CHAPTER FOUR

The room at the Hôtel Cathédrale turned out to be a two-room suite with a magnificent view of the cathedral. It had been booked in her name and prepaid for four nights. In the hotel room's safe, there was an envelope with a map of Strasbourg, a black circle around a house on Rue Geiler, and a short note from Gizella Vaszary, inviting her to visit at four o'clock. In the event that the time was not convenient, would she please contact Mr. Magoci, her lawyer, at his cell number to arrange another time. Mrs. Vaszary, however, urged Helena not to delay because there was considerable interest in the "object," and some of the interested parties were growing impatient.

Helena had come with only a small holdall. Although she hadn't anticipated a need for excessive caution, she never travelled without her thin Gerber switchblade and her Swiss mini, a handgun so tiny it could hide in the palm of her hand. These could be useful if she encountered the man who had shot the lawyer but could be a problem if she were detained by the police. She was sure every police officer in Strasbourg had her description by now. Given the number of smartphone-wielding tourists on the boat, it was likely that her photograph was also plastered all over police stations and downloaded onto cellphones. And the man might have been aiming at her, not the lawyer. She should have brought along a few of her disguises.

❧

Helena laid the man's beige coat on the hotel bed and patted it, looking for some sort of identification, but the pockets were empty. The coat was made of a light cotton-and-wool mix, soft to the touch. Silk lined. She thought it was the kind of material her Christie's colleague James liked to wear. Decidedly British, somewhat androgynous, and soft-spoken, but tough, ambitious, and uncompromising, James was always correctly dressed. He had climbed the corporate ladder to some spot above middle management at the auction house. He had assumed the role of a comfortable upper-class man, though he was neither upper-class nor relaxed. Only his chewed fingernails gave him away.

James had always seemed pleased with her work and used her expertise to make himself look efficient. Yet, despite all his effort, his career had stalled, and Helena knew that he needed a big score soon.

❧

The inside pocket had the name of its manufacturer or tailor — Vargas — in black italics sewn into the flap. A black line over the second *a*. That, too, was neatly sewn. Either a very exacting machine or a steady hand. In either case, expensive. As was the lining and the cologne she smelled when she patted the coat. *Hugo Boss? Mont Blanc?*

She called Louise and asked her to personally bring her the stylish plastic container from the office safe. Louise would know what she meant, and she would also know that something had gone wrong, or at least not as she had expected, in a routine appraisal. Could she also check for men's wear manufacturers and bespoke tailors with the name Vargas?

The TGV from Paris took three hours if there were no delays. Even if she managed to catch the next train, Louise would not arrive until seven o'clock that evening.

It was getting to be time to visit Madame Vaszary. Helena changed into a pair of black slacks, a brown sweater, a jacket with a turned-up collar, and a brown scarf with a blue cathedral on it that she had purchased in the gift kiosk outside the hotel. She replenished her stock of tissues from the bathroom, wrapped the scarf loosely around her neck so that it covered her chin, and hid her hair in the baseball cap she used for her morning runs. Then she took the stairs to the lobby. She coughed and spluttered, blowing her nose among the nearby outdoor restaurant tables, and jogged along Rue Gutenberg, then up Rue des Francs-Bourgeois across the river from where the Batorama's boats were at a standstill.

She blew her nose through the railway station to exit with a gaggle of newly arrived tourists. Much to the amusement of the cab driver, she gave the address of the Council of Europe, Avenue de l'Europe. "Everyone here knows that address, madame." She apologized for her terrible cold. The driver expressed his deep regrets and gave her his card in case she needed a cab again during her stay in Strasbourg. He offered a tour of the Château du Haut-Koenigsbourg at an excellent rate once she felt better and then suggested that he could wait till her meeting was over. She declined gratefully, tipped generously, but not too generously, and walked slowly to the entrance. She walked up the steps, looked at all the flags as if she were searching for a particular one, then turned to gaze at the field of well-cut grass.

As the cab left, she looked up at the façade, then examined the huge sign for the Palais de l'Europe, blew her nose, and sauntered slowly down to the pedestrian walkway along the river. No one followed. She joined a group of surgical mask–wearing Japanese tourists, all gazing at the massive structure. Behind them, she could see a slowly trawling police boat with four police officers scanning the entrances to the council buildings.

She crossed the river, marched along the quay, and rounded the corner onto Rue Humann where she could check her route, making sure that she was still not being followed and that no one was taking an interest in her progress. She jogged along the Avenue de l'Europe to the Boulevard Tauler and onto Rue Geiler. Number 300 was much like the other large mansions along a street, where there was nothing smaller than a three-storey French provincial, with a garden that had been fussed over and trimmed within an inch of its life. There were four security cameras pointing at different parts of the garden and the flagstone driveway. There was no police vehicle and no police officer. The only car on the street was a large SUV, comfortably far away.

She rang the bell, a commodious sound that reminded her of an orchestra's timpani, which was followed by furious barking as something solid thumped against the door. A woman in black with a white apron and a practised smile opened the door, her left hand on the chain around the rottweiler's neck. "*Semmi baj*, Lucy," she said to the dog. "You must be Ms. Marsh," she said to Helena. "We have been expecting you." Lucy, who was still grumbling under her breath, clearly didn't share the woman's polite anticipation of Helena's visit, but she backed up to leave room for Helena to enter. "Mrs. Vaszary is in the living room."

All the walls were white, the furniture was white, and there were no pictures, no decoration, no books, no potted plants, no personal touches, as if the place had been staged for a prospective buyer. Some frames wrapped in brown paper sat near the windows, suggesting the tenants were new. They hadn't had time to hang their pictures. Or, since they were divorcing, there was no point in hanging pictures.

The white curtains were open, allowing the afternoon light to fall directly onto the startlingly lifelike painting that dominated the room. At first glance, it seemed as if it were the light from the window that lit up the face of the young woman in the painting, but as Helena drew closer, she could see that the light emanated from the picture, a theatrical trick of accentuating light and dark tones to heighten dramatic tension and movement as figures emerged from the shadows. It made the young woman's round, fleshy face shine and her half-closed eyes appear to recoil from the brightness. She wore a draped blue-and-yellow dress that revealed the rise of her breasts. In her lap, there was what looked to be a human head, swarthy, bearded, mouth set in a rictus of agony, with dishevelled hair and a bloody gash where it had been severed from its body. In contrast, the woman seemed composed, at rest, her dark brown curls cascading over her shoulders, fingers of one hand entwined in the man's hair, the other hand holding a long-bladed sword, the blade bright red all the way to the hilt. Her fingers dripped blood.

"You like it?"

Helena turned from the painting with difficulty. A slim, platinum-blonde wearing an elegant white suit, a matching fur stole, and high-heeled black pumps stood in the doorway. "I am Gizella Vaszary," she said. "You prefer English or French?"

"Whatever suits you," Helena said.

Gizella continued in English. She didn't offer to shake hands. "So glad you could make it. After all that's happened." She proceeded to the white leather sofa and sat, carefully aligning her legs side by side with the knees touching. She must have been aware of her skirt riding up on her thighs. "Hilda will fetch us some coffee. Unless you would prefer something stronger. . . ."

"Coffee is fine," Helena said. "Your lawyer . . ."

"He is dead," Gizella affirmed. "But you know that, don't you?"

"I didn't wait to find out," Helena said.

"Of course not."

"The police have been here?"

Gizella shook her head. "I was not Mr. Magoci's only client, and it will take them a long time to interview every one of them. He was from Moldova. Specialized in corruption cases." She shrugged and waved her hands palm up to show she had every reason to believe that most people from Moldova wallowed in corruption. "I was maybe his least important client."

"How did you know he was killed?"

"It was on the news," Gizella said, sweeping a bit of fluff from her skirt. "I assure you, it had absolutely nothing to do with me."

Hilda appeared with a silver tray, two tiny white porcelain cups and saucers, a silver sugar bowl, a silver creamer, and matching dainty tongs. Gizella proceeded to pour the coffee with great care and circumspection. "Sugar?"

"No. Why, then, did he pursue the silly charade of meeting

me on a tour boat, pretending we didn't know each other? Seems like a lot of trouble to take over what should have been a simple appointment to appraise a painting."

"I wanted to make sure you were the right person."

"For a tour of Strasbourg? By boat?"

Gizella laughed. "Of course not. I needed the right person to give me advice about the painting. My husband and I are divorcing. We own a bit of land near Lake Balaton and an . . . *öröklakás*, how you say that, flat? condominium? in Budapest. He agreed that we would split all the valuables fifty-fifty. That's fair, since we have been married almost twenty years. We have no children. The only problem is this painting. He says it's worth maybe a couple of thousand euros, since it is a copy, and he is willing to pay me a bit more than one thousand for my share."

"I still don't see a reason for meeting me on a boat and pretending not to know me. We could have met in a café. I am told there are many excellent cafés in Strasbourg. Why the elaborate charade?"

"I was concerned that my husband would find out I am consulting you. We have been very cordial over the divorce, and I thought there was no need to be unpleasant. At least not yet." She smiled at the painting and then at Helena. "It's a very fine copy made in the nineteenth century. That's what he told me and my lawyer."

"Mr. Magoci."

"Yes. He had told me the same thing before we left Budapest."

Helena approached the painting, this time from the shady side, so she could see more of the details. The background, which had at first appeared to be solid brown, now showed faintly lit shapes that gravitated toward the central figure, hints of distorted faces, a couple with shocked, wide-open eyes. On one side, there was some mottled orange drapery with thin blue lines and dark yellow-green paint sliding downward. The hand holding the head was pale and delicate, the full, puffy sleeve of the dress pushed up to save it from the blood, the arm with the sword strong and muscular, yet there was a gold bracelet on her wrist. The woman's face, close-up, was even younger than at first glance: pink cheeks, smooth chin pointing up, as if there were nothing more gentle and natural than to be relaxing with a dead man's head in her lap. Its forehead was lit by the same theatrical light as the woman's face and her barely covered breasts.

The painting was utterly arresting. Beautiful and shocking in equal measure. The bright light that focused the viewer's eyes on the central scene suggested that the drama of this moment had already passed.

"Judith with the head of Holofernes," Helena said. Before she moved to Florence, Artemisia had specialized in painting heroic women. Susanna, Mary Magdalene, Lucretia, and Judith. There were several versions of each, and some of them had her own features. This painting might be one of them.

"So I've been told," Gizella said. "I know nothing about art," She added.

That did not sound right, Helena thought. She obviously knew enough to question what she had been told. "Your husband does?"

"He claims to."

"When did you — or was it your husband — acquire this?"

"About a year ago. We bought it from a friend who needed money rather urgently. There was a business opportunity he could not let pass, he said."

"Who was it?" Helena asked.

Gizella cupped her chin. "His name . . . ? Hmm . . . yes. It will come to me. We both thought it was an extraordinary painting. That's why I had it hung in this room, even before the rest of our furniture arrived. Don't you think it's the perfect setting?"

"Perfect," Helena said. "And you bought it as a copy?"

"Yes. For a few hundred euros."

"Your lawyer said the original was supposedly in the Hermitage?"

"That's what we were told. Except that it does not seem to be there. My lawyer made inquiries, and they do have one by her father, Orazio Gentileschi. It's possible, Magoci said, that they have not catalogued all their canvases. Did you see her signature on the bed, below the fold of her dress?"

"Yes," Helena said. Artemesia didn't always sign her full name on her paintings, and she spelled it in a variety of ways. Orazio himself had written her name with two *e*'s in some of his letters to her. But Helena had not seen a signature with the entire surname missing. When accepted into the Accademia delle Arte del Disegno, she had spelled the whole name, with Lomi added at the end: "Artemisia d'Orazio Gentileschi Lomi." Lomi, one of her relatives, was a good name to have in Florence, since he, too, had been a distinguished artist.

Helena ran her fingers over the paint, feeling where the artist had added layers of colour. She felt for the brush strokes, decisive, planned, certain. In her early work, Artemisia didn't use underpainting or even sketches on the canvas. She had been one of Caravaggio's followers — a young "Caravaggist," adopting his startling use of light and of real, unidealized models.

Artemisia shed Caravaggio's influence as her own style developed, and she began to paint in styles favoured by the courts of

Milan and Naples. She needed patrons, and the rough Caravaggist manner was thought unsuitable for a woman. The painting of Cleopatra she had presented to the Grand Duke Cosimo de' Medici was much softer, the figure more suggestive and less powerful than her earlier female figures.

"There are forty known paintings by this artist in the world," Helena said. "I think I have seen them all. I have also spent a couple of winters in the basement of the Hermitage, and I would definitely remember this painting had it been there. I have to do some tests, of course, but I do not believe it's a copy of anything in the Hermitage."

"Tests?"

"Carbon dating analysis of the canvas fibres, the pigments in the paint, the wood support of the canvas. It will take time."

"How much time?"

"It can take months if you want it authenticated. One case I was involved in took two years. If you want to be absolutely sure, you would use spectroscopy, as it allows us to determine the molecular structure of the paint . . ."

"I don't have months," Gizella said. "What can you do in a couple of weeks?" She stood and walked to the windows. "I do not think he will give me even that long. He has announced his intention to move to Brussels before the end of the month to take up another appointment. I would not be going with him."

"That does not sound very cordial. And you said the divorce was not unpleasant."

Gizella shrugged, rubbed her palms together in a strange gesture of "what can you do," and smiled out at her garden. "It's the move to Brussels," she said. "He has another, more important appointment, and he wants to settle everything before he goes."

"Presumably," Helena said, "Mr. Magoci gave you advice on that, Mrs. Vaszary. I certainly cannot, but I can tell you that a proper analysis of the painting cannot be done in such a short time. All I can do is take small samples for carbon dating and give you my best guess as to authenticity."

"There are buyers who may not demand a complete analysis, don't you think?" Gizella turned away from the window and came up to the painting. "There are some who may even accept an opinion from an expert, such as you, and not wait for the test results."

Helena said she would see what she could do. She took a number of photographs of the painting, some from a distance of three metres to encompass all of it, some up, paying particular attention to the faces, the folds in Judith's cloak, the contrasts of murky dark and brilliant highlights, the signature, and the rusty blood around Holofernes's neck. She nicked the tiniest bit of paint from the bottom left corner of the painting and put it into her handkerchief, another from where Judith's dress met her breast, and an even more miniscule sample of the signature. She examined the back of the painting for any telltale marks, felt the canvas, and cut a tiny speck from the wood. "I will let you know," she said. "Meanwhile, I have a pressing problem with the local police, who knew I was with your lawyer on the boat and seem to think I can tell them something about the man who killed him."

"And you can't?"

"I can't. And I don't want to be involved with the police here — or anywhere, for that matter. They are slow-moving and tedious. This whole situation has nothing to do with me. I didn't even know the man."

"But you did take off after the killer. It's what the television said."

"It was the right thing to do. He had just shot someone I sat with, and he was going to vanish long before the police arrived. . . ."

Mrs. Vaszary laughed. "I wouldn't have thought of running after that man."

Not in that outfit, and not in those shoes . . . "I need to borrow a scarf and sunglasses, if you have them," Helena said. "Perhaps I can give you my preliminary assessment and leave before they decide to hold me as a material witness."

"I can't imagine they would," Gizella said, and asked Hilda, who had been lingering in the doorway, to bring her silk Chanel scarf and a pair of sunglasses from the hall closet.

Helena stuffed her baseball cap into her backpack, exchanged the cheap cathedral scarf for Gizella's chic Chanel, which she wrapped over her head and throat. She put on the sunglasses and checked her reflection in the gold-framed hall mirror. Lucy, she noted, had watched her every move.

CHAPTER FIVE

Attila took a cab from the Strasbourg airport to the official residence on Rue Geiler. He asked to see Iván Vaszary. When Hilda
told him that Vaszary was not expected back from Paris until
eight o'clock, he asked whether Mrs. Vaszary could see him.
Hilda, a pleasant woman from somewhere on the Hungarian
prairies, was usually happy to see Attila. Someone from home
who had no airs and often shared old Hungarian jokes with her.
Today, however, she was as gloomy as Attila felt after his visit
with Tóth. "Mrs. Vaszary," she said, "told me to tell you that she
does not feel well."

That, Attila thought, was hardly surprising since her lawyer
had just been killed.

Attila took another cab to Magoci's office at the end of Rue
d'Austerlitz. It was in one of the new designer structures that
the city had commissioned. All glass and steel, reminiscent of

Eurométropole, with not a hint of comfort for anyone who was determined to rent there. Magoci and Associates (Les Bureaux Magoci) occupied three floors, with the entrance on the second floor, where two uniforms and a very blond receptionist surveyed Attila with no hint of a welcome.

Attila marched past the uniforms. *"Bonjour,"* he said to the receptionist with his friendliest smile. "I have an appointment with Monsieur Magoci."

"Oh," she said.

"Quel est la nature de votre relation avec Monsieur Magoci?" the taller policeman asked.

"A private matter," Attila said in English.

"Perhaps Monsieur Gilet could help you?" the receptionist asked. "He is one of our senior lawyers."

The taller policeman inserted himself between Attila and the receptionist. "No one," he said, "will go into the office today."

"Mais Monsieur . . ."

"You have not heard the news," the policeman interrupted. "Mr. Magoci has . . . he died." He accompanied his statement with a slight eye roll followed by a sad glance at his boots. "We need to know why you want to see Mr. Magoci."

"He was acting for one of our citizens in, as I said, a private matter."

"What citizen?"

"Hungarian," Attila said, as if that explained everything.

"You wait here," the policeman commanded, and left by the door behind the remarkably well-endowed receptionist. She seemed quite aggrieved by Attila's treatment but contented herself with asking for his name and telling him that she was usually Monsieur Magoci's receptionist and she would be pleased to make the introduction to Monsieur Gilet, one of Monsieur

Magoci's associates, when this was over. Her name, she said, was Mademoiselle Audet.

The uniformed officer returned with a plainclothes policeman who asked what Attila's business was and who had sent him.

"Je ne parle pas bien français," Attila said. "English?"

"Okay," the detective said. "Your name?"

"Fehér," Attila said, "and I work for the Hungarian representative at the Council of Europe, Mr. Vaszary."

"Secretarial, I assume?" the detective asked, smirking at Attila's wide shoulders and sharing the joke with the uniformed guys.

"Of course," Attila said, and returned the smirk. "But I used to be a policeman," he said.

"Hébert, Lieutenant de Police," the plainclothes policeman said, and shook Attila's hand. "Your rank?"

"Lieutenant when I left."

"And you are here because?"

Attila had considered the possibility of admitting that Magoci had been Gizella's lawyer but decided not to. "Mr. Vaszary had hoped to hire Mr. Magoci on a private matter. Not strictly embassy business. He asked me to find out if Mr. Magoci would be interested."

"Where were you yesterday?"

"In Budapest. Why?"

"Magoci was killed yesterday," Hébert said. "On a tour boat."

Attila managed to raise both eyebrows to indicate utter surprise. "On a tour boat?"

"With an arrow."

Attila whistled in appreciation of the unusual circumstances. "On the Rhine?"

"L'ill. It runs through Strasbourg. There was a man with a bow and arrow on one of the bridges."

"Have you arrested him?"

Hébert shook his head. "Monsieur Fehér, I am asking the questions. Before you came here today, did no one tell you that Monsieur Magoci has been murdered?"

Attila shook his head. Ignorance was usually the best way to extract information.

"Do you know how your boss happened to pick Monsieur Magoci for his lawyer?"

Attila shook his head again.

"Have you met him before?"

"Monsieur Magoci? No."

"Just picked him out of the phone book, did he? *Bizarre, n'est pas?* And he sent you here with no appointment? Mademoiselle Audet," he spoke to the young woman at the reception desk, "did Monsieur Fehér have an appointment today?"

Mademoiselle Audet seemed truly sorry that she had to admit "No, Monsieur."

"Isn't that a little, how you say, *négligent* of your boss? You coming here without an appointment? In your country, Monsieur Fehér, would you expect a lawyer to be available for a consultation without an appointment?"

Attila shrugged.

"I thought perhaps not, but, you know, here we are tolerant of other people's customs. How long have you been stationed in our city?"

"About three weeks," Attila said.

"You haven't taken up a bit of archery to pass the time?"

Attila laughed. "I told you I was in Budapest yesterday. You can check with Lieutenant Tóth, of the Budapest Metropolitan Police. I was meeting with him."

"All day, or just when Monsieur Magoci was killed?"

Nice try, if a bit obvious, Attila thought. "Since I don't know what time he was killed . . ."

"Of course, I forgot. *Le bateau* was approaching the Luther Bridge at around 1300 hours where the man with the *tir a l'arc* was waiting." He took a step toward Attila and looked closely at his face. Another move right out of the training book, Attila thought. "Monsieur Magoci was not alone," Hébert said.

Attila fidgeted with his cellphone, took it out of his pocket, looked at it, put it back into his pocket. Hébert, as if he had just been reminded that he had to check his own phone, pulled his out of his shoulder bag, looked at it, then the two men looked at each other. And waited.

"You wouldn't know a woman, about a hundred and seventy centimetres tall, slim, dark blond shoulder-length hair, high fore-head, very athletic," Hébert said at last. "No. More than athletic. Maybe a gymnast. Fast runner." He showed Attila the photo on his iPhone. A surprisingly good shot of Helena in the air jump-ing over someone, one foot still on the side of the boat, other foot raised for landing on the embankment. In the next shot, she was running, her arms pumping by her sides. Her dark blue running shoes floated above the pavement. It was a bright sunny day. Her profile, even from this angle, was lovely, her chin thrust forward, eyes fixed; unfortunately, an excellent picture.

"Wish I did," Attila said.

"*Moi aussi,*" Hébert said. "If, by some chance, you remem-ber who she is, or if she introduces herself to you, please let me know." He reached into his breast pocket, took out a small leather case, and extracted a card with his name, his division number, and his phone number. "How long are you staying in our city?"

"Depends on Mr. Vaszary and how long he is staying."

"If Lieutenant Tóth at Budapest *quartier general de polic-ier* is right, Monsieur Vaszary could be here for a long time. His appointment is for five years. Perhaps you should learn French. . . ."

CHAPTER SIX

She saw the car as soon as she rounded the corner of Rue Geiler and Rue Herder. A large black SUV with custom tires and front fenders that had been fitted onto its snout to make it look invincible. Was it the same car she had seen a few blocks from the Vaszarys? It was not the kind of car anyone would choose if he did not wish to be seen. That it followed her at a slow jogging pace proved the point. She stopped at the corner of Avenue d'Alsace, stood in front of the bank building where pedestrians waited for the lights to change, and waited for the SUV to catch up. The driver wore a black uniform, hat and visor, and even a striped tie. The back windows were tinted grey. When the car pulled up next to her, the back door opened, and Vladimir Azarov stepped out holding a long-stemmed red rose in one hand and a flute of what looked like champagne in the other.

"Welcome to Strasbourg, Helena," he purred. He was tall, broad-backed, with a stone-carved face, high cheekbones, stark long planes, high forehead, thin lips, and wide-set black eyes. He always had a healthy tan. She had known him for years, never trusted him, but found him interesting in spite of herself. "I had hoped to meet you here and, *mirabile deus*, here you are."

"Hardly a miracle, Vladimir, since you have been following me for three blocks."

"And such a clever disguise; it would deceive most men, but as you know I am not most men, and I am used to your inexhaustible tricks of the trade. I particularly love the glasses. Gucci, I believe."

Helena accepted the champagne. What the hell, it had been a long day, and she rarely refused good champagne. Vladimir would always buy the best. "How did you know I was here?"

"It was difficult to miss you on the news, leaping out of that boat, flying along the shore, such long strides, you have not slacked off your daily runs, have you?" he asked. "Would you care to join me? The Veuve Clicquot is in the car, and we could have a more private discussion. So much catching up to do." Vladimir was one of the less violent Ukrainian oligarchs Helena had encountered appraising Renaissance art, but he was certainly not above some very rough play when he thought it would serve his interests. Rough, in Vladimir's lexicon, ranged from simple broken bones to the more complex assassinations he may have instigated in Kiev.

"I prefer to walk," Helena said, looking at Azarov's driver, who had hauled himself out of the SUV to stand by the open back door. He was a big man. His shoulder and arm muscles stretched the fabric of his black jacket. The bulge at his side was about the size of a Glock, but Helena assumed he would be more likely to carry a Makarov. Despite the frosty relations between Russians and Ukrainians, the latter still preferred Russian manufacturers. "He seems to have recovered nicely from his misadventure in Bucharest."

"A couple of days in the hospital. A few stitches in his right hand. Your friend Marcia is one tough broad. Good thing you didn't bring her along for this little job." Vladimir gestured at the open door. "Will you?"

"I prefer to walk," Helena repeated, and set off across the road toward the river. A couple of pedestrians had stopped to peer into the car until the driver blocked them. About a year ago, Marcia, the former curator of Bucharest Museum's seventeenth- and eighteenth-century art turned fixer-bodyguard, had reduced this driver to a whimpering wreck when he was trying to steal a Titian for his boss.

"You needn't worry about Piotr. He doesn't hold grudges." Vladimir laughed. "FSB grads have unusually thick skins." The FSB, or *Federalnaya Sluzhba Bezopasnosti*, was the Russian Federation's security service, the new iteration of the legendary KGB.

"I thought he was Ukrainian," Helena said.

"Mostly," Vladimir said with a laugh. "He is also a Cossack. They tend not to belong to anyone."

"It isn't him I worry about," Helena said. "You didn't say what brings you to Strasbourg."

Vladimir caught up to her, took her empty glass and tossed it into a recycling bin, broke the stem of the rose and slipped the short end into the buttonhole of his fine linen jacket. "I think we are both here for the same reason. A rare painting that I may be interested in purchasing for my collection. It's not the sort of art I would put in my bedroom, but it could sit nicely alongside my Titian and the Raphael in the study. I told Mrs. Vaszary I wouldn't even crate it, we could drive it down the coast to Montenegro. But I would like to think it's painted by Artemisia herself. As a rule, I don't buy copies or forgeries."

Helena knew of at least one forgery Vladimir had purchased, but neither of them had ever referred to it. She assumed that had he known it was one of Simon's Renoirs, he would have mentioned it when he wanted to buy her expertise the last time. It would have served as excellent leverage. Helena had carefully guarded her flawless reputation from any connection to her father. "You are here to buy the painting," she said.

"Sadly, I am not the only one."

"How many others?" Helena asked.

"You haven't changed your mind about joining me in the car for another glass of champagne?" The SUV was following a few steps behind them, Piotr glowering over the steering wheel. "In that case," Vladimir said to her back, "perhaps we could try a riverside terrace across the way from Saint Joseph Church, in case you missed that lovely landmark on your hurried river tour earlier? You would be guaranteed a large crowd of jolly late-afternoon beer drinkers, so no concerns about being alone with me inside a car."

"That sounds fine," Helena said.

Vladimir led the way into Le Rafiot's shaded entrance and onto the deck facing the river. He ordered two Kronenbourgs on the way in. They sat on benches at a rough wooden table. "This is the local craft beer, made here since the seventeenth century," he said. "I tried to buy the factory in 2015, but they wouldn't sell. I love this city. It's so pleasantly liveable."

"How many other bidders are there for the painting?" she repeated.

"Not sure, but I saw your old friend Grigoriev at the private airport getting out of his Gulfstream, and I think Waclaw is here too. He believes this picture used to be in Poland before the war, but he has no proof. If he had papers to prove it had been there, we would not all be here wanting to buy it. Instead, there would be a battery of lawyers fighting over some ancient estate. The Poles are persistent about the ancient estates of their aristocratic *szlachta* and the priceless valuables that found their way into the hands of the occupying Germans. Remember the Lanckoroński collection? First dismembered with the partition of Poland, then confiscated by Reichsmarschall Göring when the Germans walked into Vienna. Isn't that a beautiful church?" The setting sun coloured the spires gold and amber. The central rose window shone blue and silver.

"Very Gothic," Helena said.

"If you are still here on Saturday evening, you might like to accompany me to the organ recital — one of the largest pipe organs in Europe."

"I have never heard of a Gentileschi in Poland."

"The story goes back a long way. Waclaw thinks it was bought from someone in Naples during the time when there was no Poland."

"Does he have a theory about where it's been since 1945?"

"If he does, he didn't tell me, but he did carry on a bit about the Russians and the Germans. Waclaw Lubomirski is from around Częstochowa, and one of his ancestors was a voivode, a member of the *szlachta*, the highest social class. His family goes back to the fifteenth century. They collected art through the centuries. Memling. Botticelli. There is that famous painting of Warsaw by Canaletto. As you know, Waclaw has been obsessing about stolen art from Poland for decades, and he listed a Gentileschi in an interview about missing art in Polish collections. Gizi has asked you to authenticate the painting. I assume that's why you're here. Have you any idea why the lawyer was killed?"

"No," Helena said. "Did Gizi, as you call her, say anything more about him than that he was hired for her divorce?"

"No, but Magoci had a nasty reputation. He could have been killed for some other reason than his meeting with you. On the other hand, it's possible that one of us wanted him out of the way. Or, more likely, wanted you dead. Your authenticating that painting may not be in everyone's best interest."

"The husband?"

"He, for one, but let's say I am keen to buy it for a good price. If you get involved and insist that it is by a famous artist, the price will go up, so I no longer have a bargain. In fact, your being here could cost me millions of euros, and I may not be happy with that."

"Did you, by any chance, try to have me killed?" Helena asked.

Vladimir laughed. "Would I be sitting here with you if I did? Would I be waiting for you with champagne and flowers?"

"Perhaps," Helena said.

"Would you consider giving me your best guess about the Gentileschi before you tell anyone else? For example, if you gave me just four hours' notice, I would gladly compensate you for your time. You know I am the soul of discretion, no one need know, and I would pay you double Gizi's fee." When Helena didn't reply, he continued, "Okay, make it triple."

The beer was delicious, but she did not feel comfortable sitting out in the open with Vladimir. "Thanks for the drinks," she told him, and started out toward the Quai des Pêcheurs. "I have work to do."

"Just between us, do you think it's a Gentileschi?" Vladimir asked as he rose to his feet.

Helena shrugged. "Too soon to tell."

"For a not insignificant sign of my appreciation, would you keep me informed?"

"Maybe," Helena said. "If you help me find out who killed the lawyer. And why."

CHAPTER SEVEN

Attila was equal parts concerned and pleased with his success in finding Helena. Concerned because if he could find her, others with more resources could also do so; pleased because he could warn her about the police investigation. The scarf, draped over her head and tied under her chin, was a little too colourful for a modest religious woman, and the wraparound sunglasses lent her the film star look. That it was almost dark made the sunglasses unnecessary unless they were a statement by someone famous added to the overall effect of someone who, while not wanting to be recognized, wished to be stared at. With her lithe body and high forehead, she seemed to be flaunting her desire to be mysterious.

He had been nursing an espresso at the outdoor bar facing the Hôtel Cathédrale when he spotted her striding along the square, her backpack dangling casually by one strap, stopping only to check the lineup at the cathedral's special entrance, open only for those planning to attend services. Tonight's was Evensong. There were only four people ahead of her. She waited, said something to the guard at the door, and disappeared into the darkness before Attila had a chance to stop her.

∽∘

Earlier, he had returned to the residence to check that Iván was back. The Vaszarys had been sitting in the blindingly white living room, she on the sofa, he in the armchair, both with large martinis. The only hint of trouble between them was that neither of them had been talking when he entered. He had known few other couples with such a calm approach to their impending divorce. Tonight they seemed to share a taste for vermilion — his three-piece slim-cut suit was paired with a red shirt and matching fob; her form-fitting dress with a slit up the side was also a striking red. All of it looked very expensive, if a bit theatrical. Rumour had it that she liked a French couturier, and he had his suits made by a tailor in Rome. How they could afford such luxuries on government salaries would have been puzzling elsewhere. In Hungary, everyone took it for granted that the European Union's lavish funds were siphoned off for the benefit of the party faithful.

Vaszary's appointment to the Council of Europe had been predictable for a consistently vocal advocate of the government's policies on wall-building at the southern border and ejection (by force if necessary) of all refugees. In his famous Szeged speech, he had suggested that separating children from their parents had proven to work in the United States, where the steady influx of migrants had eased once border guards put children, irrespective of age, into separate concrete holding bins. If the Americans could do it, why not the Hungarians?

Vaszary's career moves had included ordering the imprisonment of illegals who had managed to cross the border, arresting anyone who aided refugees, and fomenting the appearance of a national crisis in order to gain votes for his deeply authoritarian prime minister. Cynics in Budapest's cafés were betting that Vaszary would become the Council of Europe's commissioner for humanitarian aid and crisis management. It would be hilariously appropriate, and an exemplary way for the government to make a joke of the Council of Europe's responsibilities. That position was still open, and the prime minister was strongly urging representatives of other nations to back his choice. The Belgians and the Norwegians were stubbornly opposed.

Attila had never been involved in politics, but he loathed brutality, and he had made unhappy noises about the prisons for refugees. All the more puzzling that he had been chosen to babysit the Vaszarys in Strasbourg.

"How were your meetings in Paris?" Attila asked.

"Better than we had expected," Iván said. "The French don't much like us."

"Are you going out tonight?"

Vaszary shook his head.

"We are expecting guests," Gizella said with a little smile. "No reason not to be civil."

"We won't need you," Iván said. "It's a couple of the Brits who share our enthusiasm for Brussels."

Neither of them had mentioned the dead lawyer.

When Helena came out of the cathedral's exit door, she seemed to have lost her easy stride. In fact, she was limping. Her left arm was extended down her left side, the right arm crossed over her chest, supporting the left, as if she had walked into a door, or been hit hard. He stood up to help, but she shook her head so vigorously she almost dislodged the sunglasses.

She sat very carefully next to him, her back straight, her arm still extended, smiled, and ordered a *coup de champagne* from the passing waiter.

"What's happened?" Attila inquired.

"Other than the incident on the boat, you mean?"

"Of course the . . . incident," he whispered, "but what just happened in the church?"

"The cathedral? Not much. I had to retrieve something."

"But you are hurt," he said.

"Hurt? No. Perplexed."

"That means what?" he asked, exasperated. "You were limping just now. Did someone . . . ?"

"Perplexed means mystified, baffled, bewildered by what happened today. I barely arrive in Strasbourg — for a little job you hired me to do — and a man I am with gets killed; I discover that the painting I am to study is to be sold in three weeks or less; I then run into a very rich Ukrainian I have known who is bidding—"

"Azarov?"

"Of course. He is a collector."

"A criminal who should have an international warrant against him. But Interpol is too chicken to issue one. Perhaps now that they have a Russian at the top, it will be easier to get a warrant out on that man."

"On the other hand, it will be damned near impossible to have any warrants issued for Russians, and Vladimir told me Piotr Grigoriev is also arriving and god knows how many—"

"Vladimir?" Attila's voice rose. "Since when do you call him Vladimir?"

How had Attila become so childishly possessive? "I've always called him Vladimir," Helena said.

"My turn to be perplexed?"

"No. It's your turn to explain what the hell is going on here." Helena drank her champagne in one easy swallow. "But first I have someone to meet inside," she said, tossing €10 on the table then limping into the hotel's entrance.

Attila ordered a draft beer and settled down for a long wait.

Louise was ensconced in one of the hotel's high-backed lobby chairs, her hair held up by a couple of large pearl-tipped pins, her light mauve dress fanned out around her, her feet tucked under her, fully engrossed in her iPad. Despite her actual age of fifty-one, she looked like a child lost in a video game. When she saw Helena, she stood, turned into her businesslike self, handed her the small black plastic case with the usual variety of wigs and passports, gave her a piece of paper with the Vargas research, and suggested, quietly, that since Helena had been photographed on a tour boat with the murder victim, it would be a perfect decision for her to go home to Paris and resume working for Christie's or the Tate, since both had requested her services to confirm that a couple of Renaissance paintings were, in fact, what they seemed. James had obtained a provenance, but he didn't trust it.

"I will call him today," Helena said.

"I had hoped you would," Louise said. "I've also bought you two burner phones at the train station. They're in the bag with the rest of your stuff. Will you be coming home today?"

"Not today."

Louise offered her a small quick smile. "Saw your Hungarian friend outside," she said. "He is not very observant today. Didn't see me walk past him."

Helena suggested Louise stay the night at the Hôtel Cathédrale, but Louise had already booked a room in a B & B closer to the railway station. She had always been frugal. Besides, she planned to return to Paris early the next morning. She had travelled a great deal in her youth, and she was no longer interested in sightseeing. Helena, who was secretive about her own past, never inquired about Louise's, but during the six years that Louise had worked for her, some fragments had emerged. Several were set in India, others in Japan and Australia, Russia and Sweden. She had mentioned a man once — someone who had always brought her flowers. She was efficient, unruffled by whatever happened, and reliable, with no great interest in art except as a means of making a living. When Helena hired her, she had given "secretarial at the Orangerie" as her last job description.

Helena told the receptionist that she was checking out of her hotel, claiming an urgent business matter in Paris. She agreed that there would be no refund on Mrs. Vaszary's deposit, went to her room to change into black leggings, a long chocolate-brown shirt, a short auburn wig with hennaed highlights, and black running shoes. She inserted the Swiss mini into her belt and the knife in its holster up her sleeve. She applied a pinkish layer of Revlon cover-all makeup, orange lipstick, extra-thick eyeliner and mascara, stuffed the rest of her clothes, wigs, and passports into her suitcase, and strolled through the lobby. She was pleased that the receptionist she had spoken to less than two minutes ago gazed at her with interest but no recognition.

She checked into the Régent Petite France as Marianne Lewis, an American tourist who would stay for only a couple of nights, then she would likely take a tour on the Rhine. "I would just love to see the Château du Haut-Koenigsbourg," she said. It was not until she was settled in her pleasant room with a view of a park that she called Christie's. She told James she would accept his offer to come to London in a week and look at the painting their New York office thought was a Raphael, but, meanwhile, could he let her know whether there were some unaccounted-for Artemisia Gentileschi paintings.

"Gentileschi?" James's usually controlled voice rose on the *eschi*. "You have seen one?"

"I am not sure," Helena said. "But there is a chance."

"There is always a chance," James said, his voice giving away the effort it took for him to sound calm. "Not Orazio?"

"Some of her early work was mistaken for Orazio's, but I doubt this one is his. Why?"

"The Getty bought an Orazio for $87 million. Artemisia is worth less. But it could still be good to have one to sell."

"Will you look into it then?"

"What period?" James asked.

"From 1593 on."

"Her whole life? Including her time in Naples?"

"Yes. There are a couple of known paintings from 1612, when she was only about seventeen. This Judith and Holofernes is stylistically advanced, so, if it is hers, I have to assume she had been painting for some years, but I can't be sure, so we need to do a broad sweep. In one of his letters, Orazio claimed that she was already accomplished at age twelve."

"I'll check with Rome, Florence, and Naples," James said, "where we know there are documents about her early work. She was much discussed even then, as you know. Do you want me to have someone go back to the transcripts of the trial?"

Artemisia had been raped by her father's friend, the painter, Agostino Tassi, a fact not disputed by anyone except Tassi and the court. The legal arguments were conventional for that time. The case had been brought by her father in 1611. The charge: deflowering his daughter, thus besmirching his own good name. Artemisia was interrogated, tortured, her fingers tied to a wooden post and twisted. Tassi endured only some polite questioning, but he did have to serve a short time in jail.

"Yes, that could be helpful. It's been a long time since I looked at the transcripts. There might be some clues there. She had been working in Orazio's studio long before the rape," Helena said, "and the trial mentions a dozen paintings to explain why she was in the studio while Orazio was absent. Even if we take Orazio's boasting about her work as a twelve-year-old, I have always assumed that she was painting on her own from before the age of fifteen, I think. Otherwise Orazio would not have hired Tassi to teach her perspective. Why bother if she was not already an artist?"

"Have you seen it yet?"

"Yes."

"And?"

"I need to do some tests."

"But what was your feeling when you saw it?"

"That it's a very arresting work. I can't afford to have feelings about it. Not yet." But James was right. There was always that first impression, even before checking a painting's provenance, or submitting it to analysis. And that feeling about the Vaszarys' painting was that it was authentic.

Helena's next call was to Arte Forense in Rome. She had worked at the Rome laboratories when she was setting up a

Titian show at Vienna's Kunsthistorisches. She had had doubts about a couple of the paintings, but no one had been willing to offend the galleries that had so generously lent their works. Andrea Martinelli at Arte Forense had been the only one willing to run tests for her. Fortunately, only one had turned out to be a forgery. The other had at least been from Titian's studio and finished by his students.

Then, in 2008, they had both attended the United Nations International Conference on Organized Crime at Mont Blanc. A fine skier and eager to get away from the conference's dullest presenters, Andrea had suggested to Helena that they could escape to the mountain, and their collegial relationship grew into a friendship they both valued.

Helena knew that criminals often used art as collateral for arms, drugs, and often money laundering. She knew this might be what had happened to the Judith she was looking at, if Andrea's lab proved the painting's authenticity.

Andrea had once been on the trail of a Caravaggio purloined by a couple of thieves from the Oratorio di San Lorenzo in Palermo, Sicily. The thieves may have been acting on orders from a Cosa Nostra boss. They certainly were not sophisticated. They had cut the canvas away from the heavy frame so they wouldn't have to carry it. The crude hacking would have damaged the painting irreparably, which may be the reason no trace of it has ever been found on the black market, or anywhere else. And the hapless thieves may have incurred sufficient displeasure over the botched job to have been executed by their boss.

Andrea's research and systematic interviews of those arrested for petty crimes in the area — "in some parts of Italy, murder is not a big deal," she had told Helena — had indicated that the painting had been taken out of the country. Possibly used to make peace with the Russian mafia. Helena had been working in the Hermitage at the time, a favoured home for stolen paintings, and Andrea had asked her to keep her eyes and ears open for news of some old masters for sale. Most Russian mobsters didn't hold on to the paintings, selling them on even if they realized only a third or less of their value. Only oligarchs, like Grigoriev, enjoyed collecting art for its own sake or to display their wealth and discernment to anyone who came close enough to matter. Grigoriev kept some of his most valuable pieces in free-port storage, hauled out for special occasions such as his meetings with Saudi arms buyers.

Helena told Andrea that she needed urgent access to the lab. Of course, she would pay the "going rate" for such an extraordinary request, and, of course, she could be there Wednesday morning.

"Is it anyone we know?" Andrea asked.

"It'll wait till I see you," Helena replied.

Louise's Vargas list did not prove to be of much use. A Santa Monica Varga store sold only women's wear; there was a Mexican bakery in Barcelona, offering fresh tacos and tortillas; an ethical fashion store in Berlin but only for women; a couple of grocery stores in San Antonio, Texas — none of them looked right for a men's fine silk–lined overcoat.

She flounced — that was how Marianne Lewis proceeded in the world — back to Attila's table in Cathedral Square after making her new arrangements. Normally, he would not have waited, but he felt guilty about Helena's misfortunes since she had arrived in the city, so he stayed, ordered a plate of wieners and fries, two more beers, and, later, another espresso. When Helena dropped into the seat next to him, he said he was sorry, the seat was taken. To be absolutely sure he was understood, he repeated it in appalling French, and when the red-headed woman still didn't budge, he tried German.

"*J'ai compris, Monsieur*," Helena trilled, "*le deuxième fois*. No need to practise your German," she added in a whisper.

"Helena?" he croaked.

"Try not to look startled," she said. "You would be glad if a pretty woman sat next to you. You're here alone. She is a tourist. What better opportunity for a fling? Don't Hungarians have flings in foreign cities?"

"Perhaps you would like a drink?" Attila asked with forced joviality.

"Perhaps I would like another glass of champagne," Helena said, mimicking his tone.

"How did you . . . ?"

"I won't give away all my secrets," Helena said. "Always best to be cautious. Have you any news on the lawyer? I assume the police still have nothing? Did the lovely Gizella tell you anything?"

Attila shook his head. "Did you get hurt?"

"No."

"In the cathedral. You were limping . . ."

"Ah that," Helena said with a Marianne Lewis titter. "I went in to fetch the bow. I knew where he dropped it, and it seems no one else was interested enough to find it. It's light and only about twenty-five inches long. It fit inside his coat as it did down my side. It has wood handgrips. Looks expensive. The man who used it didn't opt for the bow because he couldn't afford a handgun. Killing with an arrow must have been his preference."

"There could be some prints on the grips?"

"Unlikely. A guy who knows enough to use one of these would also have a pair of the soft leather gloves archers like to wear. I didn't touch the grips. There is always a chance that he was careless. That's why I left the bow at the hotel for you. It's packed in newspaper and addressed to Mr. Tóth."

"Tóth?"

"Thought you'd like that."

"I will take it to the local guys. I am not even sure Tóth would be interested. The last time I spoke with him, I thought the landscape was shifting. And the lead man on the case here has already talked to him. I also find the French police lieutenant much more likeable."

"Unless they live in Paris, the French tend to be more likeable and more polite," Helena said. "Perhaps less corrupt."

"Anything else you can tell me?"

"The shooter left an expensive coat in the cathedral. The label says *Vargas*. If you could find out who or what Vargas is, we may be able to identify the man."

"Where is the coat?"

"I kept it. For now."

Attila thought that meant she didn't quite trust him, but he didn't say so.

Helena told him she would be gone for a day or two, and that she would contact him when she returned. "Meanwhile, could you ask Mrs. Vaszary the name of the man who she says sold them the painting."

"Someone in Budapest, she said."

"About a year ago, and the man was a friend in need of ready cash. She couldn't remember his name. I don't know about you, but I tend to remember my friends' names."

CHAPTER EIGHT

Attila loved the idea that the main police station in Strasbourg was called *Hôtel de Police* — police hotel. Not as grand a name as Budapest's own Police Palace, but cozier. The address on Hébert's card also included the words *Commissariat de Police à Strasbourg à 34 Route de l'Hôpital, 67000 Strasbourg.* It was an imposing, modern white building, with a long white staircase and a parking lot full of police cars. At the top of the stairs some dispirited-looking demonstrators held up a banner with demands to free four people arrested after another "*manifestation.*" They were chanting "*libérez nos camarades,*" lifting the heavy banner to their shoulders, dropping it with a thud, lifting it again, and dropping it. They made no move to hinder Attila as he passed by and entered the glass doors festooned with photographs of the missing. Many of them were months old, fly-splattered, smudged.

When Attila asked at the desk whether Lieutenant Hébert was in, he was rewarded with a broad smile and a vigorous nod by the blonde policewoman. Her attitude and her snug uniform were a pleasant change from the bad-tempered Margit in Budapest. Not that Margit's uniform wasn't snug, it was just snug in the wrong places, whereas this French police uniform fitted its wearer in a way that made Attila wonder if it had been made to measure. The dark blue pants were a perfect fit despite the extra pockets, and the top button on her blue shirt was undone. She picked up the phone and said Attila's name into the receiver, then they both waited.

Hébert arrived with a file under his arm. "In your country," he asked, "people don't bother making appointments? First at Magoci's office, now at mine. I didn't expect to see you again so soon. I assume Mr. Vaszary sent you?" He offered to shake hands.

"Is there some place we could talk?" Attila asked, ignoring the question.

"*D'accord*," Hébert said, and indicated the electronic gate and the x-ray machinery. He watched as Attila unloaded the change from his pockets, his belt, the short-barrelled police-issue handgun, and the long object wrapped in newspaper that came last. "*Intéressant*," Hébert remarked when the wrapping arrived at the other end of the screening process. Then he indicated that Attila should follow him.

The interview room was small, hot, and humid, with opaque glass walls that separated it from the rest of the squad room. There was a table in the middle, four chairs (two on each side), a decanter of water, a small computer, and four glasses. That Hébert brought him here and not to his own office indicated that he was still under suspicion and that their conversation was not going to be private. One of the glass walls was undoubt- edly a one-way mirror. Attila, in his previous life, had conducted interrogations of suspects and witnesses in rooms just like this.

"Do you mind if I record?" Hébert asked, settling into a chair across from where Attila stood.

Nicely done, Attila thought without responding. He placed the newspaper package on the table, unwrapped it carefully to avoid contact with the bow, and stood back from the table.

Hébert looked at it, looked up at Attila, then down again. Then he flicked the switch on the recorder, said his own name and Attila's, and asked with just a hint of a smile: "You are here to confess?"

"Of course not," Attila said. "I came to deliver something that could be of assistance in your investigation. Unless, of course, you have already arrested the killer but didn't want to release the news . . ."

"In this country, we are always grateful for assistance from the public," Hébert said, his eyes on the bow but his hands not touching it. "How did you get this?"

"It was found in the cathedral after the lawyer was killed."

"Found?"

"Yes."

"How *exactement* was it *found*?" Hébert pulled on a pair of plastic gloves and prodded the bow to turn it on its side. "Aluminum," he said. "Light, very expensive."

"Yes, I could see that," Attila said. "What I can't see without the proper equipment is fingerprints. I assume you have some- one here who could dust for prints?"

Hébert called to the mirror for Georges, who appeared a minute later, sweaty and ruddy faced, to pick up the bow with its newspaper wrapping and take it away.

"So, you were in the cathedral saying your prayers and happened to notice a package under your seat, took a closer look, and what a surprise, it happens to be this bow, the one that was perhaps used by the man who perhaps killed our lawyer. Is that right?"

Attila grinned. "Brilliant," he said. "How did you know?"

Hébert affected a well-practised Gallic shrug. *"Ce n'est rien,"* he said. He then opened the large envelope he had been carrying and spread its contents on the table. They were all enlarged photographs of Helena Marsh. A couple of them were a little blurry, but the rest must have been taken by tourists who had brought high-quality cameras or iPads with them on the cruise. One had captured Helena flying over a man sitting nearest the side of the boat and leaping onto the escarpment. Another showed her running full tilt over the bridge, in pursuit of a figure wearing a long beige coat and a grey hat. At the far end of the bridge, she had stopped and looked back, a motion that had been caught by the camera in a photograph that didn't do justice, Attila thought, to the perfect oval of her face, or her green-hazel eyes, but was good enough for identification. If the killer had been aiming at the lawyer, he would know that Helena had pursued him, and he could come after her. If she had been his intended target, he would certainly try again.

She could be in danger. She needed protection. He thought he should bring her to the police station to talk to Hébert. The photographs made it clear that she was not the killer. However, almost as soon as that thought leapt into his mind, he recalled how Helena responded to such admonishments. She believed she was a better judge of her own safety than anyone else, especially a police officer. Unlike the police in civilized countries, she was not hemmed in by regulations.

Perhaps Hébert had read Attila's thoughts because he said, "It's a pity she has not come to us. She would not be a suspect, but a witness. She may be the fastest runner in France, but an arrow is faster, and he may be hunting for her even as we sit here."

"You don't seem to have any photos or CCTV of the killer," Attila said.

Hébert shifted his computer so that Attila could see a very blurry image of the running man, with his long coat, his face mostly obscured by his hat. Once, as he half-turned to look behind him, there was a flash of a flat chin, a thin mouth, but even that could have been exaggerated by the strain. The man was sprinting; his face would express the kind of rictus some runners have when they are moving fast, their muscles pumping adrenalin. Attila's negative opinion of joggers had not improved since he discovered that Helena was one of them.

"Is there a widow Magoci?" Attila asked.

"They were divorced years ago."

"Was she the beneficiary?"

Hébert laughed. "I looked into that. She was not the beneficiary. He left all his money to a daughter who lives in Quebec, in Canada. She is a lawyer. The widow has married again. She seemed sad that Magoci had died, but not too sad. Said they had last spoken two years ago."

Georges came back looking considerably less overheated and proceeded to rattle off a long report that Attila managed to mostly understand. (He'd been practising his English over the past year, not his French.) There were no fingerprints. Win&Win, the manufacturer, was a Korean firm, and the bow would have cost more than €800. It was one of their high-end products. A Wiawis Nano with a recurve riser. Recommended for professionals.

"A professional would need to practise a lot," Hébert said,

switching to English. "It's not a sport you can go easy on. Takes a good eye and steady hands. Know anyone like that?"

Attila shook his head.

"If you happen to hear about someone like that, you would call me?" Hébert asked. "And if you happen to bump into the woman in these photos, you will give her my message: she can't outrun this killer."

Attila gazed at his hands to avoid Hébert's scrutiny. If Hébert thought Helena would agree with that assessment, he couldn't know much about her. That was comforting. If he knew little about her, maybe the killer knew even less.

Hébert, his hand on Attila's shoulder, accompanied him to the exit. When they were standing at the top of the steps, they stopped and faced each other again. "I have heard good things about you and that Titian in Budapest."

"From Tóth?" Attila squawked incredulously. "Lieutenant Tóth?"

"No," Hébert said. "From a Paris *flic* I've known since the academy. He said you had assisted him with a case involving a couple of lads who had been selling protection to shopkeepers in the twelfth arrondissement. Small-time criminals, but they were preying on small shops, immigrants most of them, barely making it in our City of Light. One of the shopkeepers had complained to the police in the twelfth, a busy place that didn't take the time to investigate. There are so many other crimes with higher stakes — you know what I mean."

Attila nodded. Shopkeepers in Budapest had similar problems with complaints to the police.

"*Alors*, this lot set fire to a family's corner store. One of the children happened to be inside. The gang took off for Austria, then Hungary . . ."

"I remember them," Attila said. "They had tried it in Budapest first, offering rewards for compliance. Simple stuff, like not setting your shop on fire. Your Paris *flic*, Jacques?"

"He said you tracked the buggers down, arrested them, and turned them over to his team."

"We like to think we are on the same side," Attila said.

"It so happens your Lieutenant Tóth didn't seem to agree with that sentiment. Lucky for Jacques, he was just a sergeant then. He had no time for the small stuff."

"Still doesn't," Attila said.

"My friend also mentioned something about a friend of yours, a woman who does art appraisals. She is rather unusual for an appraiser."

Attila managed to drain all expression from his face. "Hmm," he said.

"She helped my friend identify a forged Renoir. Well painted, apparently, but not the real thing."

Attila said nothing.

"You are not planning to leave our beautiful city in the next few days?" Hébert asked.

"Not as far as I know. I like it here. Rented a B & B not far from here on Rue des Prés. Small but expensive. Why the next few days?"

"I will have this murder sorted in a few days," Hébert said.

"Hmm," Attila said.

"And a last question," Hébert said, as Attila had started down the steps. "You wouldn't happen to know any Ukrainians?"

Ukrainians. Again. Attila turned and went back up the stairs. "I have met a few. Why?"

"There was one at the Colmar archery range, l'Arc et les Flêches, asking questions. Big guy, speaks lousy French."

"Worse than mine?" Attila asked, and went down again. Damn that grasping, greedy bugger Azarov.

As soon as he was out of the police station's sightlines, he called Helena's office and left a message for Louise. "Please tell your boss that her Ukrainian friend or one of his hirelings is spending time at the bow-and-arrow club in Colmar."

On Rue Geiler, Attila found only Gizella and the dog. "*Csókolom,*" he said. Not that he wished to kiss her hand, even if it was a relief to be able to speak Hungarian again.

Iván had gone to the Council of Europe, and she had planned to go shopping in Place des Halles. He thought she still seemed oddly unconcerned about the murder of her lawyer. "He was the kind of guy who collected enemies," she told him. "Most of his clients were a little shady."

"Why, then, did you hire him?" Attila asked.

"I wanted someone who couldn't be intimidated," she answered. "The wife of the Czech consul recommended him. She had managed to settle for more than twice what her husband had offered the first time; it's what I thought I wanted. You know Iván. . . ."

I don't, Attila thought. Men like Iván would never confide in men like me. "I doubt he would ever hurt you," he said.

Gizella was wearing a short white sheath dress, low cut, with a wide red belt that displayed her figure to its full advantage. She crossed the room in front of Attila, taking small steps on her stiletto heels and swaying a little with the motion. She picked up a white porcelain ashtray (Herendi, Attila thought) and a gold cigarette case from the sideboard and took them to the sofa. When she sat, her dress rode up her thigh. "I smoke when he is out," she told him. "He hates the smell of cigarettes in the house, but now that we are going to be divorced, it doesn't matter." She gently stroked the dog's neck, looking up at Attila.

He was still standing by the door, suddenly nervous. What he didn't need in this assignment was an unwanted flirtation with his client's wife. "How was your meeting with Ms. Marsh?" he asked.

Gizella lifted one shoulder, either suggestively or in an exaggerated mime of bafflement. Or both. "She didn't say much."

"She looked at the painting?"

"Yes, she did, but she gave no opinion." Gizella fitted a long cigarette into a gold holder, lit it, and inhaled, making a moue with her mouth and looking up at Attila as if he were going to audition her for a starring role in a 1950s movie. "Why don't you come in and join me?" She continued to stroke the dog.

Oh! "Did you tell her who sold you the painting?"

"No."

"Why not?"

"She didn't ask."

Attila considered the possibility of sitting down. He was an employee of her husband. Paid for by the Hungarian government, not that that made much difference: he was here to serve Iván Vaszary. A bodyguard. He had already overstepped his responsibilities by recommending Helena to Gizella for a second opinion, and he was only too aware that his interest in asking Helena to come to Strasbourg had underlying reasons, none of them related to either his job or his offer to help Gizella obtain a fair deal in her divorce. There was an old Hungarian poem about not lying to yourself, or being true to yourself, that he recited in his mind as he approached the spacious chair facing the sofa where Gizella had now crossed her legs in a way that displayed her long-muscled thighs to their best advantage.

"Perhaps I could look your friend up when I am in Budapest next week," he said. He perched on one arm of the overstuffed white chair. Uncomfortable, but not yet compromised.

He was desperate for a cigarette.

"If you like," Gizella said, taking a lingering drag. "He lives in the castle district. His name is Biro, I think. I thought you used to smoke."

"I did," Attila said. "Trying to give it up."

As soon as he could, he escaped to the street and pulled the red-and-white package of Helikons out of his pocket. They were, his mother had warned, the deadliest brand of Hungarian cigarettes, certain to reduce his life expectancy by at least ten years, but they tasted great.

CHAPTER NINE

Marianne Lewis drove to Colmar in a rented Renault, a pleasant small car that no one would notice in this pleasant little town not far from Strasbourg, where people could enjoy the feeling of being in the countryside without actually being in the country-side. Colmar seemed to have been built or, more likely, rebuilt as a tourist attraction with half-timbered houses, cobblestone streets, a well-trained, winding little river that offered old-fashioned wooden rowboat rides, bridges with hanging flower baskets, a regular market that sold regular fare you could also buy in supermarkets, and a fancy *relais* with a well-reviewed restaurant, where Helena planned to dine after she signed up for the archery course just outside the town. There was a modest ad for the place in the local paper, touting itself as a histori-cal attraction, since Strasbourg had once been a famous centre for archery. This place, the ad claimed, had been used by knights training for tournaments and for the wars of the fifteenth and sixteenth centuries. Since it was the only archery range in the area, Helena assumed it was the one Attila had alerted her to.

The plaque that marked the range (*Propriété privée, défense d'entrer*, with an appropriate *Danger!* skull-and-crossbones sign) listed a dozen knights who had been here in *les temps anciens. Malhereusement*, its heyday of happy archers had ended when the local governor banned the use of bows and arrows in the town. Helena assumed that order must have followed some very bloody altercations between various lordly factions, but she doubted the directive would have been followed by the more aggressive knights.

Crossbowmen had been an essential component of the French army. Under Charles VII, the longbow was added to their arsenal. It was a somewhat late response to the nauseating rout at Agincourt.

Helena was startled by the tall, spindly man who had been strolling along the weedy path, deep in contemplation of his black-and-tan crossbow. "Too little, too late," she said, in response to the plaque about Agincourt. "They should have had better archers, more longbows, and been a lot less terrified of the English."

The tall man, not so thin on closer inspection, was wearing full leather overalls and some sort of peaked cap that drooped over his forehead. "You do not read signs," he said, also in English. "It says 'private' and 'keep out.'" He crossed his arms, the crossbow dangling from his fingers, and stood facing her.

Helena grinned at him.

"No trespassing," he said.

"I saw that," she said, "but I am not trespassing. I was interested in your course. The *affiche* you pasted on the wall outside the market invites students who wish to study the art of archery and suggests favourable prices, starting with nothing for the first lesson if the student is serious. I am serious."

He relaxed a bit and smiled back at her. "And you are?"

"Marianne," she said.

"As in the girlfriend of Robin Hood."

"*Exactement*," she said, switching to French.

"Philippe," he said. "Why archery and when do you wish to start?"

"Today would be good. But first, can you show me the range? I was not impressed with the one in Picardy."

"Picardy," he repeated, nodding. "So, you have taken a course already."

"I didn't sign up once I saw the range," she said. "No woods. Only rocks and scrub." Thank god for Google.

Philippe led the way, explaining as he went that this area was famous for its woods and wildlife, that his students could put their skills to use hunting hare, deer, and even boar, right here without leaving the range.

There were only three other students, all men. They were profoundly engaged with the mechanics of their bows. They all had upright trays of arrows, long scopes, and leather gloves. Though it was a warm day, they all wore camouflage trousers, shirts, and padded vests. They had been practising on a target about twelve metres from their stand of trees and, by the look of the arrows surrounding the target, it had not been their best day.

Helena nodded appreciatively. "It takes time to learn," she said. "Misha said he had been here a day and was just beginning to understand the best way to address the prey."

"Misha?"

"A man who mentioned coming here."

"What man?" Philippe asked, anxiously.

Helena shrugged. "Met him in the *relais*. I think he left today."

"Oh."

"Never learned his last name."

"*Moi, non plus*," Philippe said, "and he was not interested in taking lessons. He was asking questions about other students we have had here, and he was very . . . nasty. Belligerent. Aggressive. Threatening."

"Other students?" Helena raised her eyebrows in what she hoped was a surprised expression. "Your other students?"

"Yes. It was very unpleasant."

"What other students?" Same wide-eyed expression.

"He was interested in anyone who was good."

"I guess anyone good would not be taking lessons," Helena said.

"Wrong. Everyone needs to practise. No matter how good you are, you have to keep up your skills. And his name wasn't even Misha."

"No?"

"It was Piotr. He drove a large SUV with tinted windows. I knew there was something strange about him as soon as I saw him."

It may have been the large Glock he carried, Helena thought, but she didn't say anything. She shook her head and *hmm*-ed sympathetically.

"And the man who would have interested him was already gone," Philippe said.

"Back to Russia?"

"No. Hungary. He was here for only one day."

"Not long enough, I think." Helena *tsk*ed.

"Long enough for him."

Helena signed up for the archery course, starting the next morning, paid for three lessons in advance, and drove to the restaurant A l'Échevin, where she enjoyed a perfectly prepared breast of duck with champagne sauce, a green salad, and a modest Bordeaux while she read a few pages of her new edition of *The Odyssey*. She had bought the Emily Wilson translation at Shakespeare & Company a few days before. She had always preferred the Robert Graves, but she couldn't remember where she had left it, and the Wilson turned out to be a surprisingly enjoyable rival.

There were two black SUVs in the parking lot, but neither had tinted windows or a familiar licence plate number. After lunch, she inquired of the maître d' about an old friend from Ukraine who had recommended the restaurant.

"Monsieur Azarov?" the maître d' asked with an ingratiating smile. "He has been our guest here *plusieurs fois*."

∽∾

Marianne Lewis took the 6 a.m. flight to Rome, found a women's washroom at the airport, and emerged as Helena. She took a taxi to Via Ripetta near Piazza del Popolo and presented herself at Arte Forense's main reception desk at eight o'clock. It was housed in the rather posh Accademia di Belle Arti di Roma, a former palace, reconstituted as an association of artists and a school of art, all under the Ministero dell'Istruzione, dell'Università e della Ricerca. The minister himself had an office near the central arch, but, as Andrea had told her, he rarely showed up. He preferred his more spacious offices in the Palazzo Chigi, where Italy's cabinet meet.

Andrea's section was in the research area, separated from

the main building by a series of long corridors with video cameras and two security screening machines staffed by two tough-looking, broad-beamed women who carried government-issue firearms stuffed down the outside pockets of their dungarees for easy access. Neither offered even a cursory greeting, and both carefully studied the contents of Helena's pockets and coat as they made their way through the machines. Only one of them patted her down. The other, ignoring Andrea waiting at the other end of security, asked about the nature of her business.

"We've had some problems," Andrea explained. She gave Helena a light hug and two air-kisses. She wore a red linen jacket with rolled-up sleeves, a black knee-length pencil skirt, and red sandals with no stockings. "The Cosa Nostra are sensitive about anyone investigating their major thefts, and they are incensed if they smell a rat in their own cellars."

"I assume you are still on the trail of the nativity with Saints Lorenzo and Francis of Assisi?"

"Never going to give up," Andrea answered with a smile.

She led the way down the corridor to the labs. Her own office — a spacious room with a long light table and several large colour reproductions of paintings on the walls — opened from the labs. It had only one door, fluorescent lights, and no windows. "We wouldn't want anyone to peer over our shoulders," she explained.

"And no escape route," Helena said as she made her way to the most prominent photograph. It was huge — at least six feet by six feet — embossed, with a matte finish, and it seemed to be lit from inside the manger. The Virgin's face, San Lorenzo's almost garishly bright orange cassock, and the overdressed shepherd's legs in the foreground all shone with supernatural glow. "Extraordinary! At first glance, I thought . . ."

"No. But it was made by the same people who produced the replica in the church," Andrea said. "And I don't need an escape route." She patted the left side of her stylishly loose red jacket, where a slight bulge betrayed she was carrying a gun. "However, should the need arise . . . It's best you don't know. You said this is urgent?" Andrea asked with a little crease appearing between her eyebrows, all business.

Helena showed her the photographs she had taken in the Vaszarys' living room, a couple from a distance that showed the overall composition and a dozen close-ups of the figures, the faces, Holofernes's upturned eyes, his gory neck, the spurting blood, Judith's delicate, long-fingered hand, her face turned slightly away from the man's head, the lush drapery of her gown. "I have been hired to determine whether this is a real Artemisia Gentileschi, a copy, or a forgery," she said.

"There's a great deal of interest in her since *Lucretia* was auctioned," Andrea said. "Even more with the National Gallery's retrospective."

"This painting is about four times the size of *Lucretia*."

"It looks like her, doesn't it?" Andrea said. "That tendency she had to put her own face on her heroines' necks. A bit pudgy for our times, but a beauty for the seventeenth century. And that orange with blue dashes and those reds — her colours, I think."

"She had beautiful hands," Andrea said, looking at Judith's bloodied fingers.

"Maybe," Helena said, "but I've always been skeptical of the hands being hers. Remember, her fingers had been bound and twisted when the court tried to extract a confession from her that she had lied about Tassi's rape and that she had lured him into her bed in hopes of marrying him. Tassi and her father's housekeeper both testified that she was offering her body to all comers in exchange for small favours, including hard-to-get paints. The lawyers believed that excruciating pain would induce her to confess that she was a 'harlot,' as Tassi claimed. It hadn't worked. Her hands bled for days. Still, if you're the artist, you can give yourself whatever hands you wish for."

"But I remember a drawing of her hands by another artist. It should be in one of our books. We have a big library in back — but that's not why you came to my lab."

Helena opened the small plastic bags with the three tiny samples she had taken from the painting. "I need your spectroscopic machinery to date these. I'll need it for no more than a couple of hours. I should be able to identify the pigments, the binding agents, the varnish in that time. And I am also interested in the signature. Only one of her names is on the painting, and it is misspelled. Some of her letters to her friend Galileo Galilei attest to her considerable literacy, as you know. So this could be the work of a clever fraudster, someone who tried to overpaint another signature."

One of the two Dutch artists Simon had hired for his forgeries had intentionally created spelling errors in two of his Pietro della Vecchias because the painter had been a notoriously bad speller, illiterate according to a biographer. Simon had been greatly amused by the controversy. But Andrea knew nothing of Simon, and Helena was determined to keep it that way.

"Whatever the conclusion, it is an extraordinary work," Helena said.

"Could you see the brushstrokes?"

"Yes. Not a line wasted. But that does not necessarily mean they were her brushstrokes. Some forgers do magnificent work."

"I assume you are not bringing the painting here?"

"The owner thinks she can sell it with just an unconfirmed opinion."

"Yours?"

"Apparently."

"And, of course, you will be very guarded in what you put in writing?"

"Of course."

Andrea showed Helena to the array of machinery and left to track down the books she had mentioned.

Paint and what has been used to produce it is harder to fake than brushwork. Wolfgang Beltracchi, for example, had boasted once that he could paint anything Vermeer had painted, and no one would be able to tell the difference. He was tripped up by his use of titanium dioxide white, a pigment not available until the 1940s.

In the seventeenth century, most of the pigments used today had not yet been manufactured. To get the ultramarine blue used by artists at that time, you would have had to buy lapis lazuli pebbles — more expensive, then, than gold. Once you had your lapis, you would have to grind it and use a binding agent to turn it into usable paint. Helena had been puzzled about how Artemisia could have afforded the radiant blue in Judith's dress if she painted this in her late teens. Later, once she had become successful, buying lapis would not have been a problem. The yellow and red ochre and the copper resinate were all easy to identify. She could also see a touch of saffron, white lead, and alabaster in the speck she had of Judith's skin tone. And there was the cochineal red she had identified before in a canvas of Caravaggio. Made from cochineal insects found on cacti in Mexico, it is known today as carmine and is more vibrant than the reds some other baroque artists used. Caravaggio had been a contemporary of Orazio and a visitor to his studio. Artemisia might even have been introduced to this red by him. She had certainly used it in some of her known work.

After two hours with Arte Forense's powerful microscopes and chemical scanners, its multispectral imaging and dual-laser Raman spectroscopy, Helena found nothing that indicated pigments not known in Artemisia's time. One puzzle remained unsolved: the signature. While it, too, used contemporary pigments, it was not applied at the same time as the rest of the painting. Its positioning suggested that it had been added some time after the other paints had dried, possibly much later. She would have to study the surface under the signature again.

Andrea had returned with the book she'd been seeking and had been hovering at Helena's elbow for a while, not wanting to interrupt her friend's work but ready to help if needed.

"She used a lot more blues and reds early on than I remembered. This book has some of her letters to the Duke of Alcalá demanding more funds for her paints. I think many assume that she would have been penniless when she left Rome after the trial, hurriedly married off to a third-rate artist she would barely have known." She offered to copy the letters to and from Alcalá. "And look at her hands," she opened the book to a drawing of a very delicate hand with long tapered fingers, holding a thin brush. "It's by Pierre Dumonstier le Neveu. An admirer and perhaps a lover. He certainly put a lot of effort into this drawing."

"You're right, those hands don't look like they had been bent and cut with twine, though that drawing was done at least a decade later if I remember correctly," Helena said.

"Could your painting have been done before the trial?" Andrea asked.

"No. It looks too accomplished for that. But there is a lot of pent-up rage here. Her late works are much less emotional. Perhaps soon after she arrived in Florence."

"Her hands could have healed in a couple of years, and we know she was already presenting her work in Florence two years after she left her father's house in Rome. Or maybe her lover altered her hands to please her."

Andrea suggested Giulio's for lunch. It was close and usually not too crowded with tourists. At least not in October. "During the summer, Rome has become unbearable. One can't even move along Ripetta, and I would never venture onto the Corso."

She led the way to a door at the back of the building, down a narrow street, past a couple of shoe stores, and into a dead-end alley, then back into the light at a small square. The restaurant had an unassuming exterior, but there were fine white table-cloths, waiters with white aprons, and a pleasantly effusive maître d'. He asked how Andrea's parents were, whether her father had finally decided to retire and her mother's famous roses had survived the latest heat. A disadvantage of having one of the old family names in Italy was that everybody thought they knew you, and, indeed, everybody knew just enough about you that they could engage you in cheerful, overly familiar chat-ter. Andrea was old stock, her family related to one of the popes — way back, but in Rome, ancient credentials counted. "My father will never retire," Andrea said. She added for Helena's benefit: "Been too busy for too many years and loves having all those connections. A retired lawyer in his line of law is nobody. No more 'Signore Avvocato' this, 'Signore Avvocato' that . . ."

"Didn't you almost marry a lawyer?" Helena asked.

"Lucky escape." The lawyer had followed her to the confer-ence at Mont Blanc that had cemented Helena's and Andrea's friendship. He had said he missed her too much, couldn't be in Rome without her, not even the food tasted the same when she was gone. In the evenings, he was anxious for her company, seemed eager to learn what had been said and who had said it, so eager that Andrea became concerned. It was Helena, always suspicious of men as handsome as Andrea's lawyer, who had discovered that he had been retained by one of the mafia syndicates to defend a Sicilian boss on murder charges. The chief prosecutor, the *pubblico ministero*, had been one of the conference speakers, and the lawyer was using Andrea as his ticket in.

When they had settled at a corner table, both with their backs to a wall, Helena told her friend about her adventure in Strasbourg and the dead man who had been her initial contact with Gizella Vaszary. When she mentioned Vladimir Azarov, Andrea whistled. "Him again. I had him in my sights last year for the Palermo Caravaggio. He offered to pay our boys what they wanted with maybe a little discount since it's a famous work and impossible to move. This one would be a big score for a man with an oversized ego, but no one owned up to the heist. No one has seen it. I hear Azarov has been buying stuff for his boat in the Adriatic. A couple of old masters and a Giacometti sculpture."

"That was for his new place in London. He has moved some of his art into storage at the Luxembourg airport. I am not sure how good his connections are with Volodymyr Zelensky, the new man in Ukraine's president's office, but I doubt they're strong. For one thing, Azarov was friendly with the previous president, the confections king, and Zelensky had choice words, and no time, for that man on his television program."

"I heard Azarov is selling some of his Russian shares."

"If they let him. Vladimir has always managed to keep his nose out of politics and particularly out of Putin's way. 'No sense tangling with the tiger,' he once told me. 'I am not interested in politics. Only what I can make out of them.'"

"He is a dangerous man," Andrea said, "if you get in his way. But you already know that."

They both ordered the vitello tonnato and the green salad. Then Andrea told Helena about a Rembrandt self-portrait that had been taken from the Borghese Gallery a couple of weeks before. It had not been on display, and no one was sure when it had been stolen, but the Carabinieri's art squad had taken all the employees in for questioning. It turned out that one of the employees had spent a few weeks in Montenegro, working at the seaside restaurant that caters to luxury yachts — like Azarov's.

"Is he still working at the gallery?"

"He's a she, and yes. At least, she was when she was arrested. The alarm bells for me are not just for her time in Montenegro. She's also connected to an artist's studio near Dubrovnik that we believe has turned out some excellent fakes and a few forgeries. On the surface it's just selling local art — very good local art — but that's not all it's doing. Ever come across them? Atelier Bukovar?"

Helena had first heard the name some twenty years ago. Simon, on the phone to a customer in London, had been describing a Van Gogh that would come on the market from a dealer in Dubrovnik. He claimed he could maybe offer a deal on it if his customer was willing to move fast and not ask too many questions. It was Simon at his most charming. His most convincing. Twenty years ago, when Helena thought he was just a family friend.

"Yes," she said quietly, "I believe Scotland Yard's Art and Antiquities Unit had suspected Bukovar in a fraud investigation involving a prestigious London gallery and a client who had decided he had been sold a forgery." Thank god, not one of her father's.

When they said goodbye, Helena promised to let her friend know what she concluded about the Gentileschi. If it was going to be sold, Andrea thought, the Brera should be given a chance to bid. It had risked having a big, splashy Artemisia show before anyone else had thought of it.

On the way back to the airport, using one of her burner phones, Helena called Attila's mobile. She told him she would be back in Strasbourg briefly and she needed to find the man who had sold the painting to the Vaszarys. Then she called Gizella, who was eager to find out more about the painting, so eager she would cancel a dinner date with a friend and wait at home.

CHAPTER TEN

Helena arrived at the Strasbourg-Entzheim airport on a cheap, last minute Air France ticket she had booked online. She was using her Marianne Lewis getup, including the uncomfortably tight wig, but she had left as Marianne, and she didn't want to take any chances with police officers patrolling the airport. She took a taxi to the Vaszarys'. The house was dark, but the outside lights flashed on, and Lucy barked energetically as she approached. A black Mercedes SUV sat two houses away, lights off, two heads in the front seats, both facing the Vaszarys' driveway. Neither moved when she walked toward the entrance, but both of the faces leaned forward in an effort to see her more clearly.

Probably the local police, but just as likely a couple of flunkies working for those eager art buyers who needed to know who the competitors would be.

Hilda opened the door but kept the chain on. It was gratifying that she didn't recognize Helena. She remained unconvinced when Helena said she had been sent by herself. It was Lucy who solved the problem. She inserted her nose into the narrow opening of the door, sniffed, whined, and wagged her tail. "Lucy, *az Isten fáját,*" Hilda said, but she removed the chain and let the rottweiler lick Helena's outstretched hand.

"Mrs. Vaszary is expecting me," Helena said. She removed the wig and shook her hair out.

"Oh," Hilda said.

Gizella, her smile in place, was already in the entrance hall. She wore a mid-calf black dress with a cinched waist and a slit up the side, gold choker necklace, and a dozen gold bracelets that jangled as she offered to shake hands. "You have news for me?" she asked.

"I have done some tests on the samples. They all confirm my initial impression that this is not a recent fake or a copy. I still don't know whether it is painted by Artemisia Gentileschi, but it is certainly of her time — Italian baroque. No recent copier could have matched the contemporary elements in the paints. And why would they? If what they were supplying was a copy, there would have been no need to go to the trouble of recreating the exact paints used. The frame itself dates from the sixteenth century. Now, it would be easy enough to buy an old painting by a second-rate artist and reuse the frame, but why bother if you are making a copy? I would like to take another look at the painting."

Helena followed Gizella into the living room. The lights were dim. A trolley with bottles of wine and liquor stood by the white sofa. Two cocktail glasses. One with amber liquid, the other with something colourless. The glass with the amber liquid had a distinct lipstick stain, the other did not. Since the second glass was not meant for Hilda — she didn't seem to have that kind of relationship with Gizella — there was someone else in the house. Someone, Helena assumed, who had left the room when she arrived, someone who had known to expect her, but who didn't wish to be seen. Not Iván Vaszary; he would not have stayed out of sight. Not the police. Then one of the potential buyers. Vladimir? Grigoriev? Maybe the Pole?

Helena asked for the lights over the painting to be brightened. Even in the soft light, the painting shone, but when the additional lights came on, the severed head actually seemed to bleed. The young woman's face expressed a strange combination of emotions. Rage, revulsion, triumph. Her hand holding Holofernes's head was streaked with blood, strong agile fingers, not like Dumonstier le Neveu's delicate lady's fingers, but the hand of a woman used to hard work. The knuckles were thickened, and a couple of the fingers were slightly bent. The arm itself was slender but muscular, veins throbbing under the pale skin. The maidservant was still leaning on Holofernes's chest, holding him down with all her strength.

Artemisia had boasted that she used a mixture of amber resin and walnut oil mixed in her paints to add shine and translucence. It was a technique she said she had learned from lutemakers; it made the colours glide on. She had studied Caravaggio's startlingly lifelike painting style, his use of ordinary people as models, painting them with all their physical blemishes, their dirty feet, their lack of refinement. The chiaroscuro effect, also learned from Caravaggio, was masterly, yet not as overwhelming as in some of Caravaggio's early work. If the young Artemisia had been taking lessons from her father's infamous friend, she had somehow advanced his style by softening the theatrics.

But Judith's face was a great deal more emotional than anything Caravaggio would have painted during the time he had been a guest at Gentileschi's house. In his early paintings, the women's faces showed no imperfections.

The signature remained a puzzle. It was applied over a dark red surface, a wrinkle in Holofernes's bedsheet, a drop of blood visible to its side and another above, but not under the "Artemesia." She looked closer with her loupe. Nothing to indicate that another name had appeared under this one, but it was possible, as long as it had been done before the paint completely dried.

Helena accepted Gizella's offer of a drink. She noted that the glass that had been there when she arrived was left on the tray.

"Such a relief," Gizella said, raising her glass to Helena. "We have worried that you would agree with my husband that the painting is just a copy. I never believed that. . . ."

"You are jumping to conclusions, Mrs. Vaszary," Helena said. "All I am telling you is that the painting was not made in the nineteenth or the twentieth century, and that if it is a copy, it's most likely by a contemporary of Artemisia Gentileschi's."

"We would like to believe that it's an original," Gizella said. She gestured to someone in the next room. "Your opinion is good enough for us, we think."

"Us?"

"Please be good enough to join us," Gizella said, as she patted the white sofa next to her.

Wearing a black dinner jacket, white dress shirt with long French cuffs, bow tie, and shiny, grey-and-black striped pants, Piotr Denisovich Grigoriev emerged from the shadows of the foyer. *"Rad chova vac videt,"* he said, meaning lovely to see you again, though his tight smile belied his delight. They had not seen each other since that unpleasant meeting in Budapest when

Grigoriev thought he could force Helena to let him buy a painting that belonged to another man. He seemed to have lost more hair in the intervening months. Only little tufts left over the ears; the top was bald.

"I invited Mr. Grigoriev for a viewing," Gizella explained. "You came at the best time, Ms. Marsh. Mr. Grigoriev has expressed some doubt about the painting's — how you say — source. He had met with Iván." As if that explained everything, Helena thought. Iván Vaszary would stick with the story of a late copy because that was good for his divorce settlement.

"Proiskhozhdeniye," Grigoriev said pronouncing each syllable slowly with extra emphasis. "Ms. Marsh can explain." He didn't accept Gizella's invitation to join her on the sofa. He stayed leaning lightly against the doorframe. In contrast to the very black hair on his balding head, his gaping shirt front revealed a few fine grey hairs.

"Provenance," Helena said.

Reverting to Russian, Grigoriev said he had been suspicious that this was another little hoax cooked up by someone looking for a get-rich-quick scheme. Art was perfect for money laundering and those less than scrupulous people in the former satellites had managed to hide any number of pieces when the glorious Soviet army approached their borders. *Vengerski,* meaning Hungarians — stretching his mouth wide, he made the word longer and nastier than it needed to be — had been particularly eager to bury their treasures. Moreover, he said, he was concerned about the killing of the lawyer acting for this pretty little Hungarian lady. What, he asked, could he have known that warranted killing him?

"What is that?" Gizella asked. "What is provenance?"

"The biography of a painting from as early as possible to

as recently as how it landed in your house," Helena explained, though it was fairly obvious that Gizella was not interested "Sometimes," she continued, "there are mentions of an artist working on a particular painting, letters, records of commissions, payments. All that adds up to provide some basis for assessing a painting's authenticity."

"Authenticity?" Gizella poured herself another glass of Scotch and offered Grigoriev another shot of vodka. "It's not Russian," she said, "but Finland makes an excellent substitute, don't you think?"

"No, I don't," Grigoriev said. "Finland makes smoked salmon, and that's about it." He screwed up his face again but accepted his glass from the hovering Hilda. Lucy gave a growl of warning but sat down when Gizella raised her hand.

"She did one of these paintings already," Grigoriev said in Russian, "so why would she do another?"

Helena shrugged. One was at the Capodimonte in Naples, the other at the Uffizi. Like other artists of her time, Artemisia painted the same scenes several times. If a painting was praised and sold, another wealthy collector would want one for himself and commission it. She had painted several versions of Susanna for the Borghese court. Same model. Same scene. But Helena did not owe the Russian any answers. Her client, if she was still her client, may have been in a hurry to sell the painting — although how she could do that without the husband's agreement was a mystery — but Helena did not have to be in a hurry to lend her name to the authentication. And she was not yet sure what this painting was. "Mr. Vaszary would agree to sell the painting and split the proceeds with you now?" she asked.

"I think he would, if the price was right and if he knew that I have had your opinion and an offer in hand. I mean, he could not then still insist that the painting is not worth much." She beamed at Grigoriev.

"I am going to the concert," he said. "We can talk tomorrow." Turning to Helena, he continued in Russian: "I am still your friend, Ms. Marsh," he said, "and I would cut you in on the deal if you are ready to tell me what I am buying. . . ."

Gizella rose from the sofa and hurried to accompany him to the door. "You said you would name your price, Mr. Grigoriev," she said.

"And I will, madam, I will. In the next couple of days . . . all depends on what I believe I am buying. Ms. Marsh, would you like me to drive you back to the hotel?"

"I will stay a while and study the painting," Helena said.

"This authenticity," Gizella began, after Grigoriev's car picked him up, "how do you make it?"

"You don't. You can only find it. I could maybe try if you remembered who sold the painting to your husband."

Gizella went to a box on a table that had not been there the last time Helena visited and opened it to reveal some papers. She started to rummage through the contents. "It has to be here somewhere," she said.

"Perhaps you remember the name of your friend? The one who sold your husband the painting."

Gizella looked up, hesitated for a minute or two, then she said, "You mean Biro? He lives somewhere in Buda. But I doubt he will be able to tell you much."

"Why?"

"Because he got — he bought — this one from someone else. He had it only for a short time before he decided he had to sell."

CHAPTER ELEVEN

Attila had been afraid to postpone his prearranged pickup of the girls. It was as if every delay or change of plans weighed against him on some set of scales that the ex kept in one of her brand new brilliant yellow closets (which matched the yellow brocade cover of what had once been Gustav's favourite chair). It was not as if there had been much more she could do to him, having left his life in tatters, taken the children, the curtains, all their furniture, the bookcases, and some of his favourite books. Her shelves contained a range of classics, from Aristotle to Tolstoy, but Attila doubted that she read them, though she had claimed that the purpose of books was to improve your mind. The dog-eared books in easy reach of her passing hands were about "leaning in," improving your mental retention, and practising extreme yoga.

Judging by her appearance, he figured those fine literary works had improved her body — no sign of those comfortable hips, nor the charming little pouch under her chin she had developed during their marriage. Now she looked like a woman who spent more time on a treadmill than on a sofa, reading. *What the hell, not my problem anymore*, Attila thought as he climbed the two sets of stairs to her swish new apartment and readied himself for the usual critical appraisal of his own body parts when she opened the door.

"Na végre," At last, Bea said, glancing at her expensive watch, though she would have known he was only two minutes late.

"Szia," he said with as friendly a smile as he could conjure. "Looking lovely as ever." That, he thought, should stop her in her tracks. She did, as it happened, look lovely in her tight-waisted blue dress, her matching blue high-heeled shoes with little spaces at front to display her blue-painted toes, and her hair with its frosted ends, swept up over her face. Every bit a woman pleased with her own carefully crafted appearance.

"Hmm," said Bea, and called for the girls.

They had been waiting in the overfurnished living room behind her, their backpacks at the ready, Anna's pencil case dangling from her hand, Sofi's soccer ball under her arm. They approached cautiously at first, not knowing whether there would be another fight. When they saw that their parents were peaceful, they came and hugged Attila and chorused, "Good morning, Apu."

Bea marched into the kitchen past Attila. She managed not to touch him, though it meant having to flatten herself against the wall where the girls' raincoats hung on yellow-painted hooks that blended into the wallpaper. Attila could have stepped aside to leave her room, but he didn't. He was tired of stepping aside for her. He was also tired of feeling like he should be apologizing for something. Even when he was on time. Even the last time when he had brought her flowers to apologize for being half an hour late. Or when he brought the dinner (admittedly, that was not often, but he did bring dinner sometimes). Somewhat like his mother, Bea managed to disapprove of everything about Attila's choice of work. Neither made an effort to hide her disappointment in his lack of financial stability, with no prospects for improvement as time went on. "Unlike other people's," Bea had said, "your career moves are all downward."

His mother used to chime in with, "You could at least have waited till they retired you. That would have given you a steady income. With this," she said when he visited her last week, "whatever it is you do, you can't even afford a reasonable vodka." She preferred Chopin, but only because it was the most expensive choice in Budapest stores. Attila rarely drank vodka, and when he did, he couldn't tell the difference between Chopin and any other brand. But his mother knew. As she seemed to know that the only white wine worth drinking was Olaszrizling and the only men worth knowing were former Party members who had acquired some wealth after the wall came down. At eighty-four, she was still on the lookout for new boyfriends for herself and new ambitions for her son.

"What are we going to do today?" Anna asked as she threw herself into the back of his Škoda. "Not the zoo!" she announced. *Only eleven and already past the zoo stage*, Attila thought. Another year and she would not want to get into a car with dog hair on the dog-slashed plastic seat. Gustav had stripped the back seat of its fuzzy cover and scratched the plastic into unforgiving strips in a vain effort to soften it.

"We could go swimming," Sofi ventured to loud derision from her sister.

Attila drove up Castle Hill to Mátyás Square, parked his Škoda in the Hilton parking lot, and suggested they race down to the Chain Bridge, a plan that had no attractive features other than that they had never done it before, so Anna couldn't say it was boring. It had the singular advantage of being close to where he wanted to look for Adam Biro, the man, Helena said, who sold the painting to the Vaszarys. About halfway down from the recently cleaned and buffed Fisherman's Bastion there was a park with swings, a slide, and, most important, a couple of round trampolines he thought Anna would find tempting. She was good on them. She could do backflips and aerials, and she had recently asserted that she had never been beaten in a bum war.

Biro's address, according to the internet, was 5 Fő Street, a new apartment building with a large courtyard. The architect had made an effort to fit it to the area by adding a couple of disappointing winged stone lions at the entrance and a set of marble steps that led to a heavy wooden door. Attila had left the girls at the playground (Anna was focused on the trampolines, and Sofi didn't care where she was, so long as there were other kids to play with and a slide) and pressed the buzzer for Adam Biro's apartment.

He spoke into the intercom that he was with the police department and had a couple of questions he wanted to ask Biro. *"Semmi komoly,"* nothing serious, he claimed. What with inexplicable arrests in the area since the pocket dictator moved his office here, plus parking indictments and bribe collections, most citizens were entitled to feel suspicious when a police officer rang their bell.

The man who buzzed him in was bald, about eighty, wearing fuzzy slippers and a cardigan over checkered pyjama pants.

Attila flashed his long-expired police ID and explained that he had a few questions about Mr. Biro's friend, Iván Vaszary.

Biro insisted that he knew no one by the name of Vaszary, but he was interested enough in the subject that he came out onto the landing to discuss what kind of painting he was supposed to have sold to the unknown Vaszary and why someone would have named him as the man who would have such a painting to sell.

"Who did you say this Vaszary is?"

Attila hadn't said. "He owns an expensive painting by a woman named Gentileschi that was, I am told, sold to him by you."

Biro shook his head.

"Could be a year ago. Perhaps you have forgotten?"

Biro shook his head again. "It's not the sort of thing I would forget," he said, though Attila assumed at eighty there would be quite a lot of forgotten bits lurking about in a man's brain. "How expensive is it?" Biro asked.

Attila shrugged. "I have no idea, but it's expensive enough they want the police involved." He let that float in the air without an explanation, which was fine, since Biro got the message. To underline the impression, Attila squared his shoulders and affected a menacing look.

Biro shrank back into his doorway. "I know nothing," he said defensively. Though maybe he was just disappointed to be deprived of further interesting conversation. Perhaps he would have been happy to engage in conversation with anyone at all. Maybe no one had talked with him for some years.

Attila said he would be back and returned to the playground. Anna was already waiting for him at the railing, her feet planted, her arms stretched out, practising push-ups. When he was close enough to see her face, he was surprised by how much she now resembled her mother. *"Hol a fenébe voltál?"* she demanded in a tone that was unmistakably her mother's.

"Popped in to see someone," Attila said. "I was gone for only a few minutes."

"Mom runs up and down Gellért Hill in only fifteen minutes," she said. "Flat."

"Good for her," Attila said. "Where is Sofi?"

"Sofi?" Anna asked, looking around casually. "No idea."

He felt that moment of absolute heart thumping, head-buzzing, dry-mouth panic he hadn't felt since four-year-old Anna jumped into the Dohány Street traffic chasing a strange cat. He ran over to the slide. Three small girls starting down the blue plastic tube, a boy emerging from below, a woman holding a toddler stomping about in a sandbox. "I am looking for my daughter," Attila stammered. "She was here about ten minutes ago. . . ."

"Twenty," Anna said. "But who is counting." She had materialized at Attila's elbow.

"She is wearing a pink shirt and a skirt. . . ."Attila tried to regain control of his breathing.

"Green." Anna said.

"A blue parka . . ."

"That one," Anna pointed at a kid's blue parka on a bench.

The woman, her eyes darting from Attila to Anna and back, seemed unsurprisingly confused.

Attila ran to the bench and grabbled the parka. He climbed to the top of the slide, his huge feet slipping on the kid-sized steps, peered down the chute, and, finding nothing — the little girls were again waiting their turn — he straightened and looked around the playground, shouting "Sofi!" again. It was then that he noticed Anna laughing, her shoulders jiggling with the effort to keep it in. No, she would not be laughing like this if . . . And Sofi emerged from behind the trunk of a chestnut tree.

"It wasn't my idea, Apu," she said when Attila landed on his ass near the slide. "It wasn't."

Attila picked her up and hugged her, his back to Anna. He didn't want to let her see the tears in his eyes. "Ice cream at the Ruszwurm," he managed to say, as he grabbed Anna's hand (no protests this time) and, carrying Sofi in the crook of his other arm, began the long ascent to the top of Castle Hill.

∽◯

Helena had watched the slow procession of Attila and his girls but didn't want to intercept them. She had agreed to meet him later and interrupting him while he was practising his paternal duties would be not only unwelcome but awkward. She adjusted her wide sunglasses, pulled her black hoodie over her hair, and took the winding path down to Fő Street.

Adam Biro didn't respond to her persistent buzzing.

She waited under the winged lion, made a reasonable display of texting on her burner phone (it was not connected to the internet), rummaged absent-mindedly in her large bag, and waited until a chatting couple opened the door to let themselves and Helena into the courtyard — a big, paved open space with a few small trees in containers, some boxes of flowers, and a view all the way up to the top floor of the building, with doors opening onto the terraced walkway on each level. While talking and gesticulating excitedly in French, she indicated to the couple with an upraised palm that she was too engaged to find her own key. She continued the pantomime until the couple stepped into the elevator.

She took the steps up to the third floor and rang Adam Biro's bell.

Again, no response.

She waited a few minutes, rang the bell again, and kept ringing it another couple of minutes for emphasis. When that didn't elicit a response, she slipped the knife out of her sleeve and out of its sheath, inserted its point into the lock, and opened the door. She was delighted that it took less than a minute. The last time she had jimmied a lock, she had been worried that she had lost her touch. It had taken too long and left nasty marks on the paintwork. She had been trying to see a painting offered for sale online that had been purloined from a private collection. Fortunately, Toronto's finest had set out to find a couple of young men and ignored the well-dressed woman sipping her juice on a porch. When asked whether she had seen anyone suspicious-looking in the neighbourhood, she was able to tell them that it had been a quiet evening. Rosedale liked quiet evenings.

No one would suspect that she had recovered a stolen Matisse from the lovely Georgian house with its porticoed veranda and crystal chandeliers — no one except the man who had paid the thief and the man for whom she had recovered a special gift.

The hallway was narrow and dark. She stood for a moment, allowing her eyes to adjust to the general gloom of the apartment. She walked slowly into the living room, dank, airless, curtains drawn, tall windows shut. Smell of burnt toast. Bacon. Large pieces of furniture blocking her way, a wide table with something in the middle. She slipped by the chairs and the too-wide sofa, made her way into what had to be a darkened bedroom.

Still no sounds in the apartment. Dogs barking outside but far away. She felt her way along the wall and switched on the light. It was a blue stand-up with an elaborate tasselled lampshade that failed to do justice to the multicoloured woven silk carpet under her feet or to the jumble of drawings crowding the walls. She examined them with her flashlight. There were some precise pen-and-ink nudes, some sombre faces, a few bearded hunched figures, all signed, though she didn't recognize the names. In the corner, surprisingly, a Matisse; two, maybe three Picassos over the bandy nightstand; a long horizontal etching that could have been a Rembrandt; a Renoir with orange ink shading; a Van Gogh sketch of a windmill, and another of a couple at a table with a bottle between them. *What the hell?*

The bed was a jumble of sheets and pillows, with discarded pyjamas on the art deco dresser. Flattened woollen slippers. A half-filled long-stemmed crystal glass on an ornate, perhaps Louis XV, marble-topped commode. She used her scarf to pick up the glass. It smelled of cheap, pungent brandy.

The wardrobe was of the same vintage as the commode. Two doors, curved gilt lines running around them, brass-handled drawers. There were several suits inside, dark blue, dark brown, black, and folded shirts and underwear, all white. One small pair of muddy, black lace-up shoes, worn down heels. Several large lace-up brogues; perhaps two men lived here.

A still damp towel in the bathroom. Gold fixtures, marble tub, bidet.

The living room was overfurnished, as if it were used to store pieces from another, much larger home. A bronze sculpture of a Hindu deity with four arms dancing on an old writing desk that was maybe a Napoleon III. Helena hadn't paid much attention to furniture in her art history classes, but this one did seem to be genuine, even down to the thin line of gold filigree around the edges. The drawer came out reluctantly.

Inside, there were piles of thin paper with long lists of names and dates, an example being "Cardinal Borgia by Velázquez: Prince Rupert II 1788–?, Collection of Liechtenstein 1922–1940, Knoedler Gallery 1940–1957, Colnaghi Gallery 1957–1978, Predelict Gallery 1979–2005 . . ." The next set of sheets set out the history of a harvest scene by Jacob Savery. The first date was 1567. Flicking through, she didn't see one for a Gentileschi, but she assumed there could easily be one somewhere in the apartment.

Paintings of various sizes hung on the walls. She recognized one of Rippl-Rónai's brooding Parisian women, a large canvas by Vladimir Makovsky of a group of depressed-looking peasants, and a lonely figure in vibrant colours signed by Sándor Nagy. Helena assumed the other paintings were also by eastern Europeans, until she saw a small Gauguin self-portrait with a Christ figure in the background, then an unmistakable Luca Giordano, and an unsigned Turner watercolour of a town with a river. She paused for a few moments and stared at the Turner: the lines were almost but not quite perfect, yes, it could be a fake. Maybe even one of Simon's. That would raise questions about some of the others, including the drawings. Simon's Thai artists could produce seemingly authentic watercolours.

Near the door to the surprisingly modest kitchen were unframed canvases leaning against one another.

It was, she thought, inconceivable that the person who had collected all the art in these two rooms would be so careless as to lean unframed paintings one behind the other, their surfaces touching and maybe damaging the paint. It was, however, conceivable that the person who had collected all this art would have had an Artemisia Gentileschi to sell, that the painting now in the Vaszarys' new home in Strasbourg would have come from here. Who is Adam Biro, how did he assemble his art, and, if he could afford all this, why would he share his apartment with another man?

She photographed the two rooms with special attention to art she recognized, then, as quietly as she had entered, she left the apartment, waited a few moments outside the door, then took the stairs down to the courtyard. She found a sunny spot across from the entrance, with a good view of the glass-enclosed elevator, and opened her copy of *The Odyssey*.

Who, her father had said, would suspect someone of a crime when they were reading classical literature?

She waited about half an hour and saw no one press the number three button in the elevator. The sun had dropped behind the building, creating a late afternoon shadow in the courtyard, when a youngish man in cargo pants, black lace-up boots, and an unzipped dark grey hoodie came in, hurried to the stairs, and took them, two at a time, to the third floor. He must have gone to Biro's apartment because he didn't emerge on either side of the elevator shaft. She was thinking about how long she should give him to settle in, pour himself a large drink, and not notice that anyone had been inside, when she heard running footsteps and the now hooded figure appeared in the courtyard again. He looked left, then right, reached for the main door, wrenched it open, and turned down Fő Street toward the Chain Bridge.

She had seen only a part of his face as he scanned the court-yard, but Helena had an art expert's memory for face shapes and eyes. She had no doubt that she had seen this face before, the thin lips in an almost straight line, small narrow eyes: in Strasbourg, on a bridge over the river, and later in the cathedral.

She had been close to the baby oak tree across from the main entrance, her book held high, her own hood over her head, but she thought he had seen her. She had been sitting next to his victim in the tour boat. She had followed him. He had looked right at her in the cathedral before he ran out, leaving his coat and the crossbow. He would recognize her.

She was out the door a minute after it banged shut, but he was already near the bottom of the street. Black Converse shoes running fast. He zigzagged to avoid some pedestrians, leapt into the road, jumped out of the way of a car, got back on the sidewalk, and went straight downhill, the white rims of his shoes flashing as he rounded the corner, left. Helena was also running fast now, her legs pumping to keep up, leaping side-ways to avoid people, then back, as he had done, taking long deep breaths, elbows in, hands curled. She was about forty feet behind him when he skirted the roundabout and started along the sidewalk across the Chain Bridge as Helena bounded out of the way of a bike, then a group of tourists on upright scooters. "*Scheisse!*" one of them shouted as she careened into Helena, arms flailing, feet slipping backwards as she tried to regain her balance. Helena stopped the scooter with her shoulder, grabbed the woman by the waist, and hoisted her back on the two-wheeler, avoiding another collision just as the tour leader called her group to a halt.

The grey hoodie was partway across the bridge before Helena managed to extricate herself from the Germans.

He picked up speed as he reached the end, turned up the quay, sprinted along the Danube embankment, looked back at Helena, and disappeared behind the Number 2 streetcar near the Parliament buildings. He seemed to be pacing the streetcar as it approached the pedestrian island. She waited on the other side of the tracks, where the József Attila statue had stood when she was last in Budapest. She watched the man run up to the uniformed guard and say something to him. They both laughed.

A few minutes later, he walked casually up to the side entrance of the Parliament block and disappeared inside.

Helena shook her hair loose, unzipped her hoodie, and walked to the guard's booth. He was young, pimply, and wearing a too-large uniform and a peaked cap.

"Hello," Helena said with a smile.

"Hullo," he said, also smiling.

"Could I go in here?" she asked.

He continued to smile and pointed over to the long line of tourists waiting at the main entrance.

Helena shook her head. "My friend," she said, "just came in here." She pointed to the side door.

He shook his head. "Only staff," he said.

"Oh." Helena affected a worried look. "He left his credit card on the table where we met, and I want to return it to him."

He shook his head again. "No." He motioned to the other guard at the barrier a few metres away and, when he approached, started talking to him in rapid Hungarian.

This man was older but no more comfortable with English than the first man. "You leave card," he said.

"I don't think so," Helena said rapidly. "Not safe to leave credit cards lying around and especially not safe here with you guys, whom I don't know and will not get to know in the few hours I plan to spend in your country. . . ."

Her fast talk had the desired effect. They both nodded, as if in agreement, although neither of them understood what she had said. "I will phone," she added, still smiling, as she turned to saunter across Kossuth Square. She crossed the streetcar tracks, jumped over the orange railing, and walked across to the Ministry of Agriculture's imposing colonnade. The two guards were still smiling and watching. Good to know that her ass still had that effect on men.

She stepped behind one of the columns and watched as the younger guard reached for his phone, dialled, and they all waited for the thin-lipped man to appear. Helena checked her watch. He appeared in less than two minutes. His office, if he had one, would have to be at this end of the building, and on the ground floor, or close to it.

CHAPTER TWELVE

The tour of the Hungarian Parliament building was scheduled for 4 p.m. Helena bought her ticket at the Balassi Street ticket booth, returned to the square, and bent over the rose-filled flower bed near Lajos Kossuth's large bronze statue, sniffed the petals appreciatively, and planted her knife next to the nearest rose bush. The tour would take about forty-five minutes, and tourists had eight languages to choose from. Helena picked French because there was a large, boisterous French-speaking group from one of the cruise ships, and she expected the guide would be busy keeping them under control. A few of them had already expressed a desire to find a toilet but did not want to lose their places in line. They were confident there would be toilets inside.

After a long introductory speech — well-rehearsed but in appalling French — about the Gothic revival architecture, the façade, the central dome, the statues of Hungarian and

Transylvanian leaders, military figures, and coats of arms, the guide led the way past the ornate gates and the two bored-looking stone lions into the wide entrance.

They shuffled through the security check and up the red-carpeted grand staircase. "*Le piste à splendour,*" the guide announced, and when all the tourists laughed, she changed it to "*La route de splendour,*" but it was too late: "*piste*" had reminded some of them of their bodily needs. Still, they managed to look at the hundreds of small statues and heroic frescoes along the walls with due appreciation and made it to the magnificently Gothic, red-carpeted Dome Hall. There everyone circled the bejewelled gold double crown under its glass dome and its two immobile uniformed guards. There were other, less grandiose guards around the walls and near the exits. After a requisite time of open-mouthed admiration (the French could always be moved by jewellery), the group proceeded to the Old Upper House Hall with more statuary, ornate tapestries, and fewer guards.

Two of the French women began to grouse about the lack of toilets, and when five more joined the loud demands for a pee break, the guide acceded and said she would take them to the nearest washroom while everyone else waited. There were five elegant red-and-gold settees along the corridor, and they would be allowed to sit while they waited. It was Helena's chance to slip through a door leading to the back of the building. Her problem was that, as the guide said, there were 691 rooms, 10 courtyards, and 29 staircases. There were also 27 gates or entrances. She calculated that most of them would not be used and the one that interested her would be two floors down and close to the Danube. If she kept the Kossuth Square–side windows to her left, she would likely arrive at her destination before someone noticed her absence. Since the representatives' hall was lower than the hall open to the public, she had to go down one of the numerous staircases or take the elevator. The advantage, she thought, of the elevator was that no one would expect an intruder to take an elevator. What she needed was a file folder or a stack of papers. She found both on an unguarded table. All the papers were tourist information sheets, and the folder contained lists of booked tours for the next day.

She shoved them under her arm and pushed the down button for the elevator. It opened on a man with an equally large stack of papers. He said something but, luckily, it didn't sound like a question. Helena nodded agreement, and they descended the rest of the way in silence.

It took her ten minutes to arrive at the building's entrance that the man she had followed from Biro's had used. She could see the guard booth through the leaded window. The guard at the door seemed less focused on his job than on the men at the tourist entrance, and she assumed he would be much more interested in those entering than those leaving. In any event, she gave him one of her friendliest smiles and went up the short staircase just past him. She hurried up a flight of stairs, officiously and in close imitation of how the man would have moved when he arrived an hour ago.

Two minutes later, she arrived at a corridor with a series of doors leading off in both directions. Three of them displayed thin metal signs with names. She used her cellphone to take photos of the nearest of them: two to the left, one to the right. All of them had "Dr." before their names — a wonderful middle European prefix to indicate that the individual was of considerable importance. None of the doctors she had met in the east had medical degrees, though a couple of them in Poland had offered to examine her.

She checked her watch, retraced her steps, and took the stairs two at a time, to estimate how long it took her. She descended and tried one more time to make sure her estimate of his timing was right: just under two minutes. That was how long it had taken the man to get down these stairs, out the security door, and over to the guard booth. She was satisfied that he would have come out of one of these offices. She dumped her stack of brochures on a windowsill, hurried down to the entrance, waved and smiled at the guard again, called out a cheery *"Szia,"* and left.

Outside, the pimply-faced guard in the small booth looked at her, surprised but not in the least concerned. She waved again and jumped over the streetcar tracks and the barrier, made it to Alkotmány Street and ran down Honvéd Street to Szabadság Square, where there was usually a crowd to be lost in. At the far end of the square some people with placards shouted something about liberty — a nice touch, since the translation of the square's name was liberty. She pulled up her hoodie and joined them.

She waited an hour, allowing for plenty of time for her group of tourists to leave the parliament building. Still no police siren and no one in pursuit. The French guide had not noticed her absence.

It was almost dusk when she returned to Kossuth Square to smell the roses again.

CHAPTER THIRTEEN

It was not a long walk downhill from the Ruszwurm to Tibor Szelley's remarkably pretty condominium on the Buda side of the Danube, but Attila didn't like to leave his elderly car in the Castle area in the late afternoon when the Romanian thugs started to worry about their stolen car quotas. Attila had arrested two of their mob bosses when he was still with the police, but, as it turned out, they were not prosecuted. Back then, the castle elite loved getting deals on Mercs. And back then, the Romanians would never have lifted a Škoda of any vintage. Now, Czech-made Škodas were becoming collectibles since the factory moved to India as part of Volkswagen's "rationalization" program.

Tibor shared the apartment with his mother and two white, long-haired Persian cats with a tendency to wind themselves around visitors' legs and shed. Attila was a dog lover, but he tolerated the cats because Tibor was his oldest friend and Tibor's mother plied Attila with J&B and strudel when he visited. Fortunately, in addition to the strudel, she was rarely without a tempting round of Ruszwurm Dobos torte, and Anna and Sofi loved Dobos torte as much as they loved the cats. Otherwise, after their adventure at the park, it would have been a challenge to bring them here. There had been a long lineup at the Ruszwurm with no hope of getting a table in less than half an hour.

Tibor had always been Attila's most reliable source of inside information. He had been blessed with a grandfather who was proud of his occupation as a bus conductor, his Party membership, and his ability to get Tibor's father a pleasant desk job and his grandson the best education that the "workers' paradise" could offer. As a result, Tibor spoke four languages (none of them well), excelled at maths, and made a smooth transition to the post-Communist world as a banker. He had maintained exemplary connections in the Gothic castle.

On the other hand, Attila's grandfather's pre-war occupation as a shoe factory owner proved to be a challenge in the nasty 1950s. That the factory was still turning out quality waterproof boots for the Hungarian army did not help. When the Communist government nationalized the factory and installed a politically acceptable manager, the new boots were no longer waterproof and tended to fall apart after only a few days' use, so the factory closed. Attila's grandfather had found work as a sheep wrangler. He had not been very good at it, but no one else was either because the experienced sheep wranglers had been relocated to work in factories.

Being classified as bourgeois counted against the entire family, so Attila's father found work in a leather goods factory as a machinist, and Attila could make it only to a vocational school, ideal for future factory workers. Had it not been for Tibor, Attila would not have been accepted into the police academy.

Tibor was waiting for them on the landing. He looked much younger than Attila — "all those years of healthy living," he had told Attila. As usual, he wore a cashmere sweater and light wool pants, his idea of loungewear. Entertaining guests on the landing was his opportunity to smoke one of his heavily scented Turkish cigarettes. His mother admonished him for smoking in the apartment unless he was smoking menthols, and Tibor hated menthols.

He hugged the girls and shooed them in to talk with the cats and try the Dobos torte in the kitchen. "An unexpected pleasure," he said to Attila. "Does this mean you are cancelling our afternoon at the Király?" They met most Fridays at Király Bath for Scotch, chess, and a soak in the warm pool.

"No. We'll still have lots to talk about tomorrow," Attila said. "Just a simple bit of information today."

"No information is ever simple," Tibor said, offering Attila a cigarette and the second glass of J&B he had carried out in anticipation of his friend's arrival.

Attila accepted the refill but declined the offer of cigarettes. He hated Tibor's scented cigarettes almost as much as he disliked Alexander's Sobranies. Attila had met Alexander shortly after he was first posted at the Russian embassy. They had developed a bantering friendship over Hungarian sausages, pálinka, and tracking ruble launderers. Over the years, they had shared a few investigations, mutual suspicions, and family secrets but never each other's cigarettes. "I'm trying to give up," Attila said. At least that was true. He had been trying to smoke less since he had started spending time with Helena again. "A man called Adam Biro. Lives on Fő Street in the Castle District. You know him?"

"Biro?"

"Yes."

"I think I may have met him. Why?"

"Is he some sort of art collector?"

"Not that I know. He was only a minor functionary with the ruling party. Why?"

"Do you know which ministry?"

"Industry and Commerce, maybe. And again, why?"

"The guy I'm assigned to in Strasbourg bought a painting from him that could be worth billions of forints. Maybe even millions of euros."

Tibor whistled appreciatively. "Who is the artist?"

"Some famous seventeenth century painter called Artemisia Gentileschi."

"If the guy you work for is Vaszary, he is very tight with the current kleptocratic ruling party, and very, very tight with our ruler-in-chief, all of which would be useful if you wanted to serve our great bastion of Christianity at the Council of Europe or, for that matter, any other appointed office our nation offers to those who are close to the centre of power. In other words, if he says Biro sold him a painting, Biro did, for sure, sell him a painting. We mere mortals should not be asking questions about such things. At least, not if we want to keep our heads below the parapet."

"Well, that is precisely the problem with this whole thing, Tibor. Vaszary says the painting is a copy. His wife says it's the original, and they are in the middle of a divorce. She wants her share of what the painting would sell for."

"Didn't you say just now that you worked for him?"

Attila took a cigarette from Tibor's well-thumbed package. Without his Helikons and given the direction Tibor's words were heading, Turkish was better than nothing. "I do," he said. "But I saw no harm in helping her on the side when she asked me to find her an expert to look at the painting."

"You did."

"I did."

"As I recall, you have just such an expert in your small circle of acquaintances."

"By happy coincidence," Attila said with a grin, "and she seems to like the painting for a Gentileschi. She was doing some tests on the paint and the canvas or whatever else people like her do at times like this. Meanwhile, she wanted to know more about the guy who sold it to the Vaszarys. That's why I went to see Biro."

Tibor examined Attila's face for that telltale squint he remembered from their school days, the look his friend had every time he was in some trouble with the teachers, usually at least once a day when he lied about fighting in the corridors or breaking a window, or locking someone in the boys' toilets. "What aren't you telling me?" he now asked.

Attila told him about the dead lawyer in Strasbourg and the local police's interest in Helena, and that he had gone to see Biro an hour or so ago, but the little guy wouldn't invite him into the apartment, despite Attila's flashing his old police ID, and that Biro denied he had sold Vaszary a painting. Any sort of painting, let alone a valuable one.

Tibor scratched his short-cropped grey hair, drank a bit of his J&B, and suggested they extinguish their cigarettes and sit down in the living room. "Your simple little inquiry has grown into something quite complicated, and I prefer to deal with complicated matters when I am sitting down," he said. "Besides, my mother would be delighted to see you. There is no accounting for taste."

Tibor's mother had turned on the lights and stood gazing out at the Danube, while Anna and Sofi played hide-and-seek with the cats.

"She has quite outgrown the company of young children," Tibor said, "and much of her hearing, which can be a blessing when we have young visitors. *Anyu*," he shouted, "look who has decided to grace us with his company?"

Tibor's mother turned away from the floor-to-ceiling windows and the view of the setting sun dancing red and orange on the waves and on the shiny façades of the hotels on the Pest side. "It's so beautiful," she said with a sigh. "I never tire of the view. It is always good to see you." She offered her soft, powdered cheek for a kiss and led the way into the faux-French-decorated living room with its gilt, chintz, and velvet cushioned chairs that would have made Tibor's grandfather, the former bus conductor, sneeze and make nasty remarks about bourgeois pretensions.

Tibor's mother hurried into the kitchen for the cherry strudel, her gold-rimmed plates, and the silver Attila knew she used only for special guests. Now, with fewer visitors, even the children counted as special guests. Attila didn't have the heart to tell her they didn't like cherry strudel, only apple strudel (they had already finished the Dobos), and took a very large helping for himself to make up for his children's lack of good taste. "They loved the strudel," he said, thinking they probably fed their servings to the cats but, with a bit of luck, Mrs. Szelley would not have noticed.

Attila's phone rang. "Good afternoon, Mr. Vaszary," he said.

"Not, as it happens, a very good afternoon, Attila," Vaszary said. "Where are you?"

"In Budapest."

"Why?"

"I had to check in with police headquarters," Attila said as cheerfully as he could manage. "Back tomorrow. Early."

"And it seems you had a little errand to run," Vaszary said.

"What errand?"

"You went to see someone about our painting."

"Yes." No point denying it. Biro must have called Vaszary as soon as Attila left him.

"An errand, then, for my wife, wouldn't you say? And you don't work for my wife. I was led to believe that you work for me. Or is that not the case?" His voice was cool, level, controlled. "Did you not understand that?"

"I thought—"

"You were not paid to think, Attila. You were paid to be my bodyguard, in the event that I needed guarding, and so far I haven't, but now that I do, you are not here. Not only are you not here, you are running an errand for my wife. My wife, whom I am divorcing! You went to see a man at an apartment on Fő Street. That is the errand you were on?"

"Yes."

"You went there to ask about the painting."

"Yes. But he told me nothing."

"You didn't go into this apartment?"

"No."

"But you questioned him."

"He says he didn't sell you the painting."

Vaszary was silent for so long, Attila thought he had disconnected. "You will be in my office tomorrow at nine. Sharp," Vaszary said at last, and now he did disconnect.

"Shit," Attila said.

"Can we go soon?" Sofi asked from under the Louis XVI-style giltwood settee. One of the cats was testing his claws on the embroidered upholstery above her head.

"Right after I finish Mrs. Szelley's delicious—"

"Biro," Tibor interrupted over his second J&B. "You said he was a little guy. Exactly how little did you mean? Or were you just using the diminutive to imply that he was unimportant, a negligible presence, that sort of thing?"

"No," Attila said. "I meant he is a small person. A short man. You know . . . up to my shoulder maybe. Old. He wore his pyjamas and an old sweater. Slippers. Almost bald. Bit of hair on the back of his skull. Wrinkled. Rimless glasses. He had to peer up at me when we talked. I thought he would be concerned about a police visit, but he wasn't. Even when I tried to—"

"Biro."

"Adam Biro."

Tibor stood up and paced to the window. "Adam Biro would be about 190 centimetres tall. A big guy. Maybe sixty. White hair, ruddy face, big belly."

"Biro is thin and small."

"And he died about six months ago."

CHAPTER FOURTEEN

Helena had not planned to stay overnight in Budapest. But then she had not planned to see the killer from Strasbourg here, at Biro's apartment. And now that she had seen him and he had probably seen her, she needed to understand the connections.

Having seen Adam Biro's apartment, his sale of a valuable painting made sense. He was, obviously, some sort of dealer. That he didn't appear on the list of accredited art dealers in Budapest didn't mean anything other than that he disliked paying taxes. No one likes paying taxes. There were hundreds of unregistered dealers all over Europe and the United States. Her father had kept in touch with many of them and had he not burnt his record book, she could have checked for Biro. "I don't need it any longer," he had told her. "I will give up the business." But of course, he hadn't given up the business. Had he done so, he may have stayed alive a little longer.

One of the many bits of information he had thrust on her was that unregistered dealers still kept reasonable records of what they bought and sold. Being unregistered would demand an even greater scrutiny of provenance. Her father had been not only a master purveyor of fake art, but also a brilliant creator of long, entirely credible fake provenances.

When she saw Biro's apartment, Helena was sure he would have kept the necessary papers — real or not — for all the art he had sold. But who was he?

She called James. He was more excited than usual to hear from her. "The Gentileschi . . ." he started.

"Don't jump to conclusions yet," she said. "But we know there are at least a dozen Judith and Holofernes paintings by Artemisia, documented in letters and notes, but never found. Only two are in known collections. The Duke of Alcalá had written to the King of Spain about one he had acquired in Naples. He had planned to give it to the King of England in an effort to appease him. He described it as a large canvas with lifelike figures. It has not surfaced in any museums we know of. There may have been another one in the Pighetti collection."

"None of the paintings she did in England have surfaced yet, though we know from her letters that she was busy with commissions. Can you send me a photo?"

"Could you please see if you can find an unlicensed dealer in Budapest by the name of Adam Biro?" she asked, ignoring his request. "I will call you again tomorrow. Don't want to stay here any longer than I have to." Helena had not mentioned where that was. James would, naturally, assume she was still in Strasbourg and that suited her fine. She didn't exactly distrust him, but past experience told her that his chief driving force was recognition, closely followed by money. A Gentileschi sale could bring both. The auction house had dealt with Azarov and Grigoriev in the past and, wishing to insert himself into a big sale, he could well be tempted to reveal something she had said.

She needed a place to hole up for a couple of nights while she tried to figure out who the man in the hoodie was and why he had killed the lawyer. Was he working alone, or had he been hired for the job? If he had been hired, by whom? On the way to Attila's apartment building, she checked into the Astoria. It was far from the best hotels in the city, and she thought no one would look for her there. She signed in as Marianne, and prepaid the room, that being all the proof of good intentions that the hotel required to hand her a key. She slipped the knife into its sheath and up her sleeve. She didn't bother to unpack.

She left a voicemail for Attila on his cellphone: "Please head home." She left no callback number since she was now using her other burner phone. She bought a bag of groceries — bags of groceries were always a good disguise — and walked along Rákóczi Avenue, a grittier part of the city where tourists rarely ventured and the gentrification that had overtaken much of the downtown core had not yet mounted an offensive. The building where Attila lived still had some leftover bullet holes from the Hungarian Revolution of 1956, or perhaps from the war.

No one paid attention to her opening the outside door with the point of a knife poking out of her sleeve. The long passageway to the wrought-iron elevator was dark, damp, and stank of stale cabbage and dog shit. Helena took the stairs to the apartment, settled on the top stair with the grocery bag next to her, and waited.

She could have opened his door in less than a minute, but she thought that would be overly intrusive, and, while their unusual relationship would give her the licence to intrude, the idea offended her sense of propriety. When she was last here, she had shared Attila's bed with him and his long-haired dachshund. At first, she hadn't noticed the dog at the end of the bed, or the books piled in the corners, the boxes full of dishes, the yellowing curtains, the torn-up couch, his clothes strewn over every surface. The next morning it began to bother her. She had found it all too unkempt, too redolent of disappointment. "Detritus of a recent divorce," he had explained. An evening that had been romantic, their frantic lovemaking the night before, seemed slightly embarrassing in the morning, her sleeping among the leftovers of his marriage.

Attila and his two daughters arrived shortly before eight. Laughing and yelling, the girls raced each other up the steps, and ground to a sudden halt when they saw Helena. "Hello," the smaller one said in English, panting from the exertion of trying to beat her sister.

The older one studied Helena suspiciously, her mouth turned down, her cheeks flushed, before she said "*Szia*" and edged past the grocery bag to reach the door to Attila's apartment. It had been about a year since she had last seen Helena. Chocolate ice cream with whipped cream at the Four Seasons while their father talked with Helena. Anna hadn't liked the way her father was looking at her.

"You have grown," Helena said, and continued to sit on the stairs as Attila, dishevelled, panting even more than his daughter, came into view. "I hope you don't mind my visiting," she said. "I called to tell you I happened to be in Budapest."

"Hey," he said when he recovered his breath. "I didn't expect you . . ."

"I didn't expect me either. But there was an art dealer I had to see. . . ."

"Biro?"

"The same."

"That's crazy. I went to see him."

"I know," she said, "but I need information from him that you wouldn't know how to get. Or what to look for when you found it."

Attila told her that Biro, according to his impeccable source, was dead, and that the man she had met couldn't have been Biro.

"I didn't meet anyone in the apartment," she said, "but I did look around, and whoever the guy is, whether he is alive or dead, he is, or was, an art dealer. He had paintings, drawings, some sculpture, all helter-skelter, not well stored, in fact not stored at all, out in the open, displayed like he had been in the process of selling everything. Not a collector: they are much more careful with what they have. This man was not careful. It may not even be all his own stuff. He is perhaps someone else's agent. And yes, it's quite possible he sold the painting to the Vaszarys. He may even have a provenance somewhere. I didn't stay long enough to find out. How long has he been dead? And who lives in his apartment now?"

"He's been dead about six months, and I have no idea who lives in the apartment," Attila said. "Yet. But I will find out. I actually met the guy. Would you like to join me and the girls for some supper? I have salami, sausage and bread, and peppers."

"I don't think so," Helena said.

"My place looks so much better than it did a year ago. . . ."

Helena laughed. "I believe you. And I have tomatoes, grapes, croissants, and some sort of chocolate dessert, very Hungarian. I will leave it for you and the girls. I can't stay. I came only to find out about Biro and a couple of people in your parliament."

"Not my parliament," Attila grumbled. "Hasn't been my parliament for a few years, and I very much doubt it will ever be mine again. My guys do not get elected. Who do you want to know about?" He started rummaging through her bag, looking for the tomatoes. "They would be great in a salad," he said. "You really have to stay. If you don't like the salami, I could make you Hungarian eggs, with cheese, paprika, and green peppers. I have become quite the cook since you were here last."

"Árpád Magyar, Géza Németh. Maybe Zoltán Nagy." These were names from the doorplates Helena had photographed in the parliament buildings.

"Why would you be interested in these guys? As far as I know they are not art collectors."

"Perhaps not," Helena said, biting into a croissant from her bag. "But they may have an interest in Gizella Vaszary's lawyer or in the painting I was hired to assess. I followed a man from Biro's apartment all the way to the parliament buildings. Watched him go in at the official entrance. I am fairly sure he went into one of these offices."

"You tracked him," Attila said. "How did you get into the building?"

"It was astonishingly easy," Helena said, "for a well-guarded place."

"And you picked these three names? How?"

"Five doors on that floor but only three doorplates with 'doctor.' I assumed the other two names were assistants."

"Secretaries," Attila laughed. "We're old-fashioned around here. No one calls his secretary an assistant."

"Anything you can tell me about the doctors?"

Attila sat on the step next to Helena. "Depends on what you want to know. They are all ruling party stalwarts. Magyar has been with the pocket dictator since the day he decided that democracy was bad for the people, that they were too ignorant to be trusted with it. He is the justice minister now, but he has had a smorgasbord of other portfolios. Deputy prime minister, foreign minister. Doesn't much matter. He is not in charge of anything, the pocket dictator is. Magyar has issued statements backing every one of the government's dictums. He is not a stupid man; he knows how to benefit personally from such unwavering loyalty. A journalist, working for the last vestiges of our long-gone free press, reported that Magyar now owns a large piece of real estate in — of all places — Canada. Isn't that where you are from?"

"Born there," Helena said. "But why 'of all places'?"

"My intelligence source told me that in Canada, the supervision of who buys land and with what kind of money has been absent for years. Banks don't ask questions. Sellers also don't ask, and there is a lot of real estate for sale at the right price. Big country."

"What about Németh?"

"He is known as the Parrot, reliably repeating whatever he is told by our supreme leader. Used to be a long-haired hippy, but he has shortened his hair and maybe his ambitions. He used to represent us in Brussels; now he owns a bunch of media companies and is in charge of communications on the side. He has avoided being seen as a competitor to our blessed dictator. He is the one most likely to come out with Christian religious guff, though he would know it's all bullshit. This regime is not interested in religion, except for its possible influence on Hungarians."

"And Nagy?"

"More of a dark horse. Industry and commerce portfolio. He rarely makes statements. Elected a couple of years ago. He had been flirting with the far right until then. It's fairly obvious he was offered a lot of forints — or, more likely, euros — to abandon Jobbik. No one knows how much, but it was enough for him to send his sons to school in Germany. He is also not the arty type."

"*Apu!*" Anna stood in the doorway, arms akimbo, legs apart, face set in an expression of grim forbearance. "*Mi lett a vacsora-val?*" What happened with dinner?

Helena pulled out of her bag a drawing she had made of the killer's face. "Does this look like the man in the Strasbourg police photo?" she asked.

"I think so," Attila said. "But they didn't get much of him. The hat, the coat collar . . ."

"Any luck with Vargas?"

"Not yet."

"Apu!"

"*Mindjar,*" In a minute, Attila said. "Are you sure you won't join us?" he asked Helena.

"Not tonight. I have work to do."

Then, suddenly aware of how abrupt she had been, Helena turned on the first landing. "Could I take you out to dinner tomorrow?"

"In Strasbourg?"

"Wherever."

Helena went downstairs as Gustav ran up, ears flapping, tongue hanging out, grinning with excitement, short legs pumping, tail held high ready to wag but only when he saw Attila and the girls. He gave Helena a wide berth.

CHAPTER FIFTEEN

All three of the men she was interested in lived in Rózsadomb, a green, leafy area of the city with houses far enough apart to guarantee privacy. Since Rózsadomb meant "rose hill," Helena was not surprised to see gardens full of rose bushes even now, in early October. A few dark red late-blooming roses and clusters of pink climbers were braving the chill of the evening. She wore her black jogging pants and T-shirt, her black running shoes, a bandana around her auburn Marianne wig, and earbuds — the perfect outfit for a late evening run, and exactly the sort of look that would not attract attention in a part of the city where joggers would enjoy the challenge of an uphill climb.

The Magyar residence, a three-storey art nouveau wonder with large semi-oval windows, was protected by a dense, high laurel hedge, a uniformed guard, and a wrought-iron gate. The garage door was closed, but the lights were on outside, and there were small cameras attached to the trees near the garage. The guard was on his cellphone. He paid no attention to another late evening jogger. Helena bent over, hands on her knees, hair falling forward, and panted. The guard looked at her, looked away as he kept listening on his phone, looked at her again, said something into his phone, and started to stroll toward her. Helena panted.

"*Jó napot,*" the guard said.

"*Nem beszélek magyarul,*" I don't speak Hungarian, Helena said. "English?" she asked breathily.

"Okay," he said, scratching his balls with his phone.

"It's a longer run than I thought," she whispered.

He nodded, said something to his phone, and clipped it to his belt. "You want something?" he asked.

Helena straightened up and took a good look at the house behind the guard. "What a beautiful house," she said. "Wow!"

"Villa," he said. "1900."

"Must be stunning in the daytime."

"Stunning?"

"It would be great to see the colours. Yellow?"

"And red."

She edged around him for a closer look. "Anybody home?"

"Mr. Magyar came home. Yes." He moved to block her way. "You can't go closer."

"Oh," she said. "Mr. Magyar must be very rich." She giggled.

"Yes." The guard was young, face still erupting in spots, nose florid, prominent Adam's apple on a very thin neck, ears sticking out under his cap. "He works for the government. Where are you from?"

"Australia," she said.

"If you come back tomorrow morning, I could maybe show you the villa. It's on the tours for foreigners."

"Thank you," she said, "What time?"

"Oh, around nine. He is flying to Strasbourg early tomorrow. Where are you staying?"

"Hotel," she said and pointed downhill. There was sure to be a hotel in this area. "I'll be here, and thank you." Then, as if it were an afterthought, "How about Mrs. Magyar? Won't she be here?"

"No. She is gone."

"Well, then . . ." she waved as she ran up the hill.

Németh's house was one street away, an odd-shaped white building — flat roof, cupola, tall, thin windows — that glowed in the dark. It was surrounded by a low hedge, some naked statues, more oakleaf hydrangea bushes with late-blooming flowers, a water-feature with running water she could hear and, amazingly, frogs. There was no guard, but the entrance gate was high, and there were cameras mounted on the lamppost across the street. The gate was open and a silver Mercedes sat outside the two-car garage. Someone must have just arrived or was about to leave.

Judging by the angle of the cameras, Helena could see that only the entrance and garage area were under surveillance. She took off the pink bandana, pulled a black scarf over her head, hiding her hair and most of her face, climbed over the fence, landed safely on the other side, and lay still near the pond. No alarm, no shouts, no sirens. She rose and padded softly to the house, flat against the wall, and looked in the first-storey window. Only one small lamp cast an orange light on a lot of heavy furniture, some frames on the walls. She watched as a man came into the room, looked around, and grabbed a briefcase from a table.

His face was briefly lit up by the lamp. He had put on some weight around the jowls since his internet portrait was taken, but there was no doubt this was Géza Németh. He opened his briefcase, decided he needed something else, turned, shouted, and waited. A slim-waisted woman appeared with something that looked like a pack of cigarettes, handed it to him, and kissed him on the mouth.

Helena had seen what she could and crept back toward the fence. If the archer was here, he would have to be hiding upstairs. Highly unlikely, given the hour and that Németh was leaving the house. Still, she waited until he had left. The woman stood still inside. Helena pocketed the black scarf, pulled on her pink bandana and left to check out the third residence.

Nagy lived lower down the hill in a more modest two-storey house half-hidden behind some poplars and nondescript evergreen shrubs. Even in the dark with no lights on, Helena could see that it would have been a fine addition to Rosedale, the Toronto neighbourhood where she had grown up. The stone fence was more decorative than effective. A BMW was parked on the street, and a man was sitting in the driver's seat reading. On closer inspection, the driver turned out to have a round face, low forehead, dark-rimmed half-glasses, a wide nose, thick eyebrows, and stubby fingers that hovered over his iPhone.

Helena knocked on the window and prepared her most disarming smile. It took the man a full minute to look up, and a bit longer to register that Helena was not whomever he had been expecting. *"Igen?"* he said, as he wound his window down.

"French?" Helena asked.

"Okay," he said, lowering his window all the way down. He noted her outfit, tried to see her face under the bandana, as she stepped sideways, out of the streetlamp's light and used her move to encourage him to look up, where she could see his face. It was not Nagy. And not the archer. His features were too thick, mouth too fleshy, cheekbones too high.

"Je viens voir Monsieur Nagy," she said with a heavy American accent.

"Il n'est pas . . . là," the man said with an even heavier Russian accent, pointing at the house.

"N'est pas à la maison? Mais ç'est terriblement gênant," she said very quickly and went on even faster to detail how inconvenient it was because she had a message that couldn't wait, and she wouldn't be able to come back later this evening or even tomorrow or any time, really, as far as she could tell because, for God's sake, she had to go back to Strasbourg.

As soon as she said "Strasbourg," he opened the door of the car and, emerging slowly, switched to English. "I didn't understand," he said fairly clearly with an overlay of Russian. "What did you say?"

"When?" Helena asked.

"Just now, what you said," he repeated. He had planted his feet on either side of hers and looked at her with some interest.

"About Monsieur Nagy?"

"Yes." He was becoming impatient.

Helena offered him another of her disarming smiles. "You are not Hungarian," she said.

"No. What you want with Mr. Nagy?"

"His boss — my boss — wanted to talk with him about his visit to Strasbourg."

"Who?" He shouted. "Who you work for?" There was no mistaking his tone or the bulge on the side of his jacket, but his right hand was still on the car door and his left still held the phone he had been perusing when she arrived. There were advantages to his feet straddling hers, including the obvious one: he had not yet begun to think that she was a threat.

"Mr. Magyar," she said. Judging by Attila's information about the three men, she picked Magyar as the most senior, whose name would mean something to a man in front of Nagy's house.

"And what else did you say about Nagy?" He pronounced "Nagy" with a *zh*, the Russian way: "Nazh."

"I said he was going to Strasbourg," she said with one last attempt at a sweet smile. "Tomorrow?"

The man shook his head, a gesture that reminded Helena of a dog shaking off excess water.

"He had a visit from a friend today in his office."

The man tensed. "Who are you?" he demanded.

"I am also wondering why in hell a nice guy like Nagy would need a big gorilla of a Russian thug sitting in his car, guarding his doorway," she said.

Now he reached for his holster, but not nearly fast enough. Helena shoved her knee into his groin and chopped at his left arm with her own left, and as his iPhone dropped, she positioned her knife at his throat, grabbed his gun with her right hand, and started to pull it from its holster as he lunged at her with his shoulder. A good move, but too slow. She sidestepped and let him belly flop to the ground, his gun now in her hand. She landed on his back, pulled up his head — no easy task, the man had the neck of a bull — and repositioned her knife just under his chin. It would certainly kill him if he moved.

He didn't.

"*Charoshij malchik,*" Good boy, she said.

"*Yebat tebya,*" Fuck you, he said.

'No, it's fuck you, really," she continued in Russian. "You're the one on the ground with no gun, and I am the one with your gun and a knife. Now, tell me who are you working for?"

"Nagy," he whispered.

She pushed the knife in a millimetre, just so he would feel it and worry, but not enough to draw blood. Not yet.

"Why you ask?"

"You have a silencer on the gun," she said. "A Soratnik, they are not easy to buy. FSB?"

"No," he said.

"What do you want with Nagy?"

"*Yebat tebya,*" he repeated.

She now pushed the knife in another millimetre so it would draw blood, and he would be aware of it dripping into his collar. "Wrong answer," she said.

A dog was walking with its owner along the far side of the street, maybe a couple of houses away. The owner was whistling something from *La Traviata*, and the dog was beginning to sense that there was something interesting across the street. She could hear his sniffing. The man stopped whistling to tell him to stop.

"You're out of time," Helena whispered.

"I was FSB," he said. "Not now."

"We can both get up slowly and stand by your car," she whispered. "Do not grab for the gun, or I will shoot you. What do you say?" For the first time in years, she felt grateful to her father for insisting she learn Russian and, less unusually, to her mother for insisting she take mixed martial arts classes.

"*Da,*" the man said. "Okay." She stood over him with his gun pointed at his belly as he began to stand, first his arms straightened, then both legs hopped into a crouch, and he was up, facing her knife now lowered to his abdomen, tip out, ready to plunge.

He held his hands palms up. "I am working for someone who wants to know this man's movements," he said in Russian.

"Right," Helena said. "And you sit in front of the man's house, where he and everyone else can see you. Try again."

The whistling man and his dog had passed. Remarkable lack of curiosity here about people behaving strangely.

"Complicated."

"Try me."

"I am working for Nagy and for someone else as well. That's all I can tell you."

"What do you know about this man?" Helena asked. She shoved the knife, handle first, into her sleeve and pulled her sketch of the archer from her back pocket and held it up to the light, without taking her eyes off the Russian.

"Nitchevo," he said. Nothing.

She eased the knife out from her sleeve and nudged the blade under his breastbone. His breathing didn't change. The man was a professional.

"Does he work for Nagy?"

"Ne znayu." I don't know.

"For Magyar?"

"Ne znayu," he said, his breathing a little quicker. His upheld hands shivered.

"Don't," Helena commanded. "Don't even think about it." As she pushed the blade in deeper, its point hit something hard and glanced off the man's chest. He took his chance and brought his hands down on her arm hard enough to have broken it had she resisted, but she let her arms drop and jumped back as he reached for her. She brought up his gun, pushed it into his face. No protective vest there. He hesitated for a moment too long before he reached for the gun with both hands. She hit down his hands with the knife, a fast chop that almost dislodged it, but not quite. It was pointed down, away from her chest. Suddenly, he was shouting loud enough that it almost drowned the sound of his gun going off into his own groin.

"Shit," Helena said as the man dropped sideways onto the asphalt, his hands scrabbling for his groin, his mouth open, wheezing, his shoulders shaking, a keening sound from deep in his throat. "Stupid, stupid, stupid," she said. "I am sorry. There was no need for that."

She took his iPhone from where it had fallen and placed it next to his writhing body. "So you can call for help."

CHAPTER SIXTEEN

The girls were willing to spend the evening with Gustav, watching old American movies on Attila's too small, too old TV. They enjoyed tucking into his and Helena's grocery items. The only offering they disdained was the carrots. "We have enough of those at home," Sofi said. "Carrots and cauliflower and celery. Very good for you," she added in a perfect imitation of their mother's instructional voice.

Anna made a disgusted face when Attila went to the balcony and lit one of his Helikons, but she refrained from repeating her mother's comments about Attila's smoking habits. During the first few months of their marriage, Bea had pretended to like the smell of his tobacco, but a couple of years later, she had started to cough every time he reached for a cigarette. Although he had not smoked in the apartment for some time, when she moved out, she listed the Helikons as one of Attila's more objectionable traits.

The girls spent the night in his bed, while he shared the couch with the happily farting Gustav. Hungarian salami was not ideal for a dachshund's digestive system.

Bea was still asleep when he delivered the girls to their apartment the next morning. He used their need to change out of their Sunday clothes to explain the early morning drop-off. He didn't want to mention that he had to catch the eight o'clock flight to Strasbourg or lose his job. Amazing that even after all this time separated from his wife, he was still anxious not to offend her by displaying concern for his job — concern that she thought ridiculous because he should never have become a private detective. Not that she had ever been pleased with his previous profession, but at least it was steady work. She had rarely mentioned to her friends that her husband was a police officer and tended to agree with his mother that policing was underpaid, ill-defined menial labour with few vacations and even fewer perks. The past twenty years of state-sponsored kleptocracy had offered thousands of opportunities for the men ("Yes, men! But not you!") with the right connections, and Attila had failed to take advantage of even those that had dropped into his lap. Now, Anna's jaundiced view of Bea's current boyfriend suggested that he was more enterprising but less likeable. "A lawyer," she said, making the word *ügyvéd* feel slimy, "with all the 'right connections'" (imitating her mother's tone of voice). "And, what's even more important, a very nice car."

Had there been more time for such discussions, Attila would have told his daughter that the reason her parents no longer lived together was not just her father's inability to make more money, or to buy a better car, or make the right connections, it had had more to do with having outgrown each other. Whatever had been the basis of their relationship was now foreign territory for both of them. Even their conversations were stilted, each word weighed before it was allowed to slip out. When he saw Bea, he felt like he was looking at a stranger, a lovely stranger but certainly not the woman he had lain in bed with every night for eleven years.

Perhaps there would be time for that conversation when Anna was older.

He barely made his flight and knew he would be late for his command performance at Vaszary's office, but he felt calm enough about the prospect that he didn't rush the security process and didn't run up the long staircase to his Council of Europe offices. Despite his usual abusiveness, there had been something about Tóth's demeanour that suggested Attila would not be fired. Whoever had insisted that he be sent to Strasbourg was interested in keeping him there. Otherwise, Tóth would have relieved him of the job already for not answering his phone or for any other spurious reason that occurred to him. In hindsight, whoever it was must have some serious clout. Tóth on his own would not have chosen him for something as cushy as Strasbourg. So, why did he?

Vaszary's offices were on the third floor. His secretary, a Mrs. Gilbert, occupied the small area overlooking a waiting room with grey fake-leather (faux, Bea would have said) seating for five. Only one of the seats was occupied, and its occupant seemed only half here, his ass hanging over the edge of the soft cushion, his feet neatly arranged in front, a folder held up with both hands, as if he were preparing to present it to someone or to run away. He was either smiling or his face had settled into a nervous rictus, it was impossible to tell.

Though there was no need because Mrs. Gilbert knew very well who he was, Attila introduced himself and asked whether the ambassador was already in. It was past ten o'clock. He had been ordered to be here at nine, but, he explained, the plane had been delayed. He didn't say that he had every reason to expect he would be kept waiting. Vaszary liked to show his displeasure in whatever small ways were available to him, and this time he had good reason to be displeased.

Vaszary came through the door with a stack of files balanced on both arms, his briefcase on top, his tie askew, his jacket open, and a big smile on his face. He dumped the files and briefcase on Mrs. Gilbert's desk and continued to smile as he opened his arms to the nervous visitor.

"Zbigniew," he said, much too loudly for such a small space. "I hope I didn't keep you waiting. A big day for both of our nations. I do hope your ambassador will be in the great hall for the address. Such an important — no, vital — address on the major issues that affect us both. . . ." He grabbed Zbigniew and hugged him with such enthusiasm, the smaller man and his folder collapsed against his chest. "We must. We absolutely must show them that solidarity — our solidarity, much like your historic *Solidarność* — will stand for the principles that have been our guiding stars since, well, since forever." He was speaking English with a fine Hungarian accent. He let Zbigniew escape from his embrace, but he was still holding the smaller man's shoulder with one hand and kept thumping him on the back with the other. "Middle Europe," he continued at increasing decibels, "still counts! No! It counts again, after being ignored for decades while Brussels meddled in our internal affairs, after their edicts aimed at destroying our independence, our security, our national independence, yes . . ."

"I was here to talk about today. . . ." Zbigniew said, or tried to say, but his words were half-buried in Vaszary's loud enthusiasm.

"Yes, yes," Vaszary said. "We are all here, preparing for the moment. My chief is ready. I know Slovakia is waiting for us to begin, and the Czechs are — should be — ready. Poland will be by our side. . . ."

"It is with great respect . . ." Zbignew tried again.

"As it has always been, our two noble nations facing east and west, two great bulwarks of Christianity against the hordes . . ."

Zbignew managed to extricate himself from Vaszary, tried to straighten his squashed folder, and stepped back. "There is a problem," he said.

"No problem we cannot solve. Together."

"My minister has been called back to Warsaw," Zbignew said. "He will not be at the Assembly today."

Vaszary was, for a moment, lost for words. It was only the briefest pause, but it offered an opportunity for the door to the inner office to open and another man — grey-haired, square-set, jowly — to enter the conversation. "We have counted on Poland's support," he said. "We are joined in our fight against the vermin now directly invading our countries, directed by Brussels, ready to destroy our Christian identity."

"It was unavoidable," Zbignew said.

"No," thundered Árpád Magyar, the jowly man whose many portfolios had included minister of justice, but who was now most likely still the deputy prime minister. He was in the habit of making portentous announcements. "It is not yet unavoidable. Please tell him I had planned to talk about our battles against the Turkish hordes and Bem, your great Polish general—"

"He is back in Warsaw," Zbignew said more forcefully. "He has been recalled. We are reassessing our approach to the European Union. Our party leader must consider all the implications. I am sorry. Personally, I am sorry . . ."

There was a moment of silence, then Magyar returned to Vaszary's office, banging the door shut behind him. Vaszary, with one sidelong glance at Attila, followed, leaving Zbignew, Attila, and Mrs. Gilbert to look a little embarrassed and, at least in Zbignew's case, to beat a hasty retreat. Attila stood up and raised an eyebrow at Mrs. Gilbert. She shook her head. He sat down again.

Ten minutes later, Vaszary returned. He glared at Attila. "You were late again," he said.

"Flights from Budapest . . ." Attila said, lifting his shoulders in a universal sign of helplessness.

"You will go to the police station and see captain Hébert and find out what the *fene* he wants with me. I have no time for him today. You will explain to him that this is the most important day for our country. He will understand. You will return here at one." Much less effusive in Hungarian, Attila thought as he gratefully bounced down the steps and out the glass (bullet-proof, for sure) doors.

∽◦

Helena wore the blue dress she had purchased in Rome. It was modest but slinky, swishing about her knees as she walked. She had combed her Marianne Lewis hair forward into bangs to cover the lines on her forehead, made up her eyes to seem larger and her lips to seem fuller. She used the light blue contact lenses and shaded her eyelids just enough to indicate that she had taken trouble over her appearance. Maybe she wasn't young enough to be of serious interest to the acned guard, but she could pass for a youngish, adventurous Australian, out for a good time in Budapest.

He was talking on his cellphone when her taxi drew up to the house. She waved at him even before she paid her fare. He stuck his phone into a pocket and made a great show of sauntering toward her. He must have watched a few too many westerns. Belt low on his narrow hips, the small handgun dangling in its leather holster, his ears even more prominent than last night (did he get a haircut?), but his grin was welcoming. "You are back," he shouted eagerly. "I thought you wouldn't after what happened here last night."

"What happened?" Helena asked.

"The shooting. Not far from here. A man was shot in his . . ." he stopped and blushed. "He is in hospital. You didn't hear anything?"

"No. Maybe it was after I went back to the hotel. These hills . . ."

"Come," he said. "We see the house now."

It was even more beautiful than she had imagined it would be. Painted yellow in front, with red outlines around the windows and above the doors, the lines running along the sides of the house and coming down to the edge of the garden. Brick on the side. Part Bauhaus, part art nouveau, it appeared to have been lifted out of a rich Viennese neighbourhood and dropped here. There were two small towers, one above the front door, a second above the garden entrance, and an elegant nude statue by the pool.

"Imre," the guard said, and offered his hand.

"Marianne," Helena said. "It's magnificent."

He unlocked the pale wooden front door and ushered her inside to a spacious, rusty pink living area with a winding yellow staircase leading up to the second floor, evergreens in maroon planters, a Persian rug under the grand piano, uncomfortable art nouveau chairs, and two tall paintings that looked like Rothko. Her father used to commission Rothkos like this and had gained the support of a dozen so-called experts who had been willing to swear to their authenticity. The buyers had not bothered with their own forensic analysis. She was not an expert on Rothko, but these two paintings, while beautiful, did not look right. Close up, she could see that the signature was all wrong. It seemed to have been traced, but she couldn't risk looking too closely. "These are lovely," she said. "The colours are fabulous. Must be very expensive."

"Mr. Magyar bought them to fit with the colours of the walls. Please don't touch them!" he yelled as she approached one of them.

"Wow!" Deep ochre, orange, and yellow, blending into one another at their soft edges, a white centre that seemed bruised or weeping.

"He bought them last year," Imre said.

"Here?" With no effort at all, Helena managed to sound awed.

"Yes. I helped him bring them home."

"Amazing," she said.

"Yes. We packed them into bubble plastic, and I wound more paper around them. They were very heavy to get downstairs."

"Downstairs?"

"From an apartment on Fő Street with an elevator that was too small. "

"No one else helped? Doesn't this man have a bunch of people working for him?"

"Yes, but they are all official. At the ministry. And the woman who cooks and the other who cleans."

Had they been real, these two paintings would be worth more than the Gentileschi, Helena thought. Simon had sold one of his fake Rothkos to a Dutch museum. It had been a devil of a job, he had complained to Annelise afterwards. Rothko had never discussed his methods or how he mixed his paints, so they were flying blind, trying to capture that elusive Rothko "emotional truth." The $4 million Simon received had to be split with the artists and some of the rest went for the special paints.

There were several framed photographs on the wall next to the staircase, and they continued up the stairs. All black and white, they were official shots, the participants staring at the viewer with the fixed expressions people wore when they had been asked to pose. Most of them were men in suits; some posed in front of the parliament building. Magyar displayed the same fixed smile he used for his official portraits. In all of them, the central figure was a square-built man with short hair, a little shorter than the rest.

"Our first minister," Imre said. "Mr. Magyar is a friend of his," he added with pride. "He comes here sometimes."

Apart from Magyar, the only person Helena recognized in the photos was Gizella Vaszary, and she stood next to Magyar, close but not too close, and in one photo she was looking up at him with an expression of sheer delight. Everyone else was staring into the camera.

CHAPTER SEVENTEEN

The young woman at the Strasbourg police headquarters who had smiled at him the last time gave him an even friendlier smile and waved him through the security machinery with barely a glance at his old police-issue handgun. *"Hongrois?"* she asked.

"Oui."

Attila was pondering how to ask in very polite French whether she happened to be free for dinner, but Hébert's arrival spared him the likely rejection. Just as well, Attila thought, he had more than enough trouble already managing his odd relationship with Helena. *"Désolé, mon ami, mais il n'y a aucun espoir là,"* he said as he took Attila by the arm and steered him toward the far end of the station.

"Pardon?"

"I said there is no hope there for you, my friend," Hébert said, switching to English. "She is happily married." He led the way through the phalanx of police desks and computer screens, the familiar sounds of camaraderie, the low murmurs of sharing bits of information, the stale smell of sweaty uniforms and day-old coffee. For some reason, this felt more like home than the Police Palace in Budapest.

As if he had sensed what Attila was thinking, Hébert said, "Tóth," as he opened the door to his office. Not the interview room this time, Attila noted. He may be off the list of suspects. "He is not very *charmant*, is he?"

"No," Attila agreed.

Attila's phone started buzzing. Budapest Police Headquarters. He didn't answer.

"He called. *Actuellement*, someone in his office who speaks a bit of French and more English called and talked to me while he shouted next to the phone. Must think we are deaf here in Strasbourg." Hébert indicated a chair to the side of his own desk — not facing the desk, Attila noted — and said he would bring some coffee. "It's not great but *potable*," he said.

There was a corkboard pinned to the wall on the other side of Hébert's desk. Crime scene photographs of the bridge over the river marking the place where the shooter had been, the tour boat, marking the victim's seat and the seat next to his, fuzzy pictures of the shooter running along the bridge, then the quay, the door of the cathedral and a side street near a hat shop, then some CCTV stills of a man with a long overcoat flying around his legs as he ran, and slightly clearer photos of Helena also running. In one photo, the man was seen entering the cathedral with Helena closing in. That was where he had turned, and the camera had picked up the lower part of his face. Helena's drawing was better. For one thing, in her drawing he was shown to have a low forehead and deep-set eyes.

His phone buzzed again, stopped, then started to buzz some more. Tóth. He had never been very patient. Back when he was Attila's sergeant, he favoured quick resolutions, even when that meant beating witnesses into saying they had seen stuff he thought they ought to have seen to suit his own theories of who was guilty. He liked shortcuts. He also liked incentives to walk away from cases and, less often, to charge people with offences they had clearly not committed. It would be good to know what Tóth had been offered to send Attila to Strasbourg. And why.

Hébert's desk was covered with stacks of papers and files, used paper napkins, cardboard cups, a range of pens in different colours, notebooks, a wind-up penguin, and two small grey elephants.

"Tóth was agitated that we had asked to interview your Monsieur Vaszary concerning Magoci's murder. And Vaszary's receptionist called yesterday to tell me to expect you at around nine thirty." Hébert made a production of checking his watch, handed Attila the coffee, and sat down carefully so as not to spill his own.

"When did you talk with Tóth?"

"This morning. He said you were coming back to Strasbourg today. He also reminded me that your Representative at the Council of Europe — and that would be Mr. Vaszary — has diplomatic immunity. As if I needed to be reminded. As if he needed immunity. And that made me think why."

"Why?"

"Why your police think Vaszary needs some sort of protection."

"What did you say to Vaszary?" Attila asked.

"Not much. Asked him if he could maybe come in to answer a few questions about Magoci. Since he knew the man."

"He did?"

"Does that surprise you?"

"Well . . . a little . . ." Attila said.

"When I met you at Magoci's office a couple of days ago, you said you were there for Vaszary, didn't you say that?"

"Yes," Attila said cautiously.

"I suspected you were not telling the truth. It turned out you were."

"I was what?"

"You were telling the truth. Vaszary had hired Magoci. What we want to find out is why."

"He did?" Attila asked. "Iván Vaszary?"

"*Merde!* Is there another?"

"Another?"

"Another Vaszary," Hébert said slowly, carefully pronouncing every syllable. "Is it your hearing? Or you have a problem with my English?"

Attila shook his head. "It's just that I thought Magoci was working for Mrs. Vaszary."

"As I remember, you didn't know he was working for Madame or Monsieur. You said," he flicked open his notebook, "*exactement*, 'Monsieur Vaszary had hoped to hire Monsieur Magoci on a private matter. Not strictly embassy business. He asked me to find out if Mr. Magoci would be interested.' And at that time, as we now know, Magoci had already been working for your man for six weeks. He met with Mr. Vaszary the day after he arrived in Strasbourg. *De plus*, he wrote to Magoci two weeks before then and suggested the matter should be discussed here but not in the office. He suggested a time and a place for the meeting."

"Did they meet?" Attila asked.

"*Je ne sais pas.* There is nothing else in the file. Mademoiselle Audet has been very helpful in finding this one sheet of paper, but she didn't know what happened next, only that Magoci was killed. Now," he leaned forward, his arms on his desk, his face close to Attila's. He was still smiling but only with his mouth. His eyes were serious, a look Attila knew. In every interrogation there was a moment when the good cop routine switched, and it was usually the time the suspect decided to reveal something he had managed to keep hidden.

"Time for the truth, then," Attila said. "I lied when I went to Magoci's office."

"*Evidemment.*"

"Truth is, I was there for Mrs. Vaszary. She is the one who had hired this lawyer to handle her divorce from her husband. They are disputing details of the divorce settlement: how much she gets and how much he keeps. I was helping her."

"Why?"

"Why helping her?"

"Yes. Why?"

"She thought he was going to cheat her out of what she should receive as her share of the assets."

"*Je ne comprends pas de tout.*"

"Well," Attila said, "in a divorce, the man and the woman ..."

"That I understand. It's what you were doing in this that I don't understand."

"She wanted to know the value of a painting they have acquired a few months ago."

"A painting?"

"It may be worth quite a bit, or not much at all. She wanted to know which."

"And Magoci was going to tell her?"

Attila hesitated for a second, but not so long as to make Hébert interested. "I think so," he said at last.

"Did they meet?"

"Madame and the dead lawyer?"

"They must have. At least once."

Hébert nodded and studied his fingernails. "Is there anything else you would like to tell me?"

Attila shook his head.

"Any ideas about the woman who chased the killer into the cathedral?"

Attila shook his head again.

"This guy Tóth, why the hell did he hire you if he does not think you are any good?"

"I have no idea," Attila said, and he meant it.

"That bow and arrow school in Colmar, the one I mentioned to you last time, a woman signed up for classes a few days ago. Tall. Pretty. *Cheveux auburn.* She paid for three days in advance, then she didn't show up again. Second person who wants to sign up for a course since the murder. Odd, don't you think?"

"Very," Attila said, trying to seem vaguely interested. "Did you get her name?"

"Marianne Lewis. American. You wouldn't happen to know her?"

"No."

"When you see Vaszary, please tell him we need to find out why he hired Mr. Magoci. Tell him diplomatic immunity does not mean he can refuse to answer questions. He has only been here a few weeks. Has almost five years to go, and I am pretty sure I can make his life uncomfortable. You know, parking tickets, speeding, loud noise, a string of complaints to the Council of Europe. Awkward, don't you think?"

"Very," Attila said. He, too, wanted to know why Vaszary had hired Magoci and why Gizella had misled him and Helena.

"Lovely jacket," Attila said as Hébert escorted him to the door. "I think I need to buy something more elegant to last me the next few years."

"You do?" Hébert asked, looking at Attila's jacket, the sleeves frayed, the front splattered, the vents creased up. "Yes, perhaps you do. Have a dog?"

"Yes. Why?"

"The sleeves look like something has been chewing them."

"I will bring him next time," Attila said. "Dachshund. Someone told me about a tailor called Vargas. Ever heard of him?"

Hébert scratched his chin. "No. But there is Bonhomme et Fils, not far from here; you could tell them I sent you."

⁓

He called Helena. "You're still in Budapest?"

"Yes," she said.

"Why?"

"The man I want is here. Don't call me on this phone again. I will call you." She disconnected.

Okay, so she was back on her burner phones. She had a way of making everything substantially more complicated than it needed to be. He fumed all the way down to the river. Then he called Tóth.

"*Mi a lófaszt csinálsz,*" What the fuck are you doing, "that you don't have time to pick up the phone? I've been waiting two hours for you, son of a whore, to call. What the *fuck*?!"

One advantage of working for Tóth, maybe the only advantage, was that he could go on for a long time, amusing himself with yelling at subordinates who didn't have to say anything. He didn't even have to listen: Attila had put the phone in his pocket and was enjoying the afternoon sun glinting off the river as he strolled toward Rue d'Austerlitz. He didn't pull the phone out of his pocket till he was mounting the steps. Tóth was still shouting, though perhaps less coherently than earlier.

"Right," Attila interrupted. "I am about to go into Vaszary's office, so perhaps this is a good time to tell me what the fuck is going on."

"Your fucking phone was turned off again!"

"I was in Vaszary's office, and he was talking. Very, very impolite to talk on my phone while our Council of Europe representative is talking. Then I was with Lieutenant Hébert, as instructed by Vaszary. Very, very impolite to talk to you while he is asking me questions about Vaszary and the murdered man."

"*Az istenfáját!*" Tóth yelled.

"Exactly," Attila said. "What do we know about Vaszary and Magoci?"

"We? Who we? I, for one, know nothing. That means there is nothing to know. If there were something to know, I would know. For sure." The way he had put that made it quite clear to Attila that Tóth, in fact, didn't know, that he was not happy that he hadn't known, and that he may have been covering someone else's ass. "I was calling you about the Russian on Rózsadomb."

"What Russian?" Attila's throat tightened. Rózsadomb was where the three men lived that Helena had asked him about.

"The one who was shot outside Minister Nagy's house last night."

"Shot? How?"

"Through one of his balls. Poor bastard. If he hadn't called the ambulance, he wouldn't have made it. Damn near bled to death by the time it arrived. You know anything about this?"

Attila's immediate sympathetic reaction with that involuntary grimace most men make when they hear of someone shot in the balls vanished with his next question. "How the fuck would I know something about this when I am in Strasbourg? And why would you even ask?"

"Because the poor son of a bitch works for a Russian oligarch art collector called Grigoriev. Your girlfriend had some dealings with him last time she was in Budapest. And you were not in Strasbourg last night; you were here."

"She is not my girlfriend, and she has no reason to be in Budapest." Attila did know about Helena's unpleasant encounters with Grigoriev. One of the least savoury oligarchs to have oozed out of Russia, he used enforcers to beat, kill, and threaten, and money to oil his way to his various entitlements. A year ago, Helena had run into one of his Bulgarian thugs at the Gellért hotel. "Is Grigoriev in Budapest?"

"I've no idea. Tell me your friend wasn't here last night."

"Of course not, and sadly, she is not my friend. Why would one of his thugs be at the minister's house? Is Nagy selling his rare collection of miniature Jobbik memorabilia? Or has he stolen the triple crown?"

"You are treading on thin ice," Tóth said portentously.

"Is the Russian still alive?"

"Barely. I want you to come back tomorrow after you deal with the police in Strasbourg. No way they can question one of our government guys. You make that clear."

Interesting, Attila thought, that Tóth would want him back in Budapest only to help find out who shot the Russian, if whoever gave Tóth his orders thought the Russian was connected to Vaszary or the dead lawyer, or both.

Thinking about the various possible connections including Helena's likely involvement, he walked to Les Bureaux Magoci. No police on the second floor of the building this time; only the very welcoming presence of the lovely Mademoiselle Audet, smiling when she saw Attila emerge from the staircase.

"You have decided to return," she said in impeccable English. Her white blouse was tastefully unbuttoned at the top, her silver earrings barely grazing her shoulders. She was, maybe, twenty-five years old and much too young to give him the once-over, as she did now. "Perhaps you would like to have that appointment with one of our associates, after all?"

Attila gave her the best, most winsome smile he could conjure, given that he had been awake since 5 a.m., flown, waited, been shouted at, and sweated in his heavy jacket. "I had hoped, Mademoiselle," he said, "that you would have time to talk with me for just a few moments."

"Now?"

"If it's not too much trouble, though I would prefer to invite you to lunch in the small restaurant on the river that I passed on my way here."

"Perfect," she said. She pressed a couple of buttons on her phone console and reached for her red blazer, carefully arranged on the back of her chair.

Although he had been trained to deal with the unexpected, Mademoiselle Audet's response was so astonishing that he had not even had time to back away from the reception area when she rounded the corner of the desk and arrived, expectantly, at his elbow. "Oh," Attila said. He had not expected her to accept his unintended invitation. It had been a spur-of-the-moment idea, designed to make her friendly enough to divulge some confidences.

She marched on her remarkably high heels to the elevators, pressed the down button, and turned to Attila again. "Not a busy day today," she said. "Many of our clients are staying away since Monsieur Magoci has gone." Attila noted that Magoci's murder seemed to her more like a sudden departure than a death. "I looked at that restaurant several times. People seem so relaxed there. Enjoying the sunshine, you know . . ."

Attila agreed, though he hadn't actually looked at the place and would not have been able to find it again, had Mademoiselle Audet not led the way. She walked fast for a woman teetering on seven-centimetre heels. She pulled open the door to the restaurant and went immediately to a back-corner table where there was no sunshine but a great deal of privacy. "Thought you would like this table," she told him as she gesticulated at the waitress.

"Wine?" Attila asked feebly.

"Rouge pour moi," she said. "And you can call me Monique. And you?"

"Attila." He ordered a local draft beer.

"Alors, Attila," she said, looking up eagerly. "What did you want to talk about?"

"My boss," Attila said, "Mr. Vaszary, has been quite anxious that information Mr. Magoci wrote down at their meeting would not be made public." A shot in the dark, but Attila suspected that not much happened "chez Magoci" that the very personable mademoiselle would not know.

"Ah, so your boss knew that my boss recorded everything."

"You mean his notes?"

"No. I mean his recording of his client meetings. He kept voice recordings of all the meetings. He would never say he was recording, but he didn't trust his memory on those *delicate* matters. *Une situation delicate, ça, n'est pas?* Very sensible, *n'est pas?*"

Attila nodded vigorously. "Of course those would not be in his files."

"Of course." Monique smiled prettily.

"So, they were not turned over to the police."

"No. They were not."

"But you know where they are."

"I did a lot of work for Monsieur Magoci, and he trusted me to be *absolument discrète.*"

Attila nodded even more vigorously but with less conviction than before. It seemed unlikely that Magoci would have taken this young woman into his confidence, but given the vagaries of human nature, it was possible. "Mr. Vaszary would be grateful if you would let him have the recording."

"How grateful?" Monique asked, her pretty smile in place.

Attila had no idea what would be on the recording — was there more than one? — since Vaszary had not told him about his meetings with Magoci. And now he was beginning to wonder why Iván hadn't said he knew Magoci. He thought it had been Gizella who had hired Magoci to meet with Helena on her behalf. "It depends," he said at last. "He would have to know which meeting . . ."

"All the meetings."

All? How many times could he have met this guy when Vaszary hadn't been here in Strasbourg for more than a few weeks. "And Madame Vaszary?"

"No," Monique said. "They met only once for coffee, here, in this restaurant, and I assume it was about the same matter. You think not?"

"Really, mademoiselle, I don't know what to think," Attila said quite honestly.

"But you will talk with your boss and he will tell you, right?"

Extremely unlikely, Attila thought. "Tell me what?"

"What he thinks those recordings are worth to him."

"Did you have a figure in mind?"

"A figure?"

"A sum of money."

Monique gazed out the window and sipped her wine. "This place always reminds me of Paris," she said. "I would like to live there in an *appartement*. But not too small, with a big bay window and a little patio garden, only one bedroom, I am not greedy. Maybe on Île Saint-Louis. I love those old buildings with their inner courtyards and their wide balconies overlooking the Seine. What do you think, Attila?"

"That sounds very pleasant," Attila said.

"My mother took me to Paris when I was a little girl. We stayed at a hotel called Louis or Saint Louis or Louis the Second in Saint-Germain-des-Prés. We had to carry our own suitcases up four floors to our room at the top of the stairs, but our view was wonderful. Rooftops and garden patios with flowering trees — it must have been spring. We walked along the Seine in the evening, looking at all the boats and the book vendors and thousands of swallows wheeling about our heads. It was magic. Here, the river is too narrow and not deep enough."

He was pondering how he could get more information from Monique without admitting that he was not here for Vaszary — at least not as far as he knew, and he was now sure he did not know enough about the Vaszarys' dealings with Magoci. Never had known. The recording could be the key to Magoci's murder.

"You are married?"

"What?" Attila had been planning his next attempt to find out more about Vaszary's business with Magoci, and not thinking about his marital status.

"Are you married?" Monique asked. "I mean now, are you married now?"

"No."

"I am also not married," Monique confessed.

"Oh." This may be the opening he needed, but maybe not. Still, worth trying. "A beautiful woman like you and not married."

"Haven't found the right man," she said. "You?"

"I was married," Attila said, "but it didn't last."

"Why?"

"I think she had other ideas for how she wanted to live." Well that at least was truthful even if it didn't give away much. Perhaps in this cozy atmosphere, she would think it was her turn to reveal something. "I will take your message to Mr. Vaszary, of course, but maybe you can tell me a little about the recording. For example, whether it is about a painting."

Monique *tsk*ed and wagged her finger at him. "What do you think? *Naturellement*, it is about the painting. Please tell me tomorrow what Mr. Vaszary says. I will be here again in the morning. They have a good café au lait and *pain au chocolate*. Say, eight o'clock?"

CHAPTER EIGHTEEN

Helena walked along the Danube, organizing her various bits of information. She wanted to decide what her next steps would be before she returned to Strasbourg and contacted Gizella Vaszary again.

The killer worked for one or more of the bureaucrats who resided on Rózsadomb. If he hadn't gone to one of their offices when she had been chasing him, he could not have arrived back at the guard booth so fast. He must have passed the young guard often enough for them to have become friendly. They didn't have to look up his number to call him when she told them she had something to give him.

Why there would be a lone Russian thug sitting outside Nagy's residence was a mystery. His assertion that he worked both for Nagy and for someone else would fit the notion that Grigoriev was somehow involved. But the man who had signed up for archery classes could, as easily, have been Russian as Ukrainian.

Today's *Budapest News* — the only English-language daily paper in the city — had nothing to say about the Russian, not even that he was Russian. All it reported was an accident in Rózsadomb, where the victim had been hurt but was in hospital and expected to recover. The implication was that there had been a car involved. If the man was Grigoriev's, the Russian embassy would have made whatever arrangements necessary to keep the matter out of the newspapers. Perhaps Attila's Russian contact would reveal more, but not to her.

She headed back to the hotel and asked the concierge for the name of a superior tailor in Budapest. She hadn't given up on finding the shop that had made the killer's camel overcoat.

"Someone who makes fine overcoats. I saw one that would be just perfect for my husband's Christmas present," she said.

"The best don't work fast, madam," the concierge said.

"Oh, I am not interested in speed," Helena said. "It's quality I want. A friend in Vienna recommended Vargas. It's spelled vee—"

"No need, madam," he smiled in joyful anticipation of the tip. "Mr. Vargas is two streets down, closer to the river. A walk-up. Small sign in the entrance way. Very exclusive. Coats, jackets, all made to measure, for the discerning gentleman."

Helena thanked him with a €20 tip and asked him to keep the information secret for a few days. She wanted her purchase to remain hidden from her husband and all his friends, until she surprised him at Christmas. She looked around the empty lobby and leaned in closer to the concierge's ear. "He has spies everywhere. It's a game we play," she whispered. "You wouldn't want to spoil it now, would you?"

In her room, she changed into her black pants, her black wig with the straight fringe, rimless glasses, bulky pullover, and a headband that would serve two purposes: disguising her face and keeping the wig down. The overall appearance would not have pleased Maria Steinbrunner, a woman of expensive tastes who had spent lavishly on blond and red highlights, breast implants, and facial procedures guaranteed to keep her looking youthful. But Maria had been dead for seven years, her body deposited in a vat of acid at a Vienna building site. The police had turned up no new evidence about her killer or killers, though her boyfriend, a local organized crime boss, had remained a suspect. She was not about to complain about the wardrobe choices.

Helena had acquired her passport, driver's licence, credit cards, and most of her personal history from the best document thief and forger in eastern Europe. He had been introduced to her as Michal — not his real name, of course — by her father, at a time when needing to disguise herself had been a ridiculous idea. She didn't know then that recovering lost works of art would be part of her profession, or that such work would expose her to danger, and that she, too, would one day need Michal's services.

At the time, her usual reaction to meeting her father's acquaintances was sullen indifference. She was only fourteen and still didn't know he was her father, but she was no longer flattered by his interest in her art studies. Annelise had explained his frequent presence with, "He is a good friend, we've known each other a long, long time." When he didn't visit for six months or longer, Annelise would become anxious, often tearful, retreating to her own room and smoking. When Helena persisted in wanting to understand why the fuss, Annelise said she worried about him. He went to some dangerous places. At the time, Helena had imagined the rather formally dressed Simon in South American jungles fraternizing with jaguars or in Africa being chased by wild elephants. When she was little, he would bring her small gifts of stuffed toy lions and hippos that did not look like their wild counterparts on television. Once he brought a doll with a blond wig, false eyelashes, and an elaborate wardrobe that Helena imagined would resemble his exotic wife, whoever she was. Simon didn't mention a wife and when Helena asked him, he laughed. "Not everyone has a wife or a husband. Some of us are quite happy without."

Annelise maintained that her father had vanished; she said she had never received letters. She knew he was dead only because of what he had left them in his will. There was a live-in housekeeper, and Annelise enjoyed her travel, always first class, and usually to Europe. She would spend several weeks away from home, and when she phoned, she sounded much happier.

By the time she was ten, Helena had begun to suspect that Annelise had been with Simon during her long absences. Later, when she returned with gifts for the house — a small Picasso drawing, a Renoir watercolour, a Rubens pen-and-ink — Helena had been pleased that he had such good taste in art. By then his gifts for Helena were books about artists — the life of Michelangelo, Raphael's life and loves — and museum catalogues with a few paintings highlighted. Having noted her lack of interest in them, he no longer brought her dolls.

Already he had begun to teach her how to identify fakes and forgeries and how easy it was to forge a credible provenance for a piece of art. "If you're going to succeed in this business," he had told her, "you must be smarter than they are. And the trouble is, little one, that they are very smart."

He was talking about himself, but she didn't know that then. Smart, mercurial, erudite, vain, cheerfully deceitful, restless, peripatetic, and amoral, her father was not unlike his hero, Odysseus, the man who believed he was invincible, that. he could outwit even the gods. But, unlike Odysseus, Simon had been unable to fool everybody. And while his travels were not in the jungles, they were no less dangerous. The predators he fraternized with would, eventually, turn on him.

Two years ago, she had scattered his ashes in the Seine.

∽○

She located the squat two-storey building on Kígyó Street, a half block from fashionable Váci Street, almost hidden between two restaurants, both of them displaying English menus and pictures of gypsy violinists grinning invitingly at passers-by. There was a women's fashion boutique, an insurance agency, and a travel bureau on the ground floor. A modest sign pointed upstairs to Vargas Benő. The name was in the same slanted script that had been sewn into the coat. It was repeated on the glass door that led into the tailor's entranceway to a modest, well-lit room with two large tables and bolts of cloth in different colours arranged in thick layers on floor-to-ceiling shelving that surrounded the tables. A large window faced the street, and a narrow door interrupted the shelves. One of the tables was piled high with large-format pattern books. Mr. Vargas (because that, indeed, was the man's name) emerged from an inner room. He wore a big smile, a white shirt with a cravat, and a tape measure that ran down, like suspenders, past the waist of his tidy dark trousers.

"Mrs. Lewis," he said, using her most recent name, "how nice that you have been able to find me." He approached with his hand palm up and when Helena put her own hand into his, he lifted it to his mouth for a kiss.

"Mr. Vargas?"

"Who else would be here, my dear? I am so glad that Laci called ahead, I could have gone next door for a coffee or a glass of something stronger and would have missed you altogether . . ."

"Laci?"

"Your concierge, of course. Such a good man. But how impolite I am. Perhaps you would take a coffee or a brandy with me, while we discuss the gift for your husband?"

So much for discretion by the concierge. She could not blame him for phoning Vargas, but whom else would he call? "I am in a bit of a hurry," she told him. "Only a couple of days in Budapest, but I wanted to get something special for my husband."

"A coat, I hear, my dear lady. You have come to the right place. It is what I do. Coats and suits for gentlemen. And I have customers all over the world. Why, only yesterday there was a man from Brazil . . ."

Helena let him blather on. No sense in interrupting him, and maybe something useful would drop into the monologue. She waited until he finished the story about the Brazilian and went on to someone from Chicago who ordered a morning coat, before she agreed that a coffee would, after all, be a grand idea, but perhaps they could look at some samples before they went.

She easily found the material she had been looking for and, to Vargas's considerable delight, mentioned a silk lining. Then he ushered her downstairs and out onto the street where he led the way to a café and pulled out the chair for her, bowing a little as he did. "In this country, madam, we pride ourselves on being old-fashioned," he said. "We never conclude our business without a little friendship."

She ordered a double espresso, and he asked for a brandy. Then he inquired how she had learned about Vargas.

"Someone I met in Strasbourg," she said, "had a coat I liked. His name . . . I don't remember his name, but he was Hungarian and worked for the government. Perhaps Mr. Nagy? Or Mr. Magyar?"

Vargas shook his head, sadly. "Neither of them buys his coats from me. Magyar, I hear," he leaned in and lowered his voice, "orders his in Italy. Not at all sure why he would bother to do that when we make as good here as they do there — better — and we are a lot less expensive. He and his wife holiday on the Riviera. Maybe you're expected to wear Italian there, I don't know. And Nagy? He told my friend he had his made in London. These men, they want to show off that they can spend a lot of money, and it doesn't matter because they have already made millions."

"I met Mr. Vaszary, as well, but I don't think he recommended you either."

"He is another one of the new establishment. All it takes is to belong to the right party and presto! You're rich already! Vaszary, like Nagy, has his suits made in Italy. Perhaps you mean Berkowitz, Gyuszi, he works for them, too, and he is a good customer."

Vargas nodded when Helena described the killer. "Sounds like Gyuszi," he said. "And I know he was going somewhere in Europe. He needed the coat before he left. Did Laci tell you I specialize in being on time, never delay on my commitments? If I tell you it will be ready, it will be ready."

"Mr. Berkowitz," Helena asked as casually as she could manage, "he lives around here?"

"Up in Buda, on the other side of the Danube. Why do you ask?"

"I thought I would thank him for suggesting you."

"Only if I deserve it," Vargas said, and Helena thought this was the kind of man she would really want a coat from, if she wanted a coat at all. She asked whether she could offer him an advance payment while she obtained the exact measurement, but he refused.

∽

Vaszary's initial reaction to Attila's news that Magoci had recorded their meetings was one of vague dismissal. The lawyer, he insisted, had never met with him, and he had no interest in any records he may have kept of his discussions with his wife about the divorce. What possible business was it of Attila's anyway? He had been hired to shadow Vaszary, not to interfere in his personal affairs.

After another tiresome tirade about Attila's lack of skills, let alone professional behaviour, he went on to detail the reasons why he didn't need to engage in conversations with men such as Attila, that he would complain to the home office about continuing Attila's posting here. Although Attila was deeply interested in who, exactly, Vaszary meant by "the home office," he had to interrupt with the news that Mademoiselle Audet had, actually, retained the records and that she wished to be appropriately rewarded if Mr. Vaszary didn't wish her to turn them over to the police.

"Oh," Vaszary said, sounding very much like a deflating balloon.

"She is planning to quit her job and move to Paris," Attila said. "And she wants to know what your best offer is by tomorrow morning. She has suggested we meet for coffee to discuss it."

Vaszary sat down hard and stared at Attila as if he were looking at him for the first time. "Oh," he said again. "What else did she say?" he asked quietly, looking around his spacious office as if to make sure they were alone.

"There was the matter of the painting," Attila said.

"What about the painting?"

"Not much. Only that you needed Magoci to sell it for you."

They sat in silence as Vaszary swivelled his chair so as to present his back to the room. He stared out the window at the river. "That's all she said?" he asked quietly.

Attila debated whether to keep guessing but decided it was pointless. He would be more likely to get a clear answer from Monique Audet if he pretended to play her game. "That, and her offer to sell it to you for the right price."

"Did she mention the price?" Vaszary asked faintly.

"No. She wants to hear your offer."

"I cannot meet with her," Vaszary said.

"You don't have to. She suggested breakfast at eight, and I can go for you, but you have to come up with the number. How much are you willing to pay for the recordings?"

Vaszary intertwined his fingers on his belly, and they sat that way for several minutes. "I will have to make some calls," he said, finally. "This is all very unfortunate. For all of us."

Attila was hoping that there would be some explanation of who "all of us" entailed, but there was none.

"Please wait outside," Vaszary asked politely, and he watched Attila leave the office. He was already reaching for his phone when the door clicked shut.

Not only were the walls thick, the door had been sound-proofed as well. Although Attila lingered nearby, he heard nothing. He paced and worried about Helena, stared out the green-tinted windows at the river, and tried to imagine what his daughters would have said to their mother about their time together. Would they tell her that he had abandoned them at a playground? Would they mention Helena? And if they did, would Bea seek revenge by not allowing him to take them to Strasbourg to show them his tidy room at the B & B?

To distract himself, he called Tóth to tell him that he would not be able to make it to Budapest the next morning because he had an important errand to run for Vaszary. No, it could not be put off, and Attila said he was not in a position to question Vaszary's judgment in this matter — or any other matter, really, as even Tóth would be able to understand. "Is the man who was shot in the balls still alive?"

"Yes, but our doctors say he can't be moved."

"Why would you want to move him?"

"The Russian embassy wants to move him, not me."

"Why?"

"They insist he would get better care in Moscow. And they say he has now confessed that he shot himself accidentally, that he had been confused and hallucinating. But he says there was no woman."

"He says, or they say he says?"

"The embassy says. The man doesn't speak Hungarian; barely speaks anything except Russian."

"He spoke enough to say he had been shot by a woman?"

"One of the ambulance guys spoke a little Russian. We looked at CCTV footage and no doubt there was a woman. Too dark to see much of her but she was very . . . agile. Good legs. Wore a bandana. Shortish hair, but she still looked like your friend to me."

"Not my friend . . ."

"Since you got her involved in this thing with the Vaszarys, I assume you can find her."

"I got her involved?"

"*Jeezus*, you must have known I would find out! You brought her to Strasbourg to look at the Vaszarys' painting. And one more thing. Your other friend at the Russian embassy . . ."

"Who?"

"Don't play dumb with me, Fehér! Your *haver* who likes to dress like he was some kind of European royalty. Or a model, except he is too old to be a model. Ask him why his fucking embassy wants to move this son-of-a bitch and what he knows about him. Then call me."

"If by my so-called friend you mean Alexander Merezhkov, the undersecretary for government relations at the Russian embassy . . ."

"That FSB bastard, by whatever official name. Or do you have a lot of friends to choose from at the Russian embassy?" Tóth shouted. "And one more thing, Fehér, no matter what shit you're doing for Vaszary, it would be healthy for you to remember that you work for me. He is not going to need you when all this is over."

"All this?"

Tóth hung up just as Vaszary came out of his office. He didn't look well. A film of sweat on his forehead, damp stains on his shirt front, his collar unbuttoned.

"You meet her tomorrow," he said. He made no effort to hide his anxiety, rubbing his hands together as if he had soaped them. "You will find out what she wants."

"I think the only way to find out is to offer her something and see if she accepts," Attila suggested. "The problem with bribes, Mr. Vaszary, is that people who take bribes usually want more than what you can comfortably offer." He emphasized "comfortably."

"That will simply not do," Vaszary said.

"An apartment in Paris would cost a lot, and she said she wanted one on the Île Saint-Louis, an island in the middle of the Seine in the middle of Paris. Very, very expensive, I think."

"How expensive?" Vaszary asked.

"I would think millions even for a small—"

"How many millions?" Vaszary's voice dropped to almost a whisper.

"I really don't know, Mr. Vaszary." The man was so distressed, Attila didn't want to tell him that a small apartment in Saint-Germain-des-Prés, near Helena's office, was advertised at €1.2 million a year ago when he thought he would leave Budapest to be closer to her. He had thought he could get some work from various Hungarians in Paris and that the local police might use him. He'd had the crazy notion that Helena would want him near and that Bea would agree to his commuting once a month to Budapest or, better still, the girls spending some time with him in Paris. But both Bea and Helena preferred he should stay where he was.

Bea had made her preference known by suggesting that they review the proposed divorce agreement with the lawyers and adjust them to occasional visits without sharing custody. If all he wanted of his daughters was a couple of days a month, "he obviously didn't wish to share their lives in any significant way." He thought Bea's reaction was so venomous, she must have been jealous of what she called his "liaison." Anna and Sofi declared they had not been consulted about the prospect and, frankly, loved the idea of Paris with their father. Cruise on the Seine, the Eiffel Tower, Notre Dame — Anna had read his copy of *The Hunchback of Notre-Dame*. That their notion of Paris didn't include Helena was more understandable than Bea's reaction had been. They been separated for a while, and Bea had found a new man who was much more suitable to her needs than he had been.

He had presented the idea to Helena early one morning in Budapest over coffee and croissants. They had spent the night before in his apartment. She had still been asleep when he went out to buy the coffee and croissants from the little shop around the corner where he went most mornings because they had the best coffee in the Eighth District. She had been awake when he returned; she had drawn the curtains and sat with her knees pulled up to her chin, her arms around her legs, as if she were expecting an attack of bedbugs. The place did look like it had been abandoned, books in boxes, open pizza containers on the coffee table, dishes piled up in the kitchen where Gustav was standing expectantly by his plate.

Perhaps it had not been the best time to suggest that he could move to Paris.

"Why don't we try half a million," Vaszary said.

"Euros?" Attila asked. What kind of information could possibly be worth that much to Iván Vaszary?

CHAPTER NINETEEN

When Attila called Alexander's cellphone, he thought he knew what to expect. Alexander had told him early in their friendship that a few influential Russians would remain, generally, off their list of conversational topics. Billionaires were in that category and influential billionaires — "they are all influential, or they couldn't be billionaires" — were never to be discussed. Piotr Denisovich Grigoriev was definitely in that small elite group. And, as Attila knew first-hand, he could be dangerous. Grigoriev had a nasty habit of eliminating his enemies, often using FSB or former FSB operatives to assassinate them. He lived well. He had a twenty-two-year-old wife, an eighteen-year-old girl-friend, a bunch of racehorses, a private jet, a massive boat with a helicopter pad, and a dacha close to the president's. Alexander assumed these men talked over vodka and cigars, planning how the world would be shaped when the Yanks were out of the business of thinking they still ran things and the Kremlin would finally rule. It was not a newly hatched plan. It had been centuries in the making, and wasn't it time, really, Alexander said, that somebody else had a shot at it.

Attila had anticipated a pause while Alexander switched phones — he rarely wanted to talk on his official phones — but he hadn't expected the enthusiasm Alexander exuded when he heard Attila's voice. After the usual clicking as he switched phones, he said he was amazed and delighted with Attila's timing.

"How did you know I was in Strasbourg?"

"I didn't. You are?"

"Arrived yesterday," Alexander said in Hungarian. He was obsessively proud of having learned Hungarian in only five years. It was an impossible language for an outsider, unnecessarily complicated, with a dictionary of forbiddingly unpronounceable words that were often used incorrectly or with their endings cut off. Naturally, there were some attractive incentives for FSB guys to learn the languages of countries where they were stationed, but no one, as far as Attila knew, had ever mastered Hungarian. Although, officially, Alexander was undersecretary for government relations at the Russian embassy, he had never pretended to be anything other than what he was. A spy and a fixer when something affecting Russians or Russian interests needed fixing.

"Such a grand city," Alexander continued. "Lucky for you to be sent here, my friend; there are many other much less attractive places that could use your services. Alma-Ata, for example, where your esteemed prime minister is about to deliver a speech about co-operation among the Turkic peoples. Did you even know that Hungarians are Turkic?"

"We are not Turkic," Attila said, rising to the occasion. "And it's not been so cushy these last several days."

"I knew that . . ."

"Have you been transferred?"

"Luckily, no. I love Budapest and the Hungarians, and I don't like the French, except when it comes to their wine." Alexander had an abiding interest in fine wines. "Can we meet?"

"If you haven't been transferred, what are you doing here?"

"I walked through the French Quarter today. Very pretty in a chocolate box kind of way. I thought Au Petit Tonnelier looked like something we could try. *Très français*, they claim, and it's a walk from where you are . . ."

"I thought you didn't like the French."

"This is about food, not national preferences."

"And how do you know where I am?"

"Attila, you keep forgetting that I am in the spying business. And I always do my research. Shall we say at three? A civilized time for a late lunch in France, I am told."

Attila extracted one of his Helikons from its flattened package — it had spent too long in his jacket pocket and Helikons were not known for durability — and smoked as he walked to the Petite France sector of the city. Smoking made the exercise bearable, and he thought he would need the exercise before facing another lunch.

The door, festooned with climbing clematis, of Au Petit Tonnelier was low. So low that Attila thought that the building must have been erected for very short people centuries ago. Or, it could have been the plan that anyone entering would be at a disadvantage when those waiting inside with their swords drawn were ready for a bit of carnage. A perfect ruse for your enemies. Attila ducked his head and stepped inside.

Except for one large, elegant Russian, the place was empty. He had chosen a corner table with a small window and a tall potted plant in the window's alcove. Alexander, too, preferred to have his back to the wall.

He loved clothes. Today, he wore dark brown Hugo Boss chinos, a black wool jacket with a high collar that would have looked fine on a nineteenth century Hungarian aristocrat, and a pale pink shirt with long white cuffs that peered out of his jacket sleeves. On the table, there was a basket of rolls, an open bottle of red wine, and two glasses, one of which was already half empty. When he saw Attila, he poured wine into the other glass. "A modest Pomerol," he said, "but you'll be impressed with its pretensions. Sit. Please."

"Why are you in Strasbourg?" Attila asked.

"And I thought you would be pleased to see me. Disappointing, dear friend," Alexander continued in Hungarian.

"I am usually happy to see you, but I would be much happier if I knew what you are doing in Strasbourg," Attila persisted, as he swallowed a mouthful of wine.

"You like?" Alexander inquired.

"It's okay, but didn't you know Strasbourg is famous for its craft beers? Please don't tell me you are here for the wine."

Alexander patted the plant and gazed at the ceiling next to the entrance. "You know it's wired?" he said.

Attila saw the tiny camera next to the door. It was pointed at the kitchen area. "The door?"

"Yes, but it's just an ordinary CCTV, more interested in who is coming and going than in us."

"The plant?" Attila asked.

Alexander hummed. "I think I got that earlier," he said. "but there must be more. This city lives on information. All those Europeans can't resist their desire to know more than other Europeans and the rest of us, who are not in the 'club.' All those groups, all those secrets they try to hide from one another and the press. The jockeying for positions."

"Is that why you're here? To find out what the Council of Europe is planning?"

"Not the Council," Alexander said. "We have someone else on that. I am sure you'll like the veal here. It's not as spicy as in Budapest, but it is excellent. The boeuf bourguignon is a specialty of the *maison*."

Attila didn't respond. He stared at Alexander and waited while the maître d' hovered and his friend ordered — in perfect French — the *"boeuf bourguignon avec le choucroute pour deux personnes."*

"We have a problem," Alexander began. "It's about a woman who is a master of martial arts, a talented fighter with an uncanny ability to spot Renaissance art and to distinguish between the real and the fake. She is not so discerning about people, but hey, I am happy for you both, long as you keep her well away from me and everyone I report to, because some of us are not keen on having our balls shot off."

"She didn't."

"That's not what I heard, and I had my information from the guy who was shot. Poor bugger, he shat his pants when she shot him. I got there the same time as the ambulance. Not a pretty scene." Alexander finished his wine in one gulp and refilled his glass. "There was blood everywhere and he was crying and the stench . . . you can imagine. They got him undressed and this doctor who didn't speak Russian tried to tell him in Hungarian that he had lost only one, that he could still have children, if he wanted. All that before the guy passed out from the pain, and I doubt he would have been thinking about having children just then." He drank a bit more wine and tore a bit of bread from one of the rolls in the basket. "I waited in the hospital till they stitched him up. That's when he told me he had been attacked by a woman."

"There are a lot of women in Budapest," Attila said.

"Yes, and some of them are still holding a bit of a grudge against Russians — I don't blame them, really — but very few of them could get into a fight with a trained man and win."

Still admitting nothing, Attila gazed at the CCTV camera with a vague smile.

"I know it was her, so why not cut the crap, stop playing around, and let's talk about this thing as if we were adults."

"What makes you think it was her?" Attila persisted.

"She showed the guy a drawing she had made of someone involved with this art thing in Strasbourg. It was a pretty good likeness. The woman can draw. Better than what the Russian guy had, and there was no mistaking this is the man who shot the lawyer in Strasbourg."

"And this man, does he work for you?"

"Neither man works for us, but the man who now has one ball does work for one of our beleaguered country's good friends, a very refined Russian who is close with our czar and hates this sort of violence. He is, after all, an art collector. You remember, he was trying to buy that Titian. He likes fine old paintings."

"And his man. FSB?"

"Used to be. Retired."

"He was sitting in a car outside the home of our minister of industry and commerce. Why?"

Alexander grinned. "Perfect. You've been talking with that imbecile, Tóth. What else did he tell you?"

"That you're flying the damaged FSB thug back to Moscow."

"Careful, my friend, not all FSB men are thugs. I, for one, . . ."

The maître d' served the boeuf with a Gallic flourish, checked the bottle of wine, raised an eyebrow to Alexander, who nodded, then tactfully departed.

"Okay, noted," Attila said. "I assume you're flying him back because you don't want him to talk to us?"

"Mr. Grigoriev wants him to get the best care and that would not be in Budapest. Our hospitals are not what they should be, but yours, my friend, defy reason. They are filthy, overcrowded, understaffed, and brutish. Mr. Grigoriev would not send his dog to one of them, he said, and I am sure he said the same thing to your minister of health if you still have one." Alexander dug into his food with the enthusiasm of a man long deprived and made small appreciative sounds.

"There would be no point in his talking to either Tóth or you. It's the kind of conversation that could deteriorate into a diplomatic incident, and we all know that your pocket dictator has been cozying up to our czar every chance he gets. The czar appreciates it, of course he does, someone in the European Union can have influence, but don't believe for a minute that he wouldn't squash your little fellows — *kicsi emberek* — if he was irritated. And this sort of nastiness could irritate him."

The second bottle of Pomerol arrived. Alexander sniffed the cork, swirled the wine around in his glass, tasted, and gestured to the waiter to pour. The thought of Alexander's childhood flashed through Attila's mind. He would have had to learn all this ostentation after he left his one-room home with its outdoor privy and single stove for cooking and heating, but he had learned it much better than Attila had.

"Can you say what he was doing in front of our minister's house?" Attila asked.

"He was waiting for the archery expert to show up."

"At that house?"

"That house was one of the options. Yes."

"The other?"

"Another house belonging to another minister down the street from this one. And before you ask, no, he was not planning a friendly chat with him."

"Why?"

"Why? Because Mr. Grigoriev was not pleased about the murder of the lawyer and wished to find out who ordered it and why. A simple inquiry, but he didn't get his answer because your beloved decided to shoot off one of his man's balls."

"Grigoriev didn't hire the shooter?"

"Obviously not. Hence his interest in finding out who did." Alexander finished his wine, poured some more into Attila's glass, pushed away his empty plate, and fished a gold-tipped, black cigarette from his breast pocket. A Sobranie, his preferred brand, increasingly hard to find despite its nod to the cancer scare: only 7 milligrams of tar.

"There is a no smoking sign," the maître d' protested.

"I know," Alexander said. "And there are no diners here except for me and my friend, and we will leave in two minutes. With the cigarette and without the brandy, if you insist."

The maître d' didn't insist.

"I assume your lover is interested in the same thing," Alexander said.

"She is not my lover," Attila said.

"Your once and future lover, then," Alexander said. "Or did you think we didn't know? That would be unusually simple of you. We like to know where you are and what you are doing, even when you think you are alone."

"Why in *lófasz* would I be of interest to the Russian government? I am not even of interest to my own government."

"Never mind that, Attila, I was only answering your earlier question: how I knew you were here. And it didn't take much effort to know *gospozha* Marsh was here too; the local police have the videos. She chased the shooter. She almost caught up with him along Rue de Dôme. Did you know she signed up for archery classes in Colmar? No? She doesn't share much, does she? I assume you saw her in Budapest yesterday? Did you know what she was doing there?"

Attila stared at the CCTV camera in the corner by the door.

"You can relax," Alexander said. "I took care of that already."

"I assume she was chasing the same man," Attila said. "She must have known he was in Budapest."

"Interesting," Alexander said. "If she knows his name by now, that puts her ahead of our Grigoriev and his highly paid staff. They know some of his connections but still don't have a name. And one more question: does she still think she is working for Madame Vaszary?"

CHAPTER TWENTY

"Adam Biro," James said when he finally succeeded in reaching Helena. He had been trying her cellphone (leaving messages), the Hôtel Cathédrale ("Sorry, she checked out"), and Louise ("She will call you as soon as she can") to no avail. "An interesting post-Communist case. He seems to have done well in every era, but capitalism was particularly kind to Mr. Biro."

"Did he have a lot of paintings?"

"According to my source in Vienna, he had more than a hundred. He even managed to sell a few to legitimate galleries. A Verrocchio Virgin in Stockholm, a Corot and a Renoir in Vienna, a Rippl-Rónai in Prague, some Rembrandt drawings in New York. I assume there were more."

"Didn't the government wonder how he got his loot?"

"I've no idea. But we know that in recent years he continued to sell more paintings through a guy called Kis in Budapest."

"Ferenc Kis?"

"You know him?"

"Met him a year or so ago. He was involved in the sale of a Titian that had been traded for a crust of bread in the Gulag. I wouldn't trust anything he says."

"In this case, that would have been wise advice to give Biro. One day he just disappeared, no one's seen him again."

"And the collection?"

"I assume it's still there. A few pieces are sold every year and, eventually, much like the man himself, it will all be gone. Frankly, I doubt he would have had a baroque masterpiece, if that's why you are interested in him. A Gentileschi would have been hard to hide."

"Is there a record of a Gentileschi sold sometime, years ago, to a Hungarian collector?"

"The closest I can come to a record of a painting by Artemisia in eastern Europe is a self-portrait seen in Warsaw before the war. Some nobleman, later executed by the Germans, had one that he had not wished to sell to Göring. So you think the painting in Strasbourg is a real Gentileschi?"

"Still not sure," Helena said.

"Your tests at Arte Forense confirmed it's the right era?"

"As far as we can tell."

"We?"

"Andrea Martinelli and I tested the paints used, and the canvas. Trouble is, some of the best in the fakes business have been known to use old canvases and make their own paints from the same basic materials."

"Would your client allow us to do more tests?"

"No. They want a quick opinion and a sale."

"Please tell them we could handle the sale. We have the

expertise and the experience. We are the best in the business and would get them more money than if they go on their own."

"James," Helena said, "I don't need a sales pitch. I will let you know what they decide."

She had been wondering who was selling off Biro's collection and where the money went. The old guy in fuzzy slippers Attila had met? Unlikely. Berkowitz, the archer? Very unlikely. Could he have been hired by one of the men in Rózsadomb? If so, why?

∽◯

There was only one Gyula Berkowitz listed at a Buda address. Another tree-lined street with well-kept houses, smaller than the ministers' houses but very nice. Berkowitz had part of a duplex with shared stairs, separate outside entrances, small side gardens, low fence, high windows. His side had a red-painted door, drawn blinds; the other had a couple of half-open windows and a brown door with a mezuzah on the side.

Helena rang Berkowitz's doorbell. The sound echoed inside the apartment. Few carpets and not much stuffed furniture to muffle sounds, she thought, and waited. She tried the bell again, then knocked on the door loud enough that she assumed the neighbours would hear. Still no one came.

She rang the neighbour's bell and, judging by the time it took for the response, the woman who answered must have been standing an inch from the door, looking out, waiting to see what would happen. *"Nincs otthon,"* he is not at home, she said.

"He doesn't seem to be at home," Helena said in English.

They regarded each other for a moment, before the woman said in English, "You are not Hungarian." She was short, just over five feet, with a big curly black hairdo that added some height. She wore a knee-length burgundy dress, matching lace-up shoes, and a lot of makeup for an at-home afternoon.

Helena smiled. "No. I am American," she trilled, inhabiting Marianne Lewis's personality, "I have come such a long way to see him. Very, very disappointing to say the least. I cannot imagine flying all the way home to New York without seeing him. Any idea when he will be home?"

"New York," the woman repeated.

Helena stretched out her hand. "Marianne Lewis," she announced.

"Zsuzsa Klein," the woman said, shaking Helena's hand. "That's 'Susan' where you come from. We haven't seen your friend for some time now."

"Days?"

"Two weeks, at least."

"He didn't happen to say where he was going?"

"Not really," Zsuzsa said after a moment's hesitation.

"But you have guessed?"

"I thought he may have gone to France. He travels a lot, and sometimes he asks me to pick up his mail. You know how it is: when your mail sits outside, people know you're away, and someone could try to break in."

Helena nodded. "So you have been keeping his mail for him."

"No. We put it inside. But I noticed he hasn't touched it in a long time, and a couple of small packages looked like they were from France."

"That's why you thought he was in France?"

"I thought perhaps he had bought a few things and sent them home so he wouldn't have to carry them."

"Oh."

Zsuzsa hesitated before she asked, "You are a relation?"

"Only a friend," Helena said with a small pout. Given the upper lip enhancement that being Marianne required, she could manage only a very small pout. "Gyuszi said he would be here." Vargas had called him Gyuszi — that being the diminutive of Gyula. "Perhaps, if it's not too much trouble," she asked, "you would let me have a look inside. He had invited me to stay at his place. Maybe there is a note or something for me. Like I said, he was expecting me to come. . . ."

"I didn't see a note," Zsuzsa said.

"He was" — Helena stressed the "was" — "really expecting me."

"Hmm."

"All the way from New York."

Zsuzsa rattled some keys in her pocket, selected one from a key ring, and opened the red door. She stepped back to let Helena in, and followed close on her heels.

The apartment was all open concept, airless, and smelled of disuse and disinfectant. Someone had cleaned the black-and-white tile floors and the clear plastic-backed chairs, the low plastic-top table. There was one angular brown sofa that occupied the living area. In the middle, under the table, a brown woven rug. The walls were beige. No paintings, no books, nothing that suggested someone had enjoyed relaxing here. A set of shelves with a few photographs, face down, and a copy of *Dernières Nouvelles d'Alsace* from three days ago, a photograph of the murdered lawyer on the front page.

Helena murmured something about the photographs and wondered loudly, for Zsuzsa's benefit, whether he had a picture of her, and she leafed through the black-and-white photos. One of the lawyer Magoci at an outdoor restaurant table, laughing and talking with a young woman; one of Gizella Vaszary and her husband also laughing; and another of herself half-turned toward the River Ill, close to the tickets kiosk.

There was a neat stack of mail, a local newspaper, a brown paper package, and some flyers on a side table.

"Has he lived here a long time?" Helena asked.

"About a year, I think. We hardly ever see him. He doesn't have guests. Doesn't entertain. We asked him once what he did for a living."

"What did he say?"

"He didn't. And I thought he disliked my asking. He is very . . . how you say . . . reserved. We try to be friendly," Zsuzsa said. "He thought my asking him was intrusive. Did you say you were friends?"

"Yes," Helena said with as much gusto as she could manage.

"Here he seems to have no friends. As I said, no visitors. Twice we saw a car stop, he came out, and it picked him up, but we didn't see the driver. The car had those tinted windows. One of those big black cars. Mercedes, maybe. We wondered if there was something going on with him."

"Why?"

"Well, the car that came that time had government licence plates. We thought he was in some trouble with customs, since he travels so much, and they were taking him in to ask questions. He came back the same day."

"Kind of you to worry about him," Helena said. She thought it was interesting that Zsuzsa had kept an eye on Berkowitz's movements. Obviously, there was something about him that concerned her.

"I wasn't really worried," Zsuzsa said with a smile. "He doesn't seem like someone you need to worry about, you know what I mean. Always elegant. Fine suits, good shoes."

Helena agreed with her, but she could hardly say so. What little she had seen of Magoci's killer did not suggest vulnerability. Even when he was running from her, it was more like a challenge than fear.

"Well, since he is your friend, what *does* he do for a living?" Zsuzsa asked.

"He said he worked for the government."

"That would explain the car picking him up."

They talked a little about the weather, about U.S. politics, about the elderly American ambassador (Zsuzsa thought he may be senile), and, as Zsuzsa ushered her out of the apartment, she mentioned that she had some relatives in New York. Their parents had left before the war. "Lucky for them," she added. "Maybe you would like to come back to my place for coffee?"

Perhaps it was because the two apartments were next to each other and because Helena had spent fifteen minutes looking for something — anything — personal in Berkowitz's apartment that Zsuzsa's place seemed such a glaring contrast. The walls were painted warm reds and light browns, there were worn Persian carpets covering the parquet floors, hundreds of books on packed shelves and overflowing onto low wooden tables where they shared space with a couple of calico cats that blended in with their surroundings. There were family photographs on a large sea chest in the corner; potted plants that had begun to invade the corners by the windows; and on the walls, two framed pastel Bonnard prints, a couple of Monet reproductions, an unframed print of a Turner seascape, a Hungarian National Gallery poster with Bruegel and a Kunsthistorisches Museum poster with Klimt's *The Kiss* for a major exhibition. She had seen that show.

Near the kitchen, there was a poster of the Titian exhibition she, herself, had curated at the Kunsthistorisches almost ten years ago.

The smell of browned onions and red wine cooking wafted from the kitchen.

"Delicious," Helena said, sniffing the air appreciatively. "What are you making?"

"Goulash, with a bit of wine. Have you ever had goulash?"

"If I have, it didn't smell remotely like this."

Zsuzsa laughed. "Come in the kitchen. I'll make us coffee and maybe let you try a little. It needs to sit for a while before it's done, but it should still taste okay."

The kitchen was warm and bright. A loaf of bread sat on the table with a dish of soft butter next to it. There were four chairs and four table settings with flowered plates, wood-handled cutlery, and tall glasses. Zsuzsa poured water and spooned coffee into a percolator, and pushed one of the plates aside to make room for Helena. "You know, in all that time that Berkowitz has lived next door, he has never even come over for a coffee," she said. "I invited him for dinner once, but he was, he said, too busy, and I never had a chance to ask him again. He is barely here. You said you met him in the U.S.?"

"No. I met him in France. I have just come from New York to visit."

"You came to visit him?" Zsuzsa said.

"No," Helena said. "I came for business and wanted to look him up while I was here."

"Where in France did you meet?"

"Strasbourg."

Zsuzsa wrinkled her nose. "Those guys," she said. She busied herself drying a few dishes in the kitchen and then turned around to face Helena. "Are you sure you know Berkowitz?" she asked.

"Gyuszi? Of course," Helena said.

Zsuzsa kept looking at her.

"I love your pictures," Helena said, deflecting Zsuzsa's scrutiny. "You've been to the Kunsthistorisches in Vienna?"

"Yes. And the Gemäldegalerie in Berlin, The National Gallery and the Tate in London, and the one in Warsaw . . . I love the art, but all I can afford are the posters. My grandfather loved art," she said. "He took my father to galleries when my father was just a little boy. My father took me later to the same places."

"Was he a collector?"

"My father? No. But my grandfather had been. He used to travel a lot, and, my father said, he bought paintings on his travels. Lost them all when the Arrow Cross came. All stolen."

"1945?"

Zsuzsa nodded. "He drowned in the Danube. They were running short of ammunition, tied people up so they couldn't move and threw them into the river. It was cold. I hope he died quickly."

"Did you get some of his art back?"

"No. My father tried, but there was no record of where they ended up. It was too late, I think, by the time he had grown up enough to look for them. My father was just a boy, but he remembered some of what had been lost. The furniture, he thought, had been used for firewood. Like I said, it was a long cold winter. He could have reclaimed the house, but what was the point? You couldn't own a house after the Communists ran things."

"What was your grandfather's name?"

"Alfred Klein. I kept his name after I married. Not many do that in Hungary, but since my grandfather lost everything, I thought I would at least keep his name."

"Wasn't there a restitution law?"

Zsuzsa shook her head. "My father couldn't prove anything. There were no photographs of the paintings. There was a box of family photos that had been hidden in the basement, but they were only of people. And most of them had been killed. My father would show me and say their names. I think it was to remind me to remember them after he died." She wiped her eyes with the back of her hand. "He died last year."

"Did he know anything about the Arrow Cross men who had taken your grandfather?" Helena asked.

"Not really. He was only seven or eight at the time. Hiding in that chest with a bunch of old clothes on top of him. My grandfather assumed the chest would be too heavy to move and the Arrow Cross men wouldn't think it had much value. My father didn't come out till he heard the front door bang. He was lucky that one of the neighbours took him in and hid him till after it was all over."

"Did he take anything?"

"He took a few things. Why do you ask?"

Helena had a pat answer ready: "I always wonder what people take with them when they have to escape."

Zsuzsa looked at Helena even more closely than before. If she had become suspicious of Helena's interest in her grandfather's art, she didn't say so.

Helena wrote her local cellphone number on a piece of paper, and Zsuzsa agreed to call her if she heard Berkowitz return to his part of the house.

CHAPTER TWENTY-ONE

The silver SUV was waiting for her around the corner, the engine purring, the front window down. Gennady Abramowitz, Grigoriev's so-called secretary, was seemingly enjoying the sunshine and the scent of roses. Helena slowed to a walk.

"You will please allow me to drive you to hotel," Abramowitz suggested in English.

Helena faced the car. Never turn your back on a man with a gun. Particularly if he bears you a grudge as this man still did for his humiliation of a year ago. Helena had come close to breaking his arm when he tried to push her in the elevator on their way to see Grigoriev.

"Mr. Grigoriev says he has information for you, and he hopes you have information also for him." He was hissing his *h*'s Russian style.

"I have no information for him," Helena said in Russian.

"He is not far from here," Abramowitz said a touch petulantly.

"How did he know where I was?" Helena asked.

"That is not the information he wishes to discuss. It is about the man you are . . . how you say . . . seeking."

"Tell him I am busy," Helena said, and she went around the back of the car and took the narrow alleyway between the houses, where the SUV couldn't follow, came out on Mecset Street, and climbed the steep staircase to an octagonal yellowish building with a grey metal roof. A plaque announced that it was the tomb of Gül Baba, built during Hungary's Ottoman times. She could see the red-roofed houses of Rózsadomb from the parapet. No sign of the silver SUV. But there was another car at the corner, its driver leaning out the window, peering upward at the Gül Baba monument. She had no trouble recognizing Azarov's driver, Piotr.

She ran down Rómer Flóris Street to the Danube and Margit Bridge. She crossed to the Pest side and walked down the *rakkpart* toward the parliament buildings. She took a taxi from one of the riverside hotels and returned to the Astoria. How did both men know she was in Budapest? She had been careful with her appearance. If the man in front of Nagy's house had been working for Grigoriev, as she had surmised, he may not connect the woman he had encountered with the real Helena. Or would he?

It was not so much how both Grigoriev and Azarov had tracked her down, but why they would do so. Azarov had seen the painting, and if he wanted to own an Artemisia Gentileschi, he could wait for her advice. That advice, if her sense of the painting was correct, may even be detrimental to his personal interests. He would be expected to bid exponentially more than now, while the authenticity was still questionable.

Her room had been cleaned, but her clothes had not been disturbed. The safe was locked. Inside, her second burner phone and various pieces of identification were in the same seemingly random positions she had arranged them.

She called Attila to ask him about Brankovitz.

"You are still in Budapest," he said.

"Till tomorrow," she told him.

"Why? You plan to shoot off more testicles?"

Helena took a deep breath. "I did not intentionally shoot that man," she said.

"Maybe not intentionally, but it seems he is still short a testicle after meeting you. For the first time. God forbid he run into you again. Why?"

"He attacked me," Helena said. "I had no choice. And, in any event, I did not shoot him. He shot himself."

Attila didn't say anything. Helena had saved his life in Bratislava a year ago. She threw a knife into the man's leg just as he was about to kill Attila. In hindsight, he recognized that he had been uncharacteristically careless, and that he was lucky Helena had been observing the scene.

"I was just asking him some questions. He grabbed for his gun, it let off a shot. He should have known better than to grapple for a cocked gun."

"The police suspect it was you."

"Tóth?"

"Yes, even Tóth. You have some unique talents."

"The guy is going to be all right?"

"With one ball. He is on his way to Moscow."

"Courtesy of Grigoriev?"

"Yes. Grigoriev. And I know he is more dangerous than the arrow killer, but that is no reason for you to tangle with one of his men in Budapest. As a matter of fact, that's a good reason for you to avoid all contact."

"I didn't seek him out. I had no idea Grigoriev would have one of his thugs in Budapest watching a house owned by one of your government's officials. For that matter, I am trying to figure out why someone working for a government official in Hungary would want to kill a lawyer in Strasbourg, and what that has to do with the man who may have sold a painting to the Vaszarys."

"Now you have the French police looking for you because you are a material witness to a murder, and the Hungarian police looking for you because you almost killed a Russian visitor who just happens to work for a billionaire with excellent contacts in the Gothic castle."

"What have you found out about Biro?" Helena inquired, ignoring Attila's comment.

"His father was a young Arrow Cross Nazi during the war. He accumulated a lot of paintings when he was herding Jews out of their homes down to the river to be shot. His companions went for easier or more obvious stuff to steal, jewellery, cash, furs, but Biro the elder had haunted the National Gallery as a student, and he had some idea that art would be valuable again. After the war, he became a young Communist. A lot of the little devils changed sides once the Russians took over, and, as far as I have been able to establish, the new regime was happy with their defection. They were ruthless, enjoyed inflicting pain, and the Commies needed men who did not flinch when it came to a bit of bloodshed in the service of the 'Cause.'"

"He built quite a collection," Helena said. "My colleague at Christie's says he sold many of them."

"Yes, but he had to be careful how and where he sold them because a few of the Jews he had robbed hadn't died. Some others may have known who the true owners of his collection had been, and someone could have come after him."

"And after 1989?"

"He seems to have prospered after the Soviets' party was over. He still had friends in high places. His son followed in his footsteps. Became friendly with the new regime. And took over his father's art collection. This is the Biro we've been looking for."

"Did you know that Kis sold some of the art for him?"

"I am told Kis talked a lot about the Biro collection and that some person or persons may have decided to kill Biro. No one was sad to see him vanish, but the government didn't like the idea of an investigation into how the Biro family had managed the transition from Nazi to Communist to wealthy capitalist and who had provided the protection, so the murder of the son — if it was murder — was hushed up. Biro just disappeared. There was certainly no death notice and no record of his dying. Tibor said he died about six months ago, and Tibor is usually right. He has the best connections of anyone I know in Hungary."

"That means that the real Biro junior could have sold the painting to the Vaszarys."

"He could have."

"And they reinvented him as the old guy you met? Why?"

"Tibor thinks — and never mention his name to anyone — that the people in high places wanted to continue to sell the paintings. It was good money and virtually untraceable. But why the hell would he sell the Gentileschi to them as a copy if it's the genuine article?"

"I don't know yet," Helena said, "but I plan to find out. Which takes me back to Gyula Berkowitz. That, in case you are wondering, is the name of the man who killed the lawyer on the boat. He lives here, in Budapest, and he has some sort of job with the government — at least a couple of politicians with offices in the parliament buildings."

"How did you . . . ?"

"I tracked his coat."

"His coat?"

"The one he wore in Strasbourg. Could you feed his name into some system to see if anything comes up? And those politicians I asked you about?"

"Németh, Magyar, and Nagy?"

"Yes. I am looking for the connections. Any thoughts on who was the old guy in Biro's apartment?"

"Not yet. Helena, I am responsible for your good health while you're working for Gizella. I brought you into this mess, and I am determined to restore you to Paris in one piece. I don't know why you won't leave the detective work to real detectives. Lieutenant Hébert strikes me as a man who is good at his job. And you and I are tracking the same beast. You're not safe."

"I'm probably not safe anywhere till the Gentileschi debate is resolved. I don't have time to wait until you or the Strasbourg police figure out what's going on and why."

She gave him her current cellphone number and hung up.

Helena filled out the forms at the Historical Archives of the Hungarian State Security at 7 Eötvös Street. She claimed to be Marianne Lewis, a historian working at New York State University, researching art lost during 1944–1945, after the Germans changed from Ally to Occupier and including the months that the Soviet Army was collecting booty in exchange for its victorious war against the Nazis. She was not surprised that there was no trace of Adam Biro. Some of the least savoury characters from both the Nazi and the Communist eras had successfully disappeared their own files. Attila had shared this bit of Hungarian history the last time she tried to track a man who had acquired another man's Titian. If Biro's father had murdered Zsuzsa's grandfather and stolen his paintings, he would have known how to cover his tracks. What Helena found surprising was that he had also managed to position himself as an entrepreneur with good contacts after 1989. Yet that was one of the aspects of regime change that had least surprised Attila. Corruption, he had told her, in eastern Europe is not political. It is governed by loyalties. So long as you stay loyal to your leader, you are safe, protected, but god help you if you deviate.

She did find a file on Alfred Klein and his family. They had been designated suspect individuals because Alfred had been an art collector. There were notes on his son, Sándor, who, when he finished technical school, began to ask questions about Alfred's art. Sándor did not qualify for a passport and had not been allowed to travel out of the country, even to other Republics of the Soviet Union. He had been denied a request to visit Warsaw. A small notebook contained a handwritten list of a few paintings that Sándor indicated were of interest to him but, since he had become a plumber after his schooling, there was no reason to grant him a visa to see art. According to the agent who had deposited the notebook in the "Alfred Klein" file, this was his list of the art he had planned to see when he travelled.

He had listed a Verrocchio Virgin with three angels and a child, 1476; Van Gogh, *Field with Flowers*, 1889; Renoir, *Girl with Parasol*, 1867; a Rippl-Rónai with no date and something in Hungarian; a Gustav Klimt garden, 1882. The last page was headed by several question marks followed by the name Michele Angelo Merigi de Caravaggio. The same handwriting with small slanted letters and almost no space between them went on in Hungarian for two paragraphs. Was it a list made from memory of other things Sándor's father had told him? Could he have remembered such detail from when he was a boy of seven or eight? Improbable. Much more likely, the note-book was something of his father's that Sándor had grabbed when he ran from his family's apartment after the Arrow Cross raid. Later, he would have become curious. That would explain the desire to visit art galleries. It would also explain taking his own daughter to Vienna and Paris and London after 1989, when they could, finally, travel.

Before the woman who had stood guard over her table and the Klein file folder could intervene, she took a photograph of the page.

She was about to return to the hotel, change her appearance again, and wait at the parliament buildings for Berkowitz to reappear, when she got a message from Louise: "Andrea called. She says it's urgent — she must meet you today."

"Where did she say she is?" Helena asked.

"She didn't. But she said she plans to have that fabulous chestnut purée again. And she said eight o'clock. She'll call me to confirm."

"Chestnut purée? You're sure she said chestnut purée?"

"That's what it sounded like. With whipped cream. She seemed to be in a hurry. And I heard a lot of noise in the back-ground. I thought she might have been at an airport."

"Please book me an early flight to Strasbourg tomorrow morning. And tell Andrea that I will meet her this evening as she wishes."

"As?"

"Myself, I think."

"In Budapest?"

"Well, if she said the best chestnut purée . . ."

Working on the assumption that he would stay at the Gresham Four Seasons if he were in Budapest, she called the hotel and asked to speak with Mr. Azarov. The operator connected her to his room.

∽

Since Vladimir had no problem recognizing her in her Marianne Lewis disguise, Helena again pulled on her Maria Steinbrunner fringed black wig, put on glasses, a bulky sweater, and a headband, and applied the dark red lipstick favoured by Maria. The man at the front desk gave her only a fleeting once-over, but Helena thought if she were going to continue to tangle with dangerous people, she'd better update her disguises. It would take another trip to Bratislava where Michal would construct another identity for her. These two had been perfect, down to the last detail of clothing and shoes that the deceased women would have worn, but there was no point in using an identity that no longer fooled those it had been intended to fool.

Helena locked her other passports in the safe, took the back stairs down to the lobby's back entrance, and emerged on Kossuth Lajos Street near the kitchens. Fortunately, Maria Steinbrunner had worn her hooded raincoat, because it was raining hard and steady all the way up to Szechenyi Square. She commiserated with the two wet doormen about the weather ("It's what we expect in October") and marched into the massive lobby, her feet making unmistakable sloshing sounds on the marble as she advanced to the front desk. As with most front desk people at luxury hotels, the uniformed man who was just finishing with complaints about the size of a bathroom in a guest's suite gave Helena a somewhat disapproving glance.

"It's the rain," Helena said in an ingratiating voice. "We hadn't expected rain," she added for good measure.

"Yes?" the uniform asked, as if the rain had somehow been Helena's own fault. Perhaps none of the other guests ventured out on a nasty day.

"I must freshen up before my meeting," she said, and marched to the women's ('ladies,' in the Gresham, if you please) washroom. She removed her wig and the glasses, pulled off the check pants and replaced them with her own leggings, brushed her hair, dabbed off Maria's dark makeup, put on a bit of light lipstick, and folded the now-superfluous clothing into her big purse. She walked out and breezed past the front desk with the confidence of a wealthy guest.

"Mr. Azarov is expecting me," she said to the elegant waiter at the entrance to the lobby bar.

"Mr. Vladimir Azarov?" he asked, as if the hotel were full of Azarovs.

"Indeed," Helena said.

"Did you call his room?" he asked in a tone that implied he may not want to see her even if he was in his room. But his eyes travelled to the left, past the two giant palm trees, and came to rest there for a second before returning to inspect Helena. "Perhaps you wish to leave a message?"

"Oh," she said. "I think I will just join him in the bar." Helena wove her way among the tables to the back of the bar where a pianist was attempting to entertain guests with a bit of Chopin. Vladimir was sitting alone behind one of the palms at a large marble-top table. He wore a burgundy velvet jacket that stretched over his broad shoulders. As the son of a Ukrainian prison guard at a Gulag labour camp, he would not have attended one of the Communist Party's elite schools, but he still somehow managed to accumulate a significant fortune by the time he was thirty. Not long after, Putin annexed a chunk of Ukraine where Vladimir had real estate interests. Unfazed by such small misfortune, Vladimir handed over the title to his buildings to Putin's choice of Russian oligarchs, thus establishing himself as a man to be trusted in the Kremlin.

Azarov was nursing a fat goblet of something amber that Helena assumed was brandy — his drink of choice on gloomy days, he had once told her.

He tensed when her shadow fell over his glass, but he did not look up. When she lowered herself into the leather armchair next to his, all he said was "No, madam." He took a sip from his goblet and added in a lower voice, "Maybe another day."

"Good evening, Vladimir," Helena said cheerfully. "I've decided to accept your earlier invitation. I thought it possible, just possible, that you would be inclined to share some information."

"Helena," he said with a wide grin that displayed his even white teeth. But she had known him a long time and she remembered the uneven yellowish teeth he had when they first met fifteen years ago. His teeth then had been a legacy of his impoverished childhood spent somewhere near Vorkuta, where water was scarce and wells were contaminated with coal dust from the mines. It was not the kind of place where you would eat green vegetables or fruit during the long winters and, as Vladimir had told her once, his family had not been better off than the slave labourers. "Always delighted to see you," he said. "And what information would that be?"

"I wondered whether you had managed to find the Strasbourg archer on your own? Or has your man just been following me?" she asked.

"Berkowitz? Yes. He was not so hard to find once we got his picture. I assumed he was from Hungary and, in fact, that this whole thing is some kind of Hungarian swindle that maybe we should both avoid getting mixed up in. And you do look quite lovely tonight. I don't think I have seen this outfit and it does lend you an air of — what? — mystery, maybe."

Helena didn't believe he was backing away. He rarely gave up, and he would hardly have stayed in Budapest had he decided to abandon his quest for the painting. "Have you found out more than his name?"

"You mean who he works for? I think you established that when you tracked him into the parliament buildings. Still not sure how you did that, but we saw you coming out of the politicians' and employees' entrance."

"That doesn't pinpoint whom he works for, nor does it provide a name."

"You're right. It's just a connection. It was your slicing up one of Grigoriev's men that provided the answer. You were there to find out about Zoltán Nagy. Grigoriev's man was doing the same thing."

"Looking for Berkowitz?"

"Berkowitz works for Nagy and sometimes for Árpád Magyar. He is a kind of odd-jobs man, though he has also been an enforcer. Your buddy the police officer or private dick could have told you that. Don't you wonder why he hasn't?"

"No."

"I assume he didn't mention that Berkowitz may also be connected to Vaszary? I thought not. He lurks in a lot of government news photographs, as a kind of background, like a plant or a distant view over the Danube. He is not named in the captions."

"Why did Berkowitz, or the men he works for, want to kill Magoci?" Helena asked.

"That," Vladimir said, "should be your next question. Assuming you are determined to carry on with this nonsense. If I were you, Helena, I would leave it to the professionals and go back to Strasbourg where you could maybe establish the provenance of that painting, or declare it a fake, or a copy, and go home with your well-earned reward."

"Funny, that was also my friend's advice — the private dick, as you call him."

"You are not interested in taking it," Azarov said with a grin.

"Not until I know what's going on with that painting and why."

Vladimir sighed. "Come, stay," he said as he saw Helena getting ready to leave. "Let me get you a glass of wine, and I will tell you something of what I know.

"For some people, paintings are, as you know, just another form of currency. They may not be as easy to handle as other forms, but they are an effective way to launder money. You buy a painting, and no one knows what it cost you; you sell it, and, unless you seek publicity for your sale as Christie's might to encourage other buyers or sellers, no one needs to know exactly how much you got for it. You can then reinvest your money in something clean. Like a building. Or a villa on the Mediterranean. The two gentlemen I mentioned are both richer than they have any right to be on government salaries. But once you develop a taste for owning stuff, can it ever be enough? When in doubt, my dear, I follow the money."

"Do you know anything about Magoci?"

"A little. He was an expert in making dirty money disappear and re-emerging unencumbered by its history. In his spare time, he worked for some of the boys from my own country. They sought his advice on how to seem legitimate."

"Including you?"

"Not me. I am my own most trusted advisor." He chuckled. "As for you, my dear Helena, you have skills that even I envy. You could, if you wished, tell me now whether Vaszary's painting is the real thing. You'd get paid no matter what you said. And if I had your word for it, I would gladly double your fee. Whatever it is. So long as Grigoriev doesn't find out ahead of me. I can't stomach that guy. I would like him to fill that giant mausoleum he calls his villa, near Sochi, with a hundred forgeries so everyone knows he is an idiot."

Helena wondered whether the pretty Corot fake had ended up in the villa near Sochi. He had wanted something yellow for a gift for his newest wife, no doubt to distract her from her well-founded suspicions that he had found a new, even younger mistress.

"Have I told you he has about six hundred acres?" Vladimir asked. "And a life-size replica of a Spanish galleon, complete with gold bars made to look like they had been stolen from the Inca?"

"That sounds more like your old friend Viktor Yanukovych with his estate in the middle of Kiev. Didn't you give him one of his vintage cars? Or was it the Tibetan Mastiff? There was a time you couldn't do enough to ingratiate yourself with him and his many hangers-on."

Vladimir smiled. "We live in a new era now, trying to wean ourselves off bribes. Have you seen *Servant of the People*, starring our new president, Volodymyr Zelensky? He has different ideas."

She had barely touched her glass of Puligny-Montrachet ("Nothing but the best for the young lady," Vladimir had said to the waiter) when one of her phones rang. It was Attila telling her what she already knew about Berkowitz, that he often worked for Magyar and Nagy on undefined contracts. He was described on official stationery as a "consultant." He was ex-army, occasional bodyguard for visiting celebrities, a fitness geek, frequent marathoner, and, according to his police profile, a crack shot. His hobby: archery.

$$\infty$$

"Why," Helena asked once she had walked away from Azarov's table, "would these fine upstanding citizens of your strange little country want to have a Strasbourg lawyer killed?"

"That's what I plan to find out," Attila said. He put the emphasis on I. "Soon as I can stop worrying about you and . . . where are you?"

She told him that she would be flying back to Strasbourg the next day.

She had pulled on Maria Steinbrunner's jacket and just left the Four Seasons without her wig when the phone rang again. It was Louise, confirming that Andrea would meet her at eight o'clock.

CHAPTER TWENTY-TWO

When Helena arrived at Café Gerbeaud, Andrea was already waiting. She wore a chocolate-coloured jacket, open to the ruffled neck of an off-white silk blouse that revealed her lightly tanned throat and the string of pearls that rested just an inch under the ruffles. Her cuffs extended a centimetre beyond the jacket's sleeves. She seemed to have dressed for a special occasion.

She had taken a table at the back of the dining room, close to the lush burgundy drapes that obscured the photo gallery of the Gerbeaud's history and the sign for the location of its toilets. Although the Gerbeaud had once been the best café and confectionery in Budapest, it had been so overrun by tourists that it no longer appealed to the locals. The last time Helena had been here, it was to meet Attila during the last day of their time together, and he had confessed that he still loved the old place. As a child, he had been overwhelmed by its grand decor, its nineteenth century charm, the chandeliers, the mahogany, the brocade, the long art deco tables where the patisseries were displayed behind curved glass, not to be touched by human hands until you plunged your finger or your fork into one of them. Attila had charmed the waitresses into giving him one of the prized tables by the windows. Although the occasion itself was sad, the last day of a romantic interlude, she remembered the café with sufficient fondness to have recommended it to Andrea as the place that serves the best chestnut purée in Europe, a fact confirmed by Andrea the last time she had visited Budapest.

A bottle of wine was already open on the table, and Andrea was eating goose liver on a thin slice of brown toast. "Exactly as I remember it," she said. "So warm and so Habsburg. I even ordered a local wine. It's not terrific, but it suits the place."

Helena handed her coat to the waiter and, rather than taking the chair across from her, settled into the surprisingly comfortable chair next to Andrea. It was not only because she needed to have her back to the wall, but also because she was aware of people at other tables who had watched her progression down the long red runner carpet that led to the dining area of the Gerbeaud. A good number of them could have been Russians, and any one of them could have been connected with Grigoriev.

"Lovely to see you, too, Andrea," Helena said. "Lovely but surprising. You never mentioned you were coming to Budapest."

"I didn't know that I would need to come. Tell me," she said, leaning closer to Helena, "have you made any decisions about the painting?"

"Decisions?"

"Have you concluded if it was painted by Artemisia Gentileschi?"

"The paints, as you already know, are definitely from her period. It is not an eighteenth century copy. It is not a fake. It was not painted by another artist later than the original. But you knew that already in Rome. The tests in your lab were fairly conclusive. No matter how much you love the chestnut purée, you would not have come all this way to find out what we already knew a couple of days ago. So, tell me."

Andrea took another sip of wine and smiled. "Well, you're right, there is something I wanted to tell you. In person." She waved to the waiter and ordered something from the chef's recommendations menu.

Helena told the waiter she hadn't decided yet. "I am here. In person," she said to Andrea. "So, what brings you to Budapest?"

"I had an interesting discussion with the Carabinieri's Department for the Protection of Cultural Heritage. I think you would know them as the Monuments Men. And before you ask, no, they are not all men, but they all liked that American movie with George Clooney. Who didn't? And the name stuck. They have been exceptionally busy these past few weeks, as you may have heard, with the discovery and seizure of about a hundred thousand archaeological bits and pieces, some of which are extremely valuable. But the part that interested me was that they believe they have found some trace of a lost Caravaggio. This one is described as the widow Judith with the head of Assyrian general Holofernes." Andrea's smile widened and she had a big gulp of her wine, followed by a long hard look at her friend.

"His Judith and Holofernes is in the Palazzo Barberini," Helena said. "No one has yet authenticated the second one, the one that was found under a mattress in Toulouse. I studied the two paintings side by side at the Brera and, though I was impressed by the technique, the colours, the facial expressions

— all of which seemed to be consistent with Caravaggio's style — I remain skeptical. There was something about Holofernes's pointy little teeth that seemed to me, at least, doubtful. Do you honestly think that yet one more attic has yielded a third Caravaggio Judith?"

"I am with Gian Pappi on the Toulouse painting," Andrea said. "I think it's by Finson, a talented artist and a great admirer of Caravaggio's, but not quite in his league. And you're right about those feral teeth. Never seen those in any other paintings by our bad boy of the Italian baroque."

"The Louvre turned it down," Helena said.

. Andrea finished the last bit of goose liver pâté and delicately licked her forefinger. "Still, it was snapped up for $170 million by someone who didn't need convincing. Time for you to order?"

"What kind of trace did your guys find of this missing Caravaggio?" Helena was skeptical. Undiscovered Caravaggios were rare, and his life, since he had been notorious in his own era, had been amply documented. He had fought duels; he had been banished from Rome for killing another man — a pimp, but still. He sought refuge in Naples, then in Malta, where he had been befriended by the Grand Master but fled after some altercation with the knights. He had a volcanic temper and turned nasty at the least provocation.

Helena ordered the veal medallions on Andrea's recommendation, and they chatted fondly about the catastrophe of Caravaggio's life. "There are those records of at least five canvases after he fled Malta," Andrea continued. "He was broke and desperate, even before his face was slashed by someone who had a major grudge. He had offended a lot of people. There's that persistent rumour that he was ambushed by some Knights of Malta seeking revenge for whatever he had done while he was on their island. He was hoping to be granted a pardon by Rome, and he needed new paintings to offer as gifts for the authorities, to buy his way back into the city's good graces. But he never made it, as you know, and the paintings, if there were any paintings, disappeared."

Helena tried not to seem impatient. Andrea was, obviously, building up to her story's climax.

"Okay, so those last paintings that we know, they are darker and even more violent than his earlier work. They also revisit his previous subjects. Take *The Martyrdom of Saint Ursula*. It is particularly grim, even for Caravaggio. The dark background is blacker than in the rest of his work, and the theatrical lighting ghostly: it does not illuminate, only makes the dark seem even darker. Your Judith and Holofernes is darker than Artemisia's usual work."

"It depends on when she painted it. Her early work is more violent than Caravaggio's. She had a lot to be angry about. Is there any written record, anywhere, of his having gone back to the subject of Judith?"

"Well now," Andrea whispered, leaning forward in her chair. "That's why I wanted to see you. Our Monuments Men found a credible source, something we've not seen before, a letter by a Spanish diplomat who was sailing back to Spain in 1750. This man had come to Naples to find great art, and he went home with a painting of Judith beheading Holofernes. The painting referred to in the Spaniard's letter seems to be the same one that shows up in a reference in Bratislava early in the eighteenth century, acquired by the nobleman who had bought the Rembrandts now in the collection of Warsaw's restored Royal Castle."

"Lubomirski?" Helena asked.

"No. Another collector. This man decamped for France with his art, including the Caravaggio."

"But the painting Waclaw is after is by Artemisia."

"That's what I find so interesting. The Lubomirskis did own a Gentileschi, and it, too, was of Judith killing Holofernes."

"Okay."

"But if you look at the letters, there is a record of a Caravaggio bought by a nobleman visiting the court in Madrid. According to a diary entry by a courtier, it was one of Caravaggio's last paintings. It's always been reasonable to assume that if he was killed by the Knights, they would have taken his paintings and anything else of value that they found. The Spanish diplomat's letter goes on to reveal that he bought his painting of Judith and Holofernes from a Knight of Malta."

Helena had never seen her friend so excited. Usually calm to the point of feigned indifference — a pose Italians of her class adopted to great advantage over lesser mortals — she was almost breathless, the tiny vein on the side of her neck pulsing noticeably. "I think you've found the missing Caravaggio!" Andrea said, much louder than Helena would have preferred.

"But why wouldn't he sign his name?" Helena asked. "Why does *Judith and Holofernes* have Artemisia's signature?"

"I don't know, but I have a theory. You told me there was something odd about the signature."

"Yes, but what does that prove?"

"Here is what I think happened. Artemisia was in Naples at the same time as Caravaggio. He had escaped the nasty Knights and was determined to make his way back to Rome, feverishly painting for his pardon. I think Artemisia provided sanctuary for him. She had known and admired his work since she was a child. She had even copied some of his techniques. She knew Caravaggio was hunted and that he had to keep painting. She gave him a room. I think she allowed him to put her name over his own signature on some of those last paintings in case the Knights came looking for him at her house."

"And he took it on the boat with him when he sailed from Naples."

"What do we know about the paintings he took? Yours could have been one of the four paintings said to be with him. No idea what happened to the fifth. I think that it was taken by the men who killed him and sold later to someone from the court in Madrid."

"And after that?"

"There is a June 1870 letter from a young Habsburg to his mother about buying a painting by Artemisia that he believed was really a Caravaggio. He was in France, seeking refuge after his estates were forfeited to the state for some misdemeanour. His family had wanted him out of the country."

"Where did you find the letter?"

"I didn't. It surfaced during Mendoza's research for his next Caravaggio book."

"Anything else?"

"No. We lost track of it after."

"So, it wasn't taken by Göring?"

"Not from Poland. I am coming with you to Strasbourg tomorrow. I have to see it for myself." Andrea hesitated for a moment. "If that is all right with you . . ."

Helena said there was still something she had to do in Budapest, but she could arrange for Andrea to see the painting. There was a 7 a.m. flight. "Where are you staying?"

"A boutique hotel called Aria. I booked it because I loved the name."

Helena's cellphone rang.

This time it was Zsuzsa.

"I thought you would like to know that your friend has just arrived home again," she said, putting too much emphasis on the "your friend," as if she had somehow guessed that Helena was not the friend she had pretended to be.

CHAPTER TWENTY-THREE

Helena went back to the hotel for her black hoodie, running shoes, gloves, the knife, the flashlight, and the Swiss mini. She stuffed the Marianne wig into her backpack. She had to be ready to play the part if Zsuzsa noticed her tonight. She took a cab to the cable car that led to the castle and walked the rest of the way. She didn't have much of a plan for challenging Berkowitz, but she did intend to confront him with what she knew about the lawyer's murder in Strasbourg. And she needed to know how that tied in with the Vaszarys' painting.

Berkowitz's apartment was dark. She climbed over the fence and checked the side window, but it was too dark to see inside. Zsuzsa's porch light was on, but it didn't cast its light as far as the apartment next door. There were now two small black cameras pointing toward the door. One of them blinked several times. Helena knocked and waited, but no one came. She assumed that she had triggered the security company's alarm, leaving her maybe ten minutes before they came to check. Long enough to find out whether Berkowitz was home, perhaps standing behind his door.

She used her knife to unlock the door. Waited. Still no sound. No movement. She opened the door with her foot, slowly. Still nothing. She edged the door open further. Drew the Swiss mini out of her sleeve and waited some more.

Faint notes of Mozart floated in from Zsuzsa's apartment. There was no sound inside Berkowitz's. With knees bent, shoulders squared, arms up, she slid into the darkness. János's lessons flashed through her mind. Always assume that the other person is prepared, that he is armed, that he can more than match you for strength. Still no sound. No movement. She didn't want to use her flashlight: flashlights make you a perfect target.

Flat against the wall, she edged forward to where she remembered the light switch had been. Waited. Nothing. There was again a strong smell of disinfectant or cleaning fluid.

She pushed the switch with her shoulder. Harsh yellow light flooded the apartment; the furniture floated over the black-and-white tiles. They were all just as they had been when she last saw them. No sound as she made her way toward the long brown sofa that looked like no one had ever sat on it.

On the other side of the sofa, a man lay on his stomach, his face resting on the rough woven rug, both arms over his head as if he had been stretching or reaching for something under the side table. He didn't move when she pushed her foot against his knee. She put on her gloves and reached down to feel his neck. No pulse. Some blood had pooled under his chest and seeped out onto the rug. No marks on his neck. His jacket had ridden up. There was nothing under the table. No marks on his wrists. She turned his head and looked at the face. Thin lips, low forehead. Eyebrows in a straight line. Berkowitz. A small trickle of blood had congealed in the corner of his mouth. His eyes were open.

She wanted to turn him over to see where the blood had come from, but it was too risky. She checked under the couch to find a Glock with a long silencer, its handle angled back toward Berkowitz. He could have been reaching for it, and the killer kicked it out of the way, or the killer had dropped it in his haste to leave. It had been about twenty-five minutes since Zsuzsa's call, plenty of time for the police to have arrived if Berkowitz's killer had forced his way in.

There were no signs of a struggle, no furniture turned over, the photographs were all still on the side table, as she had last seen them. Or were they? Using the tip of her knife, she pushed them face up, one after another. Only one was missing: the photo of herself. She slipped the photo of the laughing Vaszarys into her pocket.

She checked the kitchen. Tidy, clean, two clean glasses in the drying rack near the sink. Overpowering smell of disinfectant. Two glasses and an open bottle of wine on the counter, Szekszárdi Vörös. The glasses had no visible traces of red wine, but both were still wet. Someone must have washed them.

She ran upstairs. A spotlessly clean bathroom with no toothbrush or toothpaste, no shaving cream, no razor, and the bar of soap in the soap dish in the shower seemed unused. A large bedroom with a perfectly made bed, blanket corners tucked in, duvet fluffed, pillows arranged hotel-room style, the biggest at the back, the smallest in front. No pictures on the wall, no books, one jacket hanging in the closet. As she had expected, it bore the imprint of its classy tailor, Vargas, but no shirts or pants to accompany it. The small chest of drawers was empty.

Wherever Berkowitz lived, it was not here. But why would he have this apartment if he lived somewhere else?

She went back downstairs, checked the light switch for fibres from her hoodie, slipped outside, closed the door behind her, and wiped the door handle. She crossed the street and walked at a normal pace down toward Gül Baba's grave. She had reached Erzsébet Bridge by the time she heard the sirens.

◯◯

She waited for ten minutes, then walked back the way she had come, watched the police cars assemble, the ambulance arrive, and a dark sedan with no police markings park across the street.

Her phone vibrated in her pocket. Time to go.

CHAPTER TWENTY-FOUR

She was crossing the Chain Bridge when she saw that it was Zsuzsa Klein who had called, leaving a breathless message that something terrible had happened next door and that she should definitely not come to see her friend now. When Helena returned the call, Zsuzsa still sounded frightened. "You're not going to believe what has happened!" she said. "I don't know how to tell you, but your friend, Gyuszi, I mean, Mr. Berkowitz, Gyula . . . There was a break-in next door. Someone got into his apartment, and he is dead. They killed him." Zsuzsa whispered this last piece of information.

"Oh no!" Helena said, affecting a state of utter shock.

"The police are here," Zsuzsa said. "I am so sorry. I can't believe it was only today I told you about how careful one has to be around here, but I was thinking of burglars just stealing your stuff. We have never had anything like this happen, not in this neighbourhood. Killed in his own home. So terrible. So sorry . . . The police officer wants to talk to you. I told him you had come to visit Mr. Berkowitz earlier. Is it okay if I pass him the phone?" She held the phone away from her mouth and said something Helena didn't understand.

Then there was more discussion in Hungarian, and a man's voice asked, "*Ki beszél?*" Whatever that meant, Helena's reaction was to drop the burner phone into the Danube and watch it disappear.

She replayed the scene of the empty apartment in her mind, the missing photograph, and Berkowitz's inert body. In death, he had seemed younger. He had to have known the person who killed him. He would not have opened the door to a stranger. There was no sign of a struggle and two glasses in the kitchen. Everything was so clean, but that smell of clean had been there the last time she had entered with Zsuzsa. Was it stronger this time? She hadn't checked under the kitchen sink, but she felt certain that had she done so, she would have found bottles of Lysol or something Hungarian resembling Lysol.

If Berkowitz had not lived in this apartment, was there a reason why he had chosen to have a place specifically here, next to Zsuzsa's? Or was that a coincidence?

Zsuzsa would, of course, be asked about Berkowitz's visitor, and she would describe Marianne Lewis, a youngish woman, in her thirties, about 168 centimetres tall, painted nails, red-auburn hair with bangs, blue eyes, a bit flashy in an American way, not over-the-top, but you could tell she was American, and she had a loud horsey laugh. From New York. Visiting here. A friend of Berkowitz's. They had met somewhere in France. None of this would relate to Helena in the slightest, and if the police were to consult Attila, he would know this disguise, but he would say nothing.

She looked back over her shoulder at the castle above Buda, lit up for the night with thousands of small lights dancing, and the cable car's track a straight line of white lights heading all the way to the top of the hill. Arcs of lights across the bridge, reaching the lions at either end. A beautiful city in the dark. Attila had been excited to show it to her: his city in all its middle European glory, its history stamped on the buildings and on the people as indelibly as if it had been ink that the centuries couldn't wash away. That was how Attila had spoken about his city and the Buda Hills that had loomed over it while the country suffered under a range of marauders from both east and west. The Turkish pashas liked to view their dominion from the hills where Gül Baba had been buried. The Habsburg kings enjoyed the fresh air but not the winter winds, so they usually returned to Vienna's less rustic court as the temperatures fell. The Germans had liked what they saw of the hills and picked their favourite houses to live in once they arrived. Buda had been the last part of the city to be conquered by the Soviet Army and, after 1945, the Communist elite took their turn occupying the best homes in Buda, especially in Rózsadomb. Attila had not spent much time studying history, but, he said, those stories had taken root in his people's minds. "We're a small country," he had told her, "with a small history. But it runs deep."

When he stayed in her room at the Gresham Four Seasons, he loved looking across the Danube at the hills. Some nights she would wake to find him standing at the wide picture windows, gazing at the other side. In some ways, it was too beautiful, he had said. Like a postcard. With all the grit removed, it lacked reality. If she wanted to see reality, she would have to come to Rákoczi Avenue, where he shared a seedy two-bedroom with Gustav.

The apartment had been grungier than she had expected, and smelled of dog, congealed take-out, and unwashed dishes. Yet, his bed had been freshly made and his coffee was delicious, but she could not imagine living in a less inviting place. "I can't stay," she had told him when she woke up and looked at his domain.

"I know," he had said. "That's why I wanted you to see it. We inhabit different worlds, and neither of us would enjoy abandoning what we like for what we don't think we could get used to." He had seemed both sad and relieved when she packed her holdall and made her way to the door between tall piles of books, stepping over his discarded clothes and Gustav's half-chewed bones.

She nodded. Of course, he was right.

They had kissed, but it had felt strange, as if they hadn't kissed before, as if they hadn't spent some nights together. "Maybe you could come to Paris," she had said.

"Yes, maybe I could." But there was no conviction in his voice, as there had been no conviction in her invitation.

She had descended the murky staircase, making sure she didn't touch the railing. She was still holding her breath when she walked out into the noise of the road.

∽◯

She phoned Attila from the Astoria's lobby to tell him that Berkowitz had been killed.

"How?" he asked.

"It could have been a single gunshot. Or a knife. No defensive cuts on his hands. A Glock under the sofa. Silencer. There was a lot of blood under him. If it was a bullet, no exit wound."

"You didn't . . ."

"No," she said. "Of course, I didn't."

"'Of course'?"

She ignored the question. "It looked like he had let in the person who killed him. He opened a bottle of wine. May have sat on the sofa with whoever it was, but not for long because I was there about twenty-five minutes after his neighbour called to tell me that he had arrived at his apartment."

"You went in . . ."

"Obviously."

"And the neighbour had seen you."

"Not then, earlier, when I was trying to find out whether the man who had killed the lawyer was, in fact, Berkowitz."

"The neighbour would recognize you."

"Yes, but I wore a wig and stuff. She wouldn't know me as me."

"I did."

"Yes, but you have seen that getup before, and she hadn't."

"She?"

"Her name is Zsuzsa Klein. Her grandfather had been a modest art collector. Killed in 1945."

"How modest?"

"Not very. He travelled a lot, bought paintings and sculptures for his home. In a journal that had been either his or his son's, he had listed a Verrocchio and a Klimt. The journal is a tiny old-fashioned leather-bound notebook with handwritten lists of paintings and the dates they were painted. There is mention of a Caravaggio, but I couldn't tell from his Hungarian notes whether it was something he had seen or purchased."

"How did you find all that?"

"Your Historical Archives of the Communist era. It seems the Kleins were not in the regime's good graces. Maybe they had too much money before the war."

"What happened to them?" Attila remembered his own unfortunate experiences with the system that barred anyone considered a class enemy from perks such as education, travel, or a good place to live.

"Zsuzsa's grandfather — the one who collected the art — was killed by your Nazis."

"They were not *my* Nazis."

"Whatever. One of them took all the art from the house, and the only reason Zsuzsa's father survived was that his father hid him in a sea chest."

"He didn't claim any of the paintings?"

"Zsuzsa said it was impossible before 1989 and too late after. But her father did take her to galleries in Vienna, Berlin, Paris, London, Warsaw. Showed her some paintings by artists he may have remembered." As she said that, she thought of Simon taking her to the famous galleries, wanting her to see the best of the best. And later, to see the fakes no one knew were fakes that the museums displayed with pride. They are, he had told her, also great works of art, nothing phony about them, only about an art world that values objects not for their intrinsic qualities but for the names attached to them.

"Fingerprints?" he asked.

"None of mine."

"Front door handle?"

"Wiped."

"Kitchen? Bedroom? The body? Had to touch him to make sure he was dead . . ."

"Wiped everything, and I touched him wearing gloves. I think maybe he arrived with the person who killed him. There was no sign of forced entry."

"You said you were there half an hour after he came home? There may be some prints. Anything else you noticed?"

"Apart from the fact that he didn't seem to spend much time in his apartment, yes. His killer may have taken my photograph. Unless Berkowitz had pocketed it since the last time I was in his place, which is possible." Since she had not told him about it in the first place, she didn't tell Attila that she herself had removed the photo of the Vaszarys.

"I will find out more about him. And please come back to Strasbourg tonight."

"You think it's safer?"

"For you it's safer anywhere — except perhaps in Russia." Attila was thinking about Alexander's warning.

He called Tibor to ask about Berkowitz. "Anything at all that you could find out," he said. "There is nothing about him online except a couple of photographs, and even in those he is not named."

"What kind of photographs?"

"Government types standing at some sort of ceremony. He is in the background. He was killed last night."

"Not a great loss to humanity," Tibor said, "and good news for your friend, I would think. I assume the police will do their usual excellent job tracking down who did it. By the way, talking about public employees, I have a good idea who the geezer was in Biro's apartment."

"You do?"

"Szabo, the parliamentary librarian. Don't know how he got mixed up in this mess, except he needed the money. Wife is ill and his job pays nothing. My sources tell me he took a part-time job with Industry and Commerce. Bit of extra for the private clinic's bills. Only reason his wife's still alive . . ."

"Nagy?"

"Yes, the last time I checked, but portfolios don't mean much these days as long as you toe the chief's line, and Nagy does it well."

CHAPTER TWENTY-FIVE

Tibor called Attila's cellphone a little after six the next morning. "You awake?" he asked.

"Jészus Maria . . ." Attila grumbled when he had found his voice.

"Just asking. Because this is not my favourite time to call people. As it happens, it's not my favourite time to be awake, but since it's you, my friend . . ." He stressed *friend*, making it clear that he was delivering one more favour, a gift of friendship that they both knew had often been tested. Without Tibor's father's reach into the Communist power elite of the pre-1989 years, Attila would not have been able to qualify for the police academy, and without Tibor's own spectacular connections to the current power elite, Attila would not have come by intelligence that saved his career as a detective. On the other hand, without Attila's interventions, Tibor would have been beaten to a pulp by a range of boys who liked to hit smaller boys. And, without Attila's advice, he might have married the woman next door who turned out to be some sort of American spy.

"There are a few things you need to know about Gyula Berkowitz," Tibor said, "and, given this man's predilections and your own strange occupation, I am surprised you haven't come across each other already. The man is a thug-for-hire. Most of the time he works out of the Ministry of Foreign Affairs, but he has done odd jobs for other ministries. He has been employed by, among others, Árpád Magyar, our minister of many portfolios and one of the prime minister's mouthpieces. Recently, some of the guys on the second floor of the gothic castle were amazed to see him coming and going through the parliamentarians' exit as if he belonged. Why did you ask?"

"They know him?" Attila asked, not answering Tibor's question.

"Some do. He has worked for a number of our worthies, including Németh and Nagy and the deputy prime minister, but being a thug-for-hire would not, normally, offer such privileges."

"Have you any idea where he lives?"

"He has an apartment somewhere in Pest."

"Not on Rózsadomb?"

"Not as far as my sources tell me. He lives closer to the gothic castle. But given how much he gets paid for his work, he could certainly afford a house on the hill."

"Did he have any hobbies?"

"Hobbies?" Tibor's voice rose an octave. "Is this a trick question?"

"I mean hobbies like chess, or jogging, or card games . . ."

"Or archery?" Tibor asked.

"Yes, like archery."

Tibor laughed. "If you knew that already, why in hell did you waste my time? Archery, as it happens, was his only hobby. Could have let me sleep in this morning and told me all this at the Király on our usual day in the baths."

"We think he may be the man who shot the Vaszarys' lawyer in Strasbourg last week."

"We?"

"The art appraiser and I both think so, and I suspect the Strasbourg police will be able to identify him from photographs."

"But why would someone like Berkowitz kill that man in Strasbourg?"

"I have no idea, though I am beginning to guess that the minister and his ambassador to the EU may not see eye to eye about something. I think I am about to find out why it was the lawyer who got killed."

Attila called Helena, but she did not answer her phone and this one took no messages.

Attila felt his way to the kitchen area of his Airbnb. After tapping the walls unsuccessfully for several minutes, he found the light switch and later, his cigarettes. The coffee maker's ways were still a mystery, but he managed to boil water and pour it into a mug, adding a package of instant coffee. The sun had still not quite risen, but the sky had turned a soft pastel grey, so there was hope that the morning would arrive.

He called Irén next. "I will explain to Gustav," Irén said, with a giggle. "He has been waiting patiently by my door. We thought you would be here by now."

Attila apologized. He said something urgent had come up, and he would not be able to come for Gustav until the next day. He hoped Irén could manage till then. He was really more concerned about whether Gustav could manage, but he could hardly ask to speak to the dog.

"You're not about to move yourself and Gustav to France?" Irén asked anxiously. "I don't think he would like the food there. Too precious for a Hungarian dog, don't you think?"

Attila admitted to having had similar reservations for himself about the idea of his settling in France. But, he said, he had rented a dog-friendly Airbnb and would, if his assignment lasted, bring Gustav over.

He arrived early at Fou d'Café on Rue des Moulins. There was a lineup for takeout coffee and croissants. When he indicated that he wanted a table, the waitress reassured him that he would be served ahead of the line and showed him to a table with a view of the river. It was a reassuringly warm day, though thousands of leaves bobbed up and down with the waves and the wind coming off the mountains carried specks of rain. He hoped to be home by the end of October. He enjoyed being part of the October Revolution commemorations: not the ones sponsored by the government, but the ones his father's old friends joined — those who were still alive.

He ordered a café au lait and unfurled the local paper. He made a valiant effort to read the front page and reassured himself that his French seemed to be improving. One headline was about a new hate-crime investigation by the Council of Europe's Commissioner for Human Rights and another about the Roma of Gyöngyöspata. The Magoci murder had dropped off the news cycle.

Monique Audet arrived ten minutes late, perfect timing for a European lady who wished neither to offend by being too late nor to appear overly keen. She wore a red coat with large buttons over a short black skirt and the same high-heeled pumps that Attila had admired the last time they had met. Again, he was impressed by her ability to walk quickly and stay upright in shoes that would tilt someone else into a dive. She had piled her hair up into a sort of bird's nest that bounced as she walked. He had to admit it suited her face, as did the heavily accentuated eyebrows she seemed to have developed overnight. What, he wondered, had happened in the past couple of years that made some women want to look so furry? He was trying to remember Helena's early morning face, before she put on her makeup, the face she had turned to him when they woke up in his apartment. Soft light brown eyebrows, translucent eyelids, hair mussed up around her forehead.

What had he led her into? This job with the Vaszarys' painting had become dangerous, and he now suspected that he had innocently lured her here under false pretences. That she had come only because he had asked, and the person who wanted him appointed to Vaszary chose him specifically because he could be counted on to bring Helena to Strasbourg.

"C'est formidable de vous voir ici, Monsieur," Monique said as she stretched out her hand for a languid shake.

"Indeed," Attila said. He stood as she positioned herself to sit , then pushed the chair in under her bum as she sat down again. An old-fashioned gesture but he thought she would like it.

"Café au lait," she said to the waitress, *"et un petit gateau. Non, l'autre,"* pointing at a cake next to the one the waitress had selected. "Only last night, I was dreaming about that café in Paris, you know, Les Deux Magots, where Karl Lagerfeld used to go. You know, the fashion designer and many other famous people."

"Picasso," Attila suggested.

"Yes, Picasso." She took a sip of her coffee. "So," she said. "You have now talked with your boss, *n'est-ce pas?*"

"Yesterday," Attila said. "And he is interested. But you understand that it's hard for him to be convinced that you have valuable information unless you give us an idea of what exactly you are selling."

She had stopped with her fork in the air, just as she was about to place a small portion of cake into her mouth. "He said that?"

"Not his exact words but that is what he is thinking."

"And you have explained to him that I have records of all his conversations with Monsieur Magoci."

"Yes."

"All of them?"

"I don't understand."

"Did you inform Monsieur Vaszary that I have recordings of *all* his meetings with Monsieur Magoci?"

"Every one of them?" Another shot in the dark, but Vaszary hadn't been clear about what he had to fear from the mademoiselle.

"*C'est ça, monsieur.* Exactly how did you think I could transcribe what went on in the meetings if I didn't have the recordings?"

"I thought," Attila said, "you had kept his notes of the meetings."

"No, *Monsieur.* I have *tous les enregistrements audio* — that is, recordings, in your language. I told you it was the only way Monsieur Magoci could be sure to remember *exactly* what had been said. And it was important to remember what was said because he had to follow very complicated instructions from your Monsieur Vaszary. Obviously, no simple matter." She steepled her hands over the tiny cake and knitted her lush eyebrows at Attila. "Your Monsieur Vaszary speaks French *tout à fait affreux* and his English is, well, a little *infantile, n'est-ce pas?*"

"In particular," Attila said, "Mr. Vaszary may be interested in his . . . discussions about the painting."

"Surely he remembers that *all* the discussions were about the painting?"

"Well, yes," Attila said, still guessing, "about the sale?"

"Particularly about the auction. Monsieur Magoci had to contact all the possible buyers, send colour photos of the painting . . ."

"The buyers? You mean Piotr Grigoriev and Vladimir Azarov?"

"And the Pole, Waclaw something. A big scene, his shouting that the painting belonged to him. He wouldn't pay for it. Then Monsieur Magoci showed him some papers and he stopped."

"Anyone else?"

"There were others, but some dropped out early. They thought the price was too high. There were also meetings about the *monsieur* from Poland. All of these to be confidential because your minister had other ideas."

"Minister?"

"Your Minister of Justice, he was not to know about the sale of the painting. Monsieur Vaszary told us everything. How he was unhappy with the deal from the minister. This artist's last painting sold for 21 million euros, and prices go up all the time. He thought the minister was taking advantage of his position. He thought the 50 thousand was a joke, and he didn't need the job here if he had the millions. Monsieur Magoci had the contacts to set up the funds where only Monsieur Vaszary could find them."

"He had helped other people hide illegal funds," Attila suggested, hoping she would talk about the scheme to sell the painting and hide the money offshore. Hébert had mentioned Magoci's reputation for money laundering. But what was the deal between Magyar and Vaszary? Was Vaszary going to keep it all? Had Magyar hired Berkowitz to prevent the deal?

"We do not think that is illegal. If it is your money, you can do what you want with it. Monsieur Magoci believed in free enterprise."

"That was what he was hired to believe."

"*De plus*, he had to meet with the appraiser because Monsieur Vaszary could hardly do that . . ."

"Which appraiser?"

"I do not understand. You know her, yes? The one in Paris, of course."

"But Mr. Vaszary had another appraiser as well."

"That would be ridiculous. The woman in Paris — Mademoiselle Marsh — is the perfect choice for this work, she came highly recommended, and she was acceptable to all the buyers. I actually have that in writing, that every one of them agreed she was good. If your Monsieur Vaszary has lost his copies of their letters . . ." She gave him a warm, angelic smile that implied she assumed he was an idiot in the pay of someone whose memory was even less reliable than her dead boss's.

He had been the one who approached Helena for the appraisal. He had invited her to come and meet with the soon-to-be-divorced Gizella. He was trying to reconstruct what had happened just before he went to Paris. What exactly had Gizella said?

"And the divorce?" he asked.

"What divorce?"

"Mrs. Vaszary hired him to handle her divorce?"

"Monsieur Magoci knew nothing about a divorce. Monsieur Magoci had no dealings *de tout* with Mrs. Vaszary except about bringing the appraiser — Helena Marsh, *n'est pas?* — to

Strasbourg, so she could see the painting." She tapped her fork on her plate as if to make sure she had his full attention before she asked, "What is Monsieur Vaszary's offer, Attila, if I may?"

"He suggests half a million euros."

Monique Audet laughed.

CHAPTER TWENTY-SIX

When Helena arrived at the duplex, the police tape was still around Berkowitz's door, but there was no police officer in front of the house, no police car, and no one lurking behind the fence. Attila had mentioned the Budapest force was short-staffed. Since the cutbacks, the minister had called for significant redeployments in the interests of public security. That, according to Attila, meant public relations, making sure that a lot of uniforms wandered about the streets, trying to look attentive.

She wore her Marianne Lewis outfit, with a new-to-Marianne unflattering leather jacket over tight-fitting pants with rows of silver buttons down each side. She had bought the clothes in a second-hand store near the hotel. "I would not recommend you shop on Rákóczy Avenue, madam," the concierge had advised, but he would not have known how far Marianne Lewis's clothing interests stretched.

She pressed the bell on Zsuzsa's door.

Zsuzsa took her time coming to the door, and when she did, she still seemed unprepared for visitors. Her face was not made up, her dark hair hung over her shoulders in damp clusters, and she wore pink slippers and a matching dressing gown that seemed to have enjoyed finer days. Without the red shoes and high hairdo, she was a lot smaller than she had first appeared. Her music had switched from Mozart to something maudlin by Schubert. There were children's voices in the background.

"I have kept them home from school," Zsuzsa said. "Wasn't right to send them after we hadn't slept all night."

"The police . . ."

"They were here for hours. Emergency vans, a stretcher. All in white overalls like ghosts. They took the body at about eleven last night. You wish to come in?"

Concerned that someone would see her, Helena had already edged her way in but still hovered in the doorway. Though it had been very tempting, she had not wanted to push her way in until she was invited. Now that Zsuzsa opened the door wide, she grabbed Zsuzsa's hand for an enthusiastic shake and stepped quickly into the comforting warmth of the apartment. The children's voices grew louder as she approached the living room. A boy around ten and a teenage girl were playing a board game on the carpet. They were both in their pyjamas. Zsuzsa made half-hearted introductions in Hungarian. The children glanced up, then continued with their game.

"They're very tired," Zsuzsa said. "It was all so traumatic for us, as you can imagine. They were at the window when the body was rolled out, covered by a white sheet but still the shape of a man's body. I should not have allowed them to be at the window when that happened, but I didn't know.

So much noise and flashing lights and coming and going, I couldn't know when they were going to move him. And I could hardly keep them from looking." She was talking fast, anxiously glancing at the door.

"You are expecting someone?" Helena asked.

"No. No. Just checking. Maybe they are coming back."

"The police?"

"No. I worry about the man who killed him. The burglar."

"Did the police say it was a burglar?"

"No. They didn't know. They said they had to find out if anything was missing, and I told them that Mr. Berkowitz didn't have much in the apartment. He was a tidy man. Didn't need much. So they wanted me to tell them how I knew that, and I told them I used to pick up his mail and place it on that table by the door. And they asked me to go over there to show them where I had put it and to see if anything was missing. They thought it was strange that he would give a key to a neighbour."

"Did you think something was missing?"

"No. The mail was still where I had left it. Even the package I had put on top, the one that had come from France. I told you about that. It was why I thought he was in France."

"What else did they ask?"

Zsuzsa wrapped her arms around herself. "Is it cold in here?" she asked.

"Just the shock," Helena said, "and lack of sleep." She put her arm over Zsuzsa's shoulder and steered her toward the kitchen. "I could make you some tea," she suggested. "I don't know whether Hungarians drink tea, but back where I come from people drink tea to calm their nerves."

Zsuzsa gave a nervous little laugh. "Americans drink tea?"

"Sometimes," Helena said. She just realized she had slipped into her own voice and forgotten to be American. "You have a kettle?"

Zsuzsa pulled the kettle and a jar of tea off the top shelf above the stove and asked Helena to plug it in. Her hands were shaking. "The police wanted me to look upstairs, too," she said. "I told them I had never been up there, but they insisted."

"Of course, you had never been up there." Helena dropped teabags into a pot, poured in the hot water and waited. Of course, she would have been upstairs. Who could resist such a temptation? "We have to let the tea take its time," she said.

"Did the police call you?"

"Not yet."

"That's odd, I did give them your number, and I told them you were a friend of Berkowitz's. You know when the policeman in charge took the phone from my hand, when I was talking with you, he said he had asked you to come to the station."

"Why don't we sit somewhere," Helena suggested after she poured the tea into a couple of translucent white mugs and took them to the table in the living room. "Your grandfather," she said, looking at the posters and prints, "I wondered whether you had some idea of what he had collected."

"I know he loved the old masters. My father remembered one drawing that could have been by Rembrandt. Of course, he didn't know that at the time, but once he started going to the galleries, he was pretty sure it had been by Rembrandt. There was an exhibition of his drawings in Amsterdam we went to, and he said he knew then that what grandfather had on the wall in the bedroom had been a Rembrandt. And he thought there were some Van Goghs. Did I tell you we had gone once to the Kröller-Müller Museum in Holland? He pointed to one of the fields of flowers,

and he said he thought it looked just like one of my grandfather's."
She stopped suddenly, put her tea down. "Why do you ask?"

"Did he ever mention something by Artemisia Gentileschi?"

"I am not sure."

Zsuzsa's damp hair had fallen over her face as she picked up her cup again. She swept it back and stared at Helena as if she were looking at her for the first time. Her daughter's voice had risen to shout at her brother, and the boy swept the figures off the game board and came to stand near his mother. There was no mistaking his angry face or the whiny voice he used to complain. Whatever she said, made him turn around and slouch back across the room and stomp up the stairs.

"Is that the real reason you came to see me?" Zsuzsa asked. "My grandfather's paintings?"

Helena hesitated.

"Because I already told you I have none of them," Zsuzsa continued.

"I know," Helena said. "But I had hoped you would remember your father mentioning them."

"You are not really a friend of Gyula Berkowitz's," Zsuzsa stated.

"Not really," Helena ventured. "But I know something about him and something about the man who stole your grandfather's paintings. The man you said had pushed him into the river."

"Biro?"

"You knew . . ."

"We all knew. But there was nothing to be done then and nothing to be done now."

"There may be something . . ."

"Biro is dead," Zsuzsa said, cutting off whatever Helena was about to tell her.

They sat watching each other for a few minutes, then Zsuzsa asked, "What is it you actually do? Buy and sell art? You were hoping I had something of my grandfather's to sell? I had a visit from another person like that before you. But at least he was honest about his reason for coming to see me. You were not."

Helena had been trying to decide whether to tell Zsuzsa the truth. It was the kind of truth that could hurt both of them, in different ways. It was difficult to guess what the repercussions of Berkowitz's murder would be, or even who benefited from his death. But at this stage, it may be more dangerous for Zsuzsa not to know what Helena knew. How do you protect yourself and, in Zsuzsa's case, your family from something you have no idea about, only a vague suspicion that could do more harm than you realize?

Helena went to the window overlooking the porch where the yellow tape still surrounded Berkowitz's part of the house. She thought she had heard a noise, but it may have been just a man walking his inquisitive dog. Or it may have been the police returning. "I came to see Berkowitz, as I told you last time," she finally said. "But it wasn't because he was a friend. He killed someone in Strasbourg, and I wanted to know why. It was, I am pretty sure, about a painting, but I still don't know why."

"You killed him?" Zsuzsa's voice rose with the accusation, but she continued to cradle her tea.

"No," Helena said. "I didn't. I am an art appraiser. I was hired to study a painting, a baroque masterpiece that could be by Artemisia Gentileschi, and determine whether it's genuine. I was sitting next to the man Berkowitz killed. He was a lawyer acting for my client . . ." She then told her the story almost from the beginning, leaving out only some of the names. She told her about the art she had found in Biro's apartment, and how she had followed the man who had turned out to be Berkowitz. Then she showed her the page of the small notebook she had photographed in the archives. The list in that tiny, slanted handwriting that had included a Verrocchio Virgin and a child, a Renoir *Girl with Parasol*, a Rippl-Rónai, a Rembrandt drawing, a Van Gogh, and a Gustav Klimt.

Zsuzsa studied it for a while. "Not my father's handwriting," she said. "It could be my grandfather's. I have never seen his handwriting."

"Can you translate what he wrote here?" Helena asked, pointing to the Caravaggio page.

"He says, 'I bought the painting in Paris. It has no provenance. It has no date. I think it's by Caravaggio. It is his style and his use of light and dark. The signature is not his, but it may be covering his own. The man who sold it to me had been reluctant to let it go. He said he had bought it himself from a Pole who was down on his luck, living in France, off his inheritance, selling his art. I am not sure he was telling the truth, but I loved the painting, sold two of my own to pay for it and when that wasn't enough, I added two hundred francs. It was so much that I had to check out of my hotel and take the train home.' Do you think he had bought a real Caravaggio?"

"It's possible," Helena said carefully. "There are still some missing Caravaggios, and in the late thirties and early forties, he was not as highly valued as he is now." She was tempted to tell Zsuzsa about Andrea's notion that the painting she had been hired to authenticate was a missing Caravaggio, but would she be able to prove that it had once belonged to her grandfather?

When Zsuzsa asked how she had tracked Berkowitz to this address, she told her about the tailor and about her following

Berkowitz to the parliament buildings, where she had guessed whom he worked for. Strangely, that included the men who had sent her client's husband to Strasbourg.

"Did he own this building?" Helena asked.

"I don't think so. We pay rent to a numbered company. We used to have a family living next door, but they said they were moving to Pécs. The husband had some amazing offer to work at the university. I thought it was strange that I saw them on the street some weeks later, and when I asked about the job, he said, 'What job?' as if they hadn't told me they were moving to Pécs. Later, I saw the wife alone, and I asked her. She said someone had paid them to move out."

"Did she say who?"

"No. But then Berkowitz moved in. As I told you before, other than needing help with his mail, he didn't talk to us much. Not very friendly."

"Did he come to your apartment at all?"

"He didn't."

Helena jumped out of her seat and started touching the electrical outlets in the kitchen, then the light fixtures in the living room. When Zsuzsa asked what she was doing, she said, "In a minute," and continued to search until she picked up a tiny microphone attached to the underside of the sofa. There was a second one attached to the lampshade over the table where the children had been playing, and a third planted in the pot with the ferns near the windows. She collected them all and switched them off.

"He's been listening to you," Helena said, showing Zsuzsa the little gadgets.

"And now?"

"I don't know. The police may have taken his device. Or

not." She regretted now that she hadn't done a more thorough search of Berkowitz's apartment

"He could have listened to everything we said?"

"He could have."

"Why?" Zsuzsa was still incredulous. "Why would he be interested in us?"

"It has to do with that painting."

"I just can't believe he killed somebody in France. Why would he do that?"

"I don't know. But I am trying to find out. It may be important for my client. How often did you go to his apartment? I thought the place didn't look like anyone lived in it."

"He said he travelled a lot, didn't spend much time here."

"What did you tell the police?"

"I told them everything I knew. Well, almost everything. I didn't tell them that I went upstairs once. Curiosity, you know."

Helena grinned. "I do understand curiosity."

"Not much there," Zsuzsa said. "But there were some bundles of euros in a drawer. Loose bundles. I thought that was weird. Didn't tell the police because I didn't want them to know that I had been snooping."

"The person you said who wanted to talk to you about your grandfather's art," Helena asked, "was that a long time ago?"

"Maybe a month. Or less."

"Do you remember anything about him?"

"A big guy. I think, maybe Russian."

☙❧

Attila's visit to the Strasbourg police station was, again, unannounced, but the young woman at reception greeted him as if he had become part of the team. "Why not go *tout droit* to *le bureau de Lieutenant Hébert?*" she asked and waved him through the security gate. "You know where it is."

Attila wound his way along the path between the police desks toward Hébert's office where the lieutenant was standing by someone else's computer, studying photos on the other person's screen. He quickly turned, his back to the screen, and waited for Attila. "What a surprise," he said. "I have grown to expect to see you unexpectedly, but your country's customs are still a little strange for us. We are not formal here in France, but your habit of always arriving without warning is still *un peu étonnant*. I must visit your country soon. Such a joy to find everywhere people who do not make appointments, show up when they feel like . . ."

"I have something for you," Attila said and led the way to Hébert's office.

"Don't tell me, more things discovered by accident . . ."

"It's a good photograph of the man who shot your lawyer last week." Attila took the photo out of his pocket and handed it to Hébert with a flourish. It was clipped from one of the group photos taken at an official function with Berkowitz clearly visible in the background. "I may not make appointments, but I am always around when you need me. Trying to help with your investigation." Attila grinned.

Hébert spread the sheet of paper on his desk, found the photo from the video camera, compared the two and stared at Attila. "I assume you are about to tell me who he is?"

"He was Gyula Berkowitz. He was killed last night—"

"Yes. In Budapest," Hébert interrupted. "You know who his employer was?"

"Somebody in our government," Attila said.

"Well done!" Hébert exclaimed and, for emphasis, he hit the desk with the palm of his hand. "I was worried perhaps you were not going to tell me. We small provincial *policiers* in this far corner of Europe do have a modest budget for looking into this sort of thing."

"I still don't know exactly who hired him, but I do know that he had worked, in the past, with some higher-ups in our government."

"What you do not know cannot bite you on the ass, my friend," Hébert said with a wide grin. "And what is your own police going to do about this murder?"

"Maybe not much," Attila said. "The man or men who had hired him to kill Magoci have ways of shutting down investigations. If his murder is connected to what he did here . . ."

"Of that we can be certain. I don't believe in coincidences when it comes to murder. Do you?"

"I don't. Whether there will be an investigation at home depends on whether the people who hired him decided it was risky to let him live. In that case, his murder will remain suspicious but, what with budget cuts, not necessarily solved."

"Your Lieutenant Tóth is not much for sticking his neck out."

"Not much. He loves his job. It would not have taken him long to find out who Berkowitz worked for, but he may be waiting to see what he is expected to do with the information. He would usually look for ways to enhance his paycheque. I assume you have no such constraints. That's why I came to you. Perhaps you will be able to shed some light on the who and the why."

"You were also *désireux de me dire* how your breakfast went with the beautiful Mademoiselle Audet?"

"You had me followed?"

"*Ça va sans dire, mon ami,*" Hébert said. "You are, as they say in police language, still 'a person of interest.'"

Attila hesitated. He wasn't sure how much to tell Hébert. He knew now that he had been chosen for this stint in Strasbourg because of his relationship with Helena. The Vaszarys had asked for him specifically because he would be able to bring Helena here. Iván Vaszary was also responsible for Helena's presence on the tour boat that day, and Berkowitz worked for the same people who had provided this cushy Council of Europe job for Vaszary.

The savvy mademoiselle had told him that Vaszary was planning to sell the Gentileschi painting for a very large sum of money. Since Vaszary had hired Magoci to invite bidders and conduct an auction for the Gentileschi, he would hardly have had him killed before the sale was concluded. Attila could not see how selling a painting, however valuable, would be a police matter, unless it involved theft or some other kind of criminal activity.

Whatever it was that the mademoiselle was selling, it was worth more — perhaps a lot more — than half a million euros.

That he blamed himself for inviting Helena to Strasbourg made the decision to withhold information more difficult, but withhold it he did. It had been, as he told himself, a tough judgment call. He was sure that there were still gaping holes in his understanding of what the Vaszarys or their slippery employers in the Gothic castle had planned. What he thought he knew was that the original plans, whatever they were and whoever had devised them, had gone off the rails. Vaszary would not be offering a bribe to silence Mademoiselle Audet, unless she had something of value beyond convening buyers for the painting.

"She offered to give some information to Iván Vaszary in exchange for money," he finally said. "It's information she hadn't shared with you and was not interested in sharing with me, but I don't believe it's of the kind that implicates Vaszary in your lawyer's murder. As far as I can tell, it would have been against Vaszary's best interests to have the guy killed because the painting he was hired to sell had not yet been sold. However, it may be the end of Vaszary's career as our esteemed representative to the Council of Europe and of my fascinating stay in your magnificent town."

"How much money are we talking about?"

"For Vaszary, maybe twenty-four million. At least that was what the last painting by this artist fetched."

Hébert whistled. "That's a lot of money for a painting."

"Apparently not if it's by Artemisia Gentileschi."

"Who?"

"She was, apparently, a baroque master. Italian. Not many women artists in her time, so she is rare. But don't ask me how these things are valued, all I know is they usually go for more than the last time a painting by the same artist was sold."

"What was Magoci's take?"

"No idea. But the mademoiselle would know, and she expects a substantial chunk to keep or destroy the tapes of Vaszary's dealings with Magoci."

"You don't think whatever their meetings were about would be of interest to the police?"

"I am not sure yet."

"You know Magoci was good at money laundering."

"Yes, and it's possible that his work for Vaszary included a bit of that."

"That could have been the reason he was killed. Someone or someones didn't want him to take the money out of the country."

"We need to know who would have benefited from Magoci's death and how."

"That is now," Hébert said, "the starting point of the rest of my investigation. What happens in Budapest with this man Berkowitz is only of interest to me as far as it relates to our crime. After I find out who hired Berkowitz to kill Magoci, I will not care whether Tóth wants to find Berkowitz's killer or not. I will think that is a purely Hungarian matter."

Hébert scratched his head, walked around his office, poured them both coffee from his little espresso machine, and stood facing the window with his hands clasped behind his back. It was still a beautiful day in Strasbourg. The linden trees across the street had turned deep shades of ochre. A light wind played in the branches and what you could see of the sky was blue. When Hébert turned, he was smiling.

"I plan to take my wife and kids to the mountains this weekend," he said. "You still have some mountains in your country. Perhaps you could take someone for a holiday."

A great idea, Attila thought. But whether Helena would agree to a cabin in the lower Carpathians was hard to know. She would probably prefer the French Alps. "I will suggest it to her," he said.

Hébert shook Attila's hand. "That's why I want to close this case before the end of the day. We both need a holiday. Do you think you are willing to help?"

CHAPTER TWENTY-SEVEN

Attila drove to the steel-and-glass monstrosity that billed itself the Palace of Europe. He parked in the employees parking lot close to the human rights building, ran up the stairs, and made his way along the corridors to the office of Hungary's Permanent Representation. It was an odd label for a member's office in this rather utopian setting, where nothing seemed permanent, not even the short-cropped blue-green grass that still showed signs of having been laid in slabs.

He was surprised that Mrs. Gilbert, Vaszary's long-suffering secretary, was not at her desk. It was even more surprising that the door to the inner sanctum was open and the minister of many portfolios, Árpád Magyar, was sitting at Vaszary's rather ornate leather-covered desk. He wore an exceptionally fine blue linen jacket, its sleeves rolled up, his hands steepled, his lightly tanned face composed, mildly expectant, eyebrows raised when Attila entered.

"We have been expecting you," he said with a pleasant smile as he waved Attila into the room. Attila looked around to see who else had been included in the minister's plural, but there was no one else there, not even Iván Vaszary, the only person who had any reason to expect to see Attila here today. "Come in, come in," the minister said, indicating a wide-armed chair across from the desk.

"Why?" Attila asked.

"Perhaps it is a conversation we should have had already, but no time like the present," the minister said, still smiling. Attila thought that, what with the fine suit, the tan, the restrained but friendly smile, Árpád Magyar managed to look more like an Italian actor than a middle European bureaucrat, but since he was known for mixing with the rich when he and Mrs. Magyar were on vacation, he had come by the look honestly.

"Your salary, for starters, is not — how shall we put it? — adequate for your *lifestyle*." Magyar said the last word in English. Perhaps, Attila thought, so few Hungarians could afford one that there was no need for a translation.

"My what?" Attila asked.

"You are divorced," the minister said, his voice taking on a shade of regret. "Your wife, as I understand it, had desired more than you could offer her, and she left you for a more . . . more interesting companion, a better life, really, wouldn't you say, Attila?"

"More interesting?"

"Money, as you know, makes for better options. She needed better options than your limited means could offer."

"I don't think my divorce is any of your business, Mr. Magyar," Attila said.

"That's exactly why we are having this discussion, Attila. I can very easily make it our business. You have two lovely daughters, for example. Wouldn't you like to give them more of the things that little girls desire? My daughters, for example, have a keen sense of fashion. They like to wear pretty clothes. They like to go on interesting vacations. You see, there is that word again, interesting. Little girls can be quite demanding. Haven't they told you they are tired of the zoo? It's a great zoo in Budapest, one of the best in the world, but they must get bored with it, Attila. And aren't you bored with your car?"

Attila had an overwhelming desire to slap the minister's jowly face but held back. Waiting.

"I thought so," Magyar said, with growing confidence. "I think you would find us very understanding. Very generous. And not too demanding. A few little things, maybe, from time to time that you could do for us. No, nothing onerous, I assure you." He had his hand up as if to ward off whatever objections Attila offered.

"For example," Attila prompted.

"For example," Magyar repeated. "There is a small, irritating local matter," Magyar said.

"What sort of small matter?"

"The matter of Magoci's unwelcome interference in something that did not concern him. A business matter, really. You know he had the nastiest reputation. Money laundering. He worked, you must know this by now, for the Sicilians. Dirty, small-time crooks. The man had no sense of honour." He breathed a long sigh and waited for Attila's response.

Attila composed his face into what he hoped was sufficiently keen, without being an easy mark. The longer he held out, the more the minister would reveal. He was already close to admitting that he had Magoci killed.

"What is it, exactly, minister, that you are offering, and what are you expecting of me?"

"Well now," Magyar said, leaning back in Vaszary's chair, he knew how to sink into this sort of negotiation. "We wanted the . . ." Was he searching for the right word or playing for time? He settled on "elimination" and smiled, "of this unsavoury character. Usually, you understand, Attila, we would be on the side of law enforcement, but this is a completely different matter. The man was a pariah. A waste of fresh air."

"I am not sure I understand," Attila said, drawing out the moment and building Magyar's confidence.

"It's like this," Magyar said. "He had interfered in what was none of his business."

"The painting," Attila prompted.

"The sale of the painting — which did not belong to him; therefore, he had no right."

"Vaszary's painting?"

"Vaszary's?" Magyar snorted. "That's the point I am trying to make here, Attila. Not Vaszary's. That fool . . ."

"He told me he bought it from Biro."

"That's another thing we need to settle, Attila. We were surprised you took it upon yourself to track down Biro, and then your little friend" — emphasis on the *little* — "followed our man in Budapest. We hadn't expected her to get into the middle of this. But we are willing to overlook that. For your sake."

"Berkowitz was working for you," Attila said.

Magyar sighed ostentatiously, as if he had finally succeeded in making his point with his rather thick pupil.

"So, it was you who had Magoci killed," Attila said.

Magyar placed an envelope on the desk in front of Attila. They both stared at it for about a minute before he motioned toward it with his chin and said, "You can look inside."

Attila picked up the envelope. It was full of purple euro notes.

"You can count it," Magyar said. He rose from Vaszary's chair, walked around to Attila's side of the desk, and stood, his butt leaning against the desk, looking down at Attila.

Attila stroked the flap as he positioned the envelope back on the desk, slowly, hesitantly, still staring at it. He thought there could be at least forty banknotes inside. Twenty thousand euros.

"I need to think," Attila said.

"Not much to think about, but if you need a couple of hours, that's okay. For the little we expect. All you need do is stop mucking around in this business. That local policeman who has been asking questions, you can convince him this thing has nothing to do with Hungary. It's not the place for him to look. We told that idiot Tóth, but I am not sure your man, Hébert, will listen to Tóth. Get him to look for other suspects. There are a lot of people this son of a bitch dealt with who could have wanted him dead."

Attila was nodding.

"Two hours," Magyar said, sweeping the envelope off the table and pocketing it.

⁑

When Attila drove to the house on Rue Geiler, it was overcast with a sprinkle of rain. He had suggested to Helena that she should arrive about fifteen minutes after him. That would give him a chance to talk to the Vaszarys in Hungarian about Mademoiselle Audet's dismissive attitude to Iván's generous offer. The question was, What had Vaszary been saying to Magoci that was worth more than half a million euros? And how exactly did Magyar fit into the picture? Now that he knew that the hit on Magoci had been engineered by Magyar (and whomever he had included in this "we"), what was Magyar's expectation of the painting? Attila had called Hébert, but he did not mention Helena. He was reluctant to drop her into the soup Magyar and his cohorts were cooking.

Hilda, not wearing her full maid's uniform today — no apron, only the black dress — opened the door. "I think, finally, I will be able to visit my mother in Karcag," she said. "She has been ill for the past week, but they wouldn't give me time off until I told them I would quit if they didn't. I have not had one day free since we came here. Why do you work for these *elfajult rohadékok*?" she asked.

"Same as you, I think," Attila said. "I need the money. And did you quit?"

"Not yet. I agreed to stay if they give me the bonus they promised when we moved to this wretched place and I get two weeks off to go to Karcag. They were all excited about some higher-up's visit. They wanted little sandwiches and cakes. I think they would have given me much more if I had had sense enough to ask."

"Then you are coming back?"

"Not if I can get another job."

Lucy followed Attila into the living room, sniffing loudly

up and down Attila's trouser legs from the ankle to below the knees at about Gustav's full height. It was not a friendly sniff. Ignoring Hilda's warnings, Lucy accompanied him to the living room.

The room was strangely still and murky with the rain now beating on the windows. No one had turned on the lights. The Vaszarys were sitting on the sofa, holding hands. A third person, a tall man wearing a suit with an old-fashioned long jacket, stood facing the painting, his back to the door. He did not turn when Attila entered.

"We were not expecting you," Iván Vaszary said in Hungarian. "At least not here." He spoke so quietly that Attila had to approach the sofa to hear him. "You were supposed to come to my office." He looked down at his wife's fingers woven through his own.

"I did," Attila said, "but you were not there."

"So you came here," Vaszary said, stating the obvious.

"I assume you are not getting divorced," Attila said.

"We changed our minds."

"Mademoiselle Audet told me that Mrs. Vaszary had not hired Magoci."

"What else did she tell you?"

"That your offer was insufficient."

"Insufficient," Vaszary repeated in a whisper. "How?"

"I think she imagined that your painting would sell for enough money that you could afford to give her a much bigger slice of the proceeds. At least as much as you had agreed to pay Magoci to find the buyers and conduct the sale." Attila was now close enough to the sofa to see Vaszary's face, damp with perspiration, his shirt front wet and stuck to his chest.

"I had already paid a retainer. The rest was not due till the deal was concluded, and it has not been concluded."

"I don't think she cares about those details, and she didn't get any part of the retainer."

"We were going to pay him a percentage."

"Mademoiselle Audet may not be willing to wait for her share."

"I have nothing to give her now," Vaszary said.

"You know Gyula Berkowitz?" Attila asked, changing tack. Vaszary's face remained impassive, but Gizi looked scared.

"I don't think I . . ." Gizi began before Vaszary squeezed her hand, then she stopped.

"We don't know anyone by that name," Vaszary said.

"That's strange. He had a photograph of you in his apartment."

"Me?" Gizi squawked.

"Both of you."

The man who had been facing the painting in the murky room now turned and stood looking at Attila, then he walked over to the standing lamp near the sofa and turned on a light. He had a pale, narrow, doleful face with a pronounced brow. "Waclaw Lubomirski," he said. *"Et vous êtes?"*

"Attila works for me," Vaszary said in English. "He used to be a policeman and now he is my bodyguard. He is also a close friend of the appraiser, Helena Marsh. We were expecting her today."

"In that case, we can conclude today," Waclaw said. He didn't offer to shake Attila's hand. Perhaps he thought bodyguards were beneath him.

"Everything has gone wrong," Gizella whined. "Everything."

"You know Magoci was murdered," Vaszary said to Lubomirski.

"I don't see how that changes our arrangement," Lubomirski said. "Magoci was dead more than three days ago and that's when you told me to proceed with the payment, and I have moved the funds you required into your account in Canada." He spoke almost perfect English.

"There was a delay with Miss Marsh's report . . ."

"We have already discussed that as well. I accept your word for what she has already told you."

"Miss Marsh," Hilda said with a hint of a smile as Helena, Lucy the rottweiler, and another woman entered the room. Lucy was showing an unhealthy interest in the other woman's bottom. "Lucy," Hilda warned, and tried to pull the dog away from her quarry. The tall woman with the ruffled shirt and chocolate-coloured jacket slapped the dog's snout with her matching purse.

Waclaw already had his hand stretched out as he bore down on the two women, his face expressing sheer delight. "Such an honour," he said, pumping Helena's hand. "Waclaw Lubomirski," he announced. "And I have been wanting to meet you for so, so long, Miss Marsh. I hope we can entice you to come to Warsaw to see our collection. So many more works since you were last there and this one," he indicated the painting he had been studying, "this one will, of course, be the new star of the museum. We plan a whole show around its acquisition. We will feature some of Artemisia Gentileschi's other works. A great retrospective exhibition. We are contacting the galleries that have lent works to her show in London, and we plan to assemble the entire lifetime of Artemisia's art. She is such a seminal figure in the baroque. Maybe as soon as next summer, and you would be an honoured guest with us, maybe we could persuade you to be a speaker at the opening of the exhibition itself . . ."

"There may be a problem," Helena said, extricating her fingers from Waclaw's grasp.

"No problem we can't overcome, Miss Marsh," Waclaw rushed on. "We understand if you have a conflict. If the timing does not entirely suit you, we could reschedule your lecture as part of our planned series of talks and a film about the baroque and that could be any time while the exhibition is open to the public."

"That isn't the problem," Helena stopped Waclaw's torrent of plans. "I came to tell the Vaszarys that the painting may not be by Artemisia Gentileschi, after all." She approached the seated Vaszarys. "Good afternoon," she said. "I assume you have reconciled your differences and the divorce is off? Hmm. I thought so."

Iván Vaszary stood to greet Helena. He still seemed ill at ease, but it was as if he were relieved to hear Helena's words about the painting. "It's not by her?"

"It may not be," Helena said. "I did warn Mrs. Vaszary that unless I tested the entire painting in laboratory conditions, we couldn't be sure."

"But you had tested the paints, and they were of her time," Waclaw shouted.

"I haven't introduced my colleague," Helena said, ignoring Waclaw's outburst. "*Dottore* Martinelli works at Arte Forense in Rome. She was kind enough to allow me to run the tests of the paints used in the Judith and Holofernes. And they are, indeed, of the right era. We couldn't be sure that they were used by Artemisia Gentileschi, but these were certainly the kinds of paints she would have used."

"Exactly!" Waclaw said, still confident. "And Vaszary showed me the provenance."

"Provenances can be faked," Andrea said. She had been standing next to Helena, but now she walked toward the painting. She stopped a couple of metres from it, stepped closer, then took out her scope and started examining the picture from top to bottom.

"I am sure you have heard or read about cases where forgers were able to produce provenances that convinced even the archivists at the Tate," Helena said. "John Drewe forged provenances for paintings he had commissioned himself and sold, on the basis of those provenances, as original work by such artists as Giacometti and Nicholson."

"But Adam Biro was not a forger, Miss Marsh," Waclaw protested. "He has sold the highest quality of art to museums and collectors for decades."

"You are right, Mr. Lubomirski," Helena said. "He may not have been a forger, but he was certainly a thief, a killer, and a war criminal. Also, he has been dead for some time, as has his son who followed in his footsteps. No one is sure how long the younger Biro has been dead because his death has been covered up so that he can continue to sell paintings his father stole."

"We had no idea that Biro was dead," Vaszary interrupted. "We were told he had a painting to sell, that he was short of funds. I bought it, and we brought the painting to Strasbourg when I was appointed to the Council."

"You never met him?" Attila asked.

"No, I did not. But he was recommended by the then Minister of Justice."

"Mr. Magyar," Helena said.

"Yes. He is a trusted friend of our prime minister's," Gizella added.

"How much did you pay for it?" Helena asked.

"A thousand euros. We were told it was a copy of a painting by Gentileschi. He was specific about that — a nineteenth century copy."

"What about the provenance?" Waclaw interrupted. "You showed me the provenance for this Gentileschi. Not a copy. The original painting. The one that had been in my family's home. I was buying it back to honour my family. It was to be . . ."

"You decided it wasn't a late copy?" Helena interrupted.

"Monsieur Magoci told us," Gizella blurted.

"When?"

"When we invited him here to meet with us. He said it looked like a baroque painting by someone very, very good. He asked whether we were interested in having him do some research. Then he called to say he was sure that it was by Artemisia Gentileschi. His firm had looked into its history."

"He must have been one of your first visitors," Attila said in Hungarian. "Why?"

"You hired him," Helena asked, "as soon as you came here? What was he going to do for you?"

"It had nothing to do with the painting," Vaszary said.

"Other investments?" Helena suggested.

"We were investing in real estate, if you must know," Gizella said. "No laws against that and, as Iván said, nothing to do with this painting."

"Real estate?" Helena asked. She remembered Vladimir's talk about laundering money.

"How did this man get a provenance?" Andrea asked.

"He wrote up what he had found out about the painting's history," Vaszary said. "That's what provenance is, right?" He was looking at Andrea.

"Then why did you ask me here?" Helena asked.

"Magoci advised us that we needed someone to verify his research," Gizella said.

"So you could sell it," Helena said.

"Yes, so we could sell it. He knew how to do that. Knew the market for a painting like this."

Andrea, who had been studying the painting with a flashlight and a magnifying glass, turned to face Helena. "Nothing for sure," she said, "but I think the signature may be covering up another signature and it's possible, just possible, that this is a lost painting by Caravaggio."

"Caravaggio?" Waclaw shouted. "It can't be. The painting we lost is by Artemisia Gentileschi."

"In that case," Helena said, "this may not be your painting. There is only one way to find out. We have to study the signature using infrared light and a microscope. We cannot risk scraping the paint here. Unless we take the painting to Rome, we cannot be sure."

"No," Waclaw shouted. "You can't take my painting to Rome. We have concluded our deal . . ."

"You are not taking this painting anywhere," said the short man with bristly white hair who had come into the room. No one, not even Lucy, had noticed.

"*Miniszter ur,*" said Vaszary and rose to his feet again. "We were not expecting you," he added, still in Hungarian.

"*Nyilván.* Obviously," Magyar said to Vaszary, then he turned to Attila. "You didn't say you were coming here."

"Okay," Waclaw said in English, "I really don't care what you say in your language. This painting is coming with me to Warsaw. I paid for it . . ."

"It is not," Magyar said. "Do not worry, your deposit will be returned in full. You have been the victim of a fraud, my friend; this painting does not belong to these people. Therefore they are not able to sell it to you — or to anyone else, for that matter. It is the property of my government, and it is not going anywhere except home to Hungary."

"Ah," Helena said, "Mr. Magyar."

Árpád Magyar offered to shake her hand, but Helena pretended to look for something in her backpack and ignored the gesture.

"You told us you planned to buy it from us later," Gizella said in Hungarian. She was looking at Magyar. "After we brought it out of the country. You said we would even make a bit more on the side, if all went well, you said, and Iván never asked any questions when it came to what you wanted. He took orders. It's the way it is."

"That's ridiculous, my dear." Magyar snickered. "No one would believe such a fanciful story." Turning to Waclaw, he added in English, "I apologize on behalf of my government. As I said, your money, sir, will be refunded in full. Mr. Vaszary will send you a letter withdrawing any claim he imagined he had to the painting, and we shall rely on your goodwill as a gentleman to let this pass. I know it is difficult to forgive, but I promise you that if we decide to sell the painting, your bid will receive the most favourable consideration. And now, I must insist that Vaszary and I are left alone to clear up this mess."

CHAPTER TWENTY-EIGHT

"You didn't take the money?" Lieutenant Hébert inquired.

Attila shook his head.

"You left twenty thousand euros on the table, just like that?" he snapped his fingers. "Regrets?"

"Not yet," Attila said. "Maybe when I get home and begin to wonder whether I will be hired again."

They were sitting at one of Le Rafiot's wooden tables on the riverside terrace across from Saint Joseph's church. It was a warm autumn afternoon, the scent of damp leaves, the recent rain on the boardwalk, the drifting algae where the waves from passing boats hit the banks of the Ill. Though the Ill was much narrower and shallower than the Danube, the scent reminded Attila of late summer evenings in Leányfalu, where one of his aunts had a cottage and he used to take the girls for a lazy dip. Despite the beauty of the French Quarter's multicoloured buildings leaning in to admire their own reflections, and despite his recent encounters with the great man wrapped in the mantle of his country's current kleptocracy, he felt oddly homesick.

"I am not sure they would know enough to blame you for what happened after you left," Hébert said. "I did not even have to produce the recording of Magyar's conversation with you. I showed Magyar a typed version, and when he asked whether I had the right to invade the privacy of a foreign government's office, I told him I had obtained the necessary paperwork. I think he imagined that we had bugged Vaszary's rooms. We had certainly bugged the house. That young woman they brought along as a maid proved to be enormously helpful. Magyar knew that we had enough evidence to arrest him. Except for his diplomatic immunity. But, you know what, Attila, I will make sure the other members of the *Conseil* know that this man paid to have a French citizen killed."

"Given how our government works, I doubt that he would suffer much," Attila said. "Maybe he would not get another major appointment for a couple of years."

"I made sure the papers will have the story."

"That won't make a difference in Hungary. The government controls almost all of the press, and whatever your papers say, they can label it fake news. I suppose the International Criminal Court is too busy to get around to small cases of individual murders when they have mass murderers still walking around free."

"Not to mention all those Russians killed by friends of Putin or friends of friends of Putin."

"Maybe he could go on one of those lists that would prevent his travel to civilized places."

"That rarely happens to anyone in government."

"And Magyar will be protected by his friends in our so-called parliament."

"Do you think getting the painting out here was his idea, or was he working for someone else?"

Attila shook his head and ordered another drink. "That, *mon cher*, we'll never know. But the way our system works, he would have had to split the millions from the sale of the painting with others — we have an expression in my language, *Kéz kezet mos.* 'Hand washes hand' in English."

"Something like protecting each other?"

"There is an English expression that might fit: taking turns scratching each other's backs."

Hebert laughed. "We have a lot of that going on in France too. Do you know what they plan to do with the painting?"

"No."

"I talked with Tóth about Berkowitz's murder."

"Since Berkowitz worked for Magyar, I assume that will be unsolved for at least a dozen years and by then everyone will have forgotten about him. There are no witnesses, and Vaszary will be too busy keeping his nose clean in Ulaanbaatar . . ."

"Is that where they are sending him?"

"It was that or Tashkent. The bastard will have lots of time to think about why he tried to rip off Magyar and his cohorts."

"Why? For €21 million or more. Enough to buy him and his pretty wife one-way tickets to anywhere they fancied, change their names, live in clandestine luxury for the rest of their lives. It would be tempting for a pair tired of taking orders."

"A pleasure to meet you in person, Madame Marsh," Hébert said standing up when Helena came toward the table. "You may enjoy meeting my friend, here," he added, pointing at Attila. "For the past two weeks, he insisted he didn't know you."

Helena kissed Attila on both cheeks and shook Hébert's hand. "I have some good news, at least," she said, taking a sip from Attila's wineglass. "They will have to bury Biro now, and his confiscated collection will no longer benefit your elite little clique in Hungary. I reported the case to the Stern Foundation, and they will send in their own people. I assume the Washington Principles on Nazi-Confiscated Art will apply the rules. Maybe Zsuzsa Klein will receive an inheritance, after all. There was proof in the archives that her grandfather had bought a Caravaggio, and we may yet be able to identify the Vaszarys' painting as the one stolen from him." She called the waiter and pointed at Attila's glass. "I like your taste in wine," she said.

CHAPTER TWENTY-NINE

A large bouquet of roses greeted Helena at her office on Rue Jacob in Paris. Louise had unwrapped it and found a vase almost big enough to accommodate its girth. The leftovers — all yellow flowers — were on Louise's own desk in a much smaller vase. A thick yellow envelope sat leaning against Helena's vase. The writing was a bit smudged but still legible: "Mademoiselle Helena Marsh, Personal."

When she ripped it open, she found three micro voice recorders, a photograph of herself, and a letter on a stiff sheet of white paper.

My dear Helena,

I would have destroyed all these, but I didn't want you to worry that they had fallen into the wrong hands. Or about who killed your archer. Accept this, too, as a gift from an admirer.

Yours, as ever, Vladimir

P.S. If your friend decides she wants to sell the Caravaggio, please let me know.

I am grateful for the encouragement Susan Renouf provided even before I began to write this book, her editorial comments after she first read the manuscript, and her eagle-eyed spotting of small embarrassments after the second read.

A heartfelt thanks to Julian, who introduced me to Baroque art and to the story of Artemisia Gentileschi.